Dear Reader,

You've seen the news re[...]
New Orleans. A police for[...]
breakdown of law and order. Citizens cowering in
their homes after dark. The old and infirm preyed
upon by roving bands of thugs.

For Detective Evangeline Theroux, it's just another
day in the Big Easy...until death becomes personal.

A body covered in snake bites is found in an
abandoned house in the Lower Ninth Ward. A
connection to a notorious child killer is eventually
uncovered. Throw in a Pandora's box of family
secrets, murder and insanity, and you've only
scratched the surface of Evangeline's story.

Known as the Ghoul Girl because of the cold and
emotionless way she approaches even the most
gruesome crime scenes, Evangeline has worked
hard to be accepted as an equal by her male
colleagues. She's aloof, analytical and tenacious—
traits that are sometimes at war with her Southern
upbringing.

On a personal level, she's a grieving widow
and a single mother, the sister of an ex-con
and the daughter of a couple whose forty-year
marriage is disintegrating. But more important,
Evangeline Theroux is a fighter. A survivor.
A woman who will not go quietly into the night.

And for me, the writer, she is a character who
refuses to say goodbye.

Welcome to her world.

Amanda Stevens

Also by

AMANDA STEVENS

THE DEVIL'S FOOTPRINTS
THE DOLLMAKER

AMANDA STEVENS

the whispering room

MIRA

MIRA

Recycling programs
for this product may
not exist in your area

ISBN 13: 978-0-7783-2628-1
ISBN-10:   0-7783-2628-4

THE WHISPERING ROOM

Copyright © 2009 by Marilyn Medlock Amann.

www.MIRABooks.com

Printed in U.S.A.

For Pat and Lefty

And these signs shall follow them that believe; In my name shall they cast out devils; they shall speak with new tongues; They shall take up serpents; and if they drink any deadly thing, it shall not hurt them; they shall lay hands on the sick, and they shall recover.
—*Mark* 16:17, 18

One

July, 1976

The swamp bustled with the sounds of a summer morning. Mosquitoes buzzed in the shade, mockingbirds trilled from the pecan trees and in the distance, an outboard motor chugged toward the oyster beds and the shallow fishing waters of the Atchafalaya Basin.

But the house was quiet.

Too quiet, Nella Prather thought uneasily as she walked up the gravel driveway.

Something black and sinewy slithered through the grass, and she gave it a wide berth as she headed across the yard to the porch.

Slowly she climbed the steps and knocked on the screen door. When she didn't get an answer, she cupped her hands to the sides of her face and peered inside.

The interior was so dark she couldn't see anything beyond the shadowy front hallway, nor could she hear so much as a whisper from any of the children.

That's strange.

Her cousin's five offspring ranged in ages from eight years all the way down to thirteen months. With their blond curls and wide blue eyes, they looked like perfect little angels.

But even angelic children made some racket.

Despite the silence, the family had to be home. It was still early, and Mary Alice's old station wagon was parked under the carport. They lived too far out in the country to walk to town or even to the nearest neighbor.

Besides, Mary Alice rarely left the house. She'd converted the back sunporch to a classroom so that she could homeschool the two older children, Ruth and Rebecca. If they were out there now, she mightn't have heard the knock, Nella decided.

But she hesitated to call out in case the boys—Joseph, Matthew and baby Jacob—were still sleeping.

Turning, she glanced out over the bayou, where the lily pads were bursting with purple blooms. The air smelled of mimosa, moss and the wet green lichen that grew on the bark of the cypress trees lining the banks.

It was beautiful out here. So calm and peaceful. And yet apprehension fluttered in Nella's heart.

Where are the children?

Except for an overturned tricycle in the dense

shade of a cedar tree and a tiny, forgotten sneaker at the top of the steps, the place looked immaculate. Baskets of ferns hung from the porch rafters, and the lawn was painted with patches of red and yellow four-o'clocks and pink peonies.

Nella couldn't imagine how her cousin managed to keep everything so orderly, especially now that her husband had left her. According to Nella's mother, he'd just up and walked out months ago, leaving Mary Alice to fend for herself and the children.

Thank goodness she had a small inheritance from her father to fall back on, but that wouldn't last long, what with feeding and clothing five little ones. Nella worried how her cousin would cope once the money ran out.

I should have come sooner. She's my own flesh and blood, and I couldn't be bothered to drive out here and lend a helping hand.

But she and Mary Alice hadn't been close in years, not since the summer Nella had come home from her first year at LSU to find her cousin engaged to Charles Lemay, a dark, taciturn man fifteen years her senior.

Charles was extremely handsome, Nella would give him that. And she supposed there were some who might even consider him charming. But the way he'd flattered and cajoled and later browbeat a besotted Mary Alice had disgusted Nella.

And then the babies had started coming, some barely a year apart. Throughout her pregnancies, even the difficult ones, Mary Alice had worked like a dog caring for the house and children and making sure her husband was properly pampered.

Charles had put the family on a rigid schedule—dinner on the table by six and bedtime at eight, except on nights when they all attended church service together.

His church, naturally.

Mary Alice had been raised Catholic, but Charles would never allow his wife and children to drive all the way into Houma to attend mass at St. Ann's, where she'd received First Communion. Instead, they'd joined a rural, nondenominational congregation that met in an abandoned gas station near the highway.

Nella had never gone to one of the prayer meetings, but she'd heard talk of snake-handling. Rumor had it one of the members had nearly died the year before when he'd been bitten by a pit viper.

A chill wind swept over Nella, an early breeze from the storm clouds gathering out in the gulf. Or so she thought.

But then she realized that the Spanish moss in the live oaks was completely still, the porch so silent she could hear the drone of a fly trapped on the inside of the screen door.

The cold breath that blew down her back wasn't the wind, she realized. It was dread.

She pulled open the screen door, no longer concerned with whether or not she woke the boys. Something was wrong. She could feel it.

"Hello? Anyone home?" The door creaked as it snapped shut behind her. "Mary Alice?"

Nella's flip-flops slapped against the old hardwood floor as she walked down the long hallway, glancing first in the parlor, then hurrying through the dining room to the kitchen.

She stood for a moment, gazing around in wonder. The room was pristine. Not a speck of dust or a crumb to be found anywhere.

But there was another fly in the window and, mindful of the loathsome insect, Nella placed the basket of food she'd brought on the table and made sure it was covered before she walked out back to the enclosed porch.

Here, the chalkboard was blank, the textbooks and lesson plans neatly stacked in the shelves. Nothing was out of place. No reason to think anything was amiss.

And yet Nella's trepidation deepened as she retraced her steps to the front of the house. Something drew her attention to the cramped room beneath the stairs. The door was closed, but she'd heard a sound… a whisper…

A tremor of fear raced up her spine as she placed a hand on the knob. The door opened quietly and for a moment, Nella saw nothing inside.

Then, as the door swung wider, a shaft of sunlight fell across a child sitting cross-legged on the floor.

Head bowed, light haloing her golden hair, she cradled a doll in her arms as she rocked back and forth.

Mary Alice's daughters were only a year apart, and they looked so much alike that it was hard to tell one from the other.

"Ruth?" Nella said softly.

No answer.

"Rebecca?"

Only silence.

"Where's your mama?"

The little girl looked up then, her blue eyes eerily serene.

Slowly, she lifted a finger to her lips. "Shush. She'll hear you."

The hair at the back of Nella's neck lifted as she leaned down. She'd meant to offer comfort to the child, but when the doll moved in the little girl's arms, Nella recoiled in shock.

It wasn't a doll, she realized in horror, but a newborn baby bundled in a towel and still bloody from the birth canal.

She heard a thud against the floor upstairs and she whirled, more terrified than she'd ever been in her life. Something was so very wrong in this house.

"I'll be right back," Nella whispered to the child. "You stay put, okay?"

Heart hammering, she closed the door and started up the stairs.

Mary Alice's bedroom was right off the landing. The door was open, and as Nella reached the top of the stairs, she saw a bloody handprint on the wall outside the bedroom and a trail of wet footprints on the hardwood floor.

But Mary Alice was nowhere to be seen.

Nor were the other children.

Trying to fight off a wave of panic, Nella followed the tracks to a room down the hallway. The door was ajar and she could see something moving against the wall. She couldn't tell what it was at first, and then comprehension struck her so hard she staggered back, fist pressed to her mouth.

Her stomach churned as she stared in horror at the shadow of a noose swinging back and forth against a sunny yellow wall.

Out of the corner of her eye, she saw someone at the end of the hallway and she spun.

One of the little girls stood in front of the window, and the sunlight spilling in made her seem nebulous and golden, like a ghost child.

Without a sound, the girl started toward Nella.

"Are you okay?" Nella called softly, trying not to frighten the child.

When the girl didn't answer, Nella said a little more urgently, "Where's your mother?"

The child wore a blue dress with a matching hair

ribbon. She looked angelic and sweet and it was only when she drew closer that Nella saw the blood-stains all down the front of her dress.

"Honey, are you hurt?"

The little girl shook her head. "Jacob got it on me when he grabbed my dress."

"Is Jacob hurt?"

"No, he doesn't hurt. Not anymore."

Her soft voice was melodic, a tinkling bell, but the shock of her words stole Nella's breath. "What do you mean?"

The girl's movements were so lethargic she seemed under a hypnotic spell. She stared up at Nella with the same eerie calm as her sister. "Jacob was bad. They were all bad. Mama said they had the evil in them just like my daddy. It wasn't their fault, but they had to be saved just the same."

Nella drew a ragged breath, trying desperately not to let the horror of the moment overwhelm her. "Where are they?"

"Shush." The child put a tiny finger to her lips, mimicking her sister. "It's still here."

"What is?"

"The evil. Can't you feel it?"

Nella's heart flailed like a trapped bird inside her chest as she stole a glance over her shoulder. Some-where down that long hallway, a floorboard creaked.

Had someone come up behind her? The other girl?

For a moment, Nella could have sworn she saw

something hovering at the top of the stairs. A giant shadow that was there one moment, gone the next.

The child's gaze was transfixed, as if she could see something that Nella could not.

It was all Nella could do not to snatch the child up and run screaming from the house. Something terrible lurked in those shadowy rooms, in the beguiling depths of that little girl's wide blue eyes.

She bent and put her hands on the child's arms. "Where are your brothers? You have to tell me so that I can help them."

The little girl's gaze strayed to the room where the noose swung in a draft. "Mama carried them down to the swamp."

Oh, dear God. "Can you take me to them?"

"I have to find my sissy first."

She reached for Nella's hand. Her tiny fingers were warm, but the fear that slid down Nella's spine was ice cold.

Together they descended the steps, and Nella opened the door beneath the staircase.

The other girl was gone, but the baby lay wriggling on the floor. Nella reached for the tiny body.

I have to get them out of here. Lord, please help me save them....

But when she glanced over her shoulder, the hallway behind her was empty.

Ruth and Rebecca Lemay had vanished.

Two

Present day

There is no odor in the world like that of rotting human flesh, Detective Evangeline Theroux thought as she climbed out of the car.

The scent hung heavy on the hot, sticky air, an insidious perfume that stole her breath and turned her stomach. It was all she could do to stifle her gag reflex.

A group of uniformed officers stood in the overgrown front yard of the deserted house and Evangeline could feel their eyes on her. It was like they could smell her weakness and were anticipating with relish a mortifying display.

Jerks.

As if she would ever give them the satisfaction.

A female police detective wasn't much of an

anomaly these days, but there were those in the New Orleans PD who still clung to their good-ol'-boy mentality. Evangeline was accustomed to hostile scrutiny from some of her male colleagues, and she knew better than to give them any unnecessary ammunition.

Turning away from those condescending glances, she swallowed hard, though she pretended to survey her surroundings—a ghost street in the Lower Ninth Ward. A no-man's-land of abandoned vehicles and tumbledown houses that served as an enclave for the city's crack merchants and the homeless.

This was the section of New Orleans hit hardest by the floodwaters, and it was also the last neighborhood in the city to be rebuilt. Some referred to it as the "bad" side of the Industrial Canal because of the crime rate. Others called it Cutthroat City.

Her late husband, Johnny, had once called it home.

Evangeline mopped her brow as she waited for Mitchell Hebert to get out of the car. The swampy heat was not helping her queasy stomach. Earlier, clouds had drifted in from the gulf, bringing a cool breeze and a quick shower, but now the purplish banks had given way to a robin's-egg-blue sky. At ten-thirty on a June morning, the temperature was already in the high nineties and the steam rising from the drying puddles felt like a sauna.

"You smell that?" Mitchell asked as he climbed out of the car. "That's dead-body smell."

"You think?"

The older detective eyed her suspiciously. "You don't look so hot this morning."

That was an understatement if she'd ever heard one. Evangeline had been up half the night with the baby, and she looked and felt like a hundred miles of bad road. But lack of sleep was the least of her problems. With the impending anniversary of Johnny's death, she was finding it harder and harder to emerge from the dark cloud that had hovered over her since the funeral.

A year ago, her life had been as close to perfect as she could imagine, and now it lay in ruins, the joy and sunlight replaced by a cold, gray loneliness. Happiness was a concept she barely remembered. Now she awakened each morning to the stark reality of a future without Johnny. Sometimes she felt so hopeless and lost, she had to pull the covers over her head and weep before somehow mustering the strength to swing her legs over the side of the bed and begin another day without him.

But Evangeline's lifestyle didn't allow for a breakdown. She was a cop and a single mother. She had her and Johnny's son to think about, plus all the responsibilities that her job entailed. Lives were on the line. She couldn't afford the luxury of wallowing in despair, no matter how much she might wish to.

Mitchell was still sizing her up. "You're not gonna faint or something, are you?"

She gave him a thin smile. "Have you ever known me to faint?"

"And that, in a nutshell, is your problem, girl."

"I didn't realize I had a problem."

"You don't always have to work so damn hard to prove how tough you are."

Oh, yes, I do.

But all she did was shrug.

She knew that wasn't the end of it, though. Mitchell had that fatherly look on his face, the one that signaled he was about to impart a necessary but unpleasant truth.

He nodded toward the officers. "They're not the enemy, you know."

"Sure feels that way sometimes."

"Maybe you just need to lighten up."

"If by lighten up you mean let a bunch of infantile ass-clowns humiliate me so they can feel good about themselves, then no thanks."

"You know something? It might actually help if you let them see you toss your cookies at a crime scene once in a while. Li'l ol' thing like you. You make them look bad."

"That's their problem. Besides, I don't see you upchucking in the bushes to get brownie points." Placing an icy can of Dr Pepper on the car's fender, Evangeline tightened her blond ponytail. Her hair felt damp and lank even though she'd shampooed it in the shower that morning.

"Different situation," Mitchell said. "I'm a man. We're supposed to be hardcore."

Evangeline cut him a look. "You did not just say that."

In spite of the teasing quality in Mitchell's tone, Evangeline knew there was an element of truth in what he said. She did try too hard to be tough and cold and cynical, and her stoicism in the face of blood and gore—and in the wake of Johnny's death—made some of the officers uncomfortable. Of course, they didn't see the reflection of a devastated woman that stared back at her from the mirror each morning. All they knew was the facade she erected for work and so they didn't know what to make of her. Here she was, a mere slip of a woman with the constitution of a vulture, as she calmly and methodically picked through human remains.

Someone had called her a ghoul girl once and the nickname stuck. On the surface, the teasing had seemed good-natured, but there was a disturbing undercurrent of scorn in the murmurs and stares that accompanied her arrival at every crime scene. Especially since Johnny's death.

Evangeline had discovered a long time ago that a woman in her position was damned if she did and damned if she didn't. Showing weakness might make her more palatable to some of her macho colleagues, but it would also cost her their respect.

She would never admit it, even to Mitchell, but

her cast-iron stomach was an illusion, just like the fragile veneer that hid her desolation. Her insides were still recoiling from the smell, and she would have liked nothing better than to join the young patrolman throwing up at the corner of the house, their smirking comrades be damned.

But instead she swallowed the bile in her throat and squared her shoulders as she walked across the yard. The sick officer looked up in embarrassment as he wiped a hand across his mouth.

"Here." Evangeline handed him what was left of her Dr Pepper. "It'll help a little."

He took the drink with a shaking hand and held the cold can to his face. "Thanks."

"Softy," Mitchell teased as they climbed the porch steps.

"Shush. Someone might hear you."

"And wouldn't that be a shame?" He paused, as if bracing himself before they entered the house. "You ever think about getting out of this racket, Evie?"

"At times like this, yeah."

"I've told you about my uncle, right?"

"The one who owns the security firm in Houston?"

"He's getting on in years and he needs somebody he can trust to put in charge of his operation."

"Meaning you?"

"That's the plan. You play your cards right, there might be a place in Houston for you, too."

Evangeline sighed. "It's a nice thought, but I have too many ties here. I'm not going anywhere."

Not to Houston, anyway. It was hotter than hell in Houston, just like in New Orleans.

If I move anywhere, it'll be to someplace with snow, she thought wistfully as sweat trickled down her back.

"Just give it some thought is all I'm saying."

"You're like a dog with a bone," she grumbled.

"I'm trying to look out for you, kiddo. A city like Houston has a lot to offer a smart gal like you. Might be a good place for you and J.D. to start over."

"J.D. is barely five months old. He doesn't care where we live."

"Yeah, but police work's not such a hot profession for a single parent. With Johnny gone, you're all that boy has left."

And just like that, with his name spoken aloud, Evangeline's dead husband was right there with them on the dilapidated porch.

She couldn't see him, of course, but for a moment, his presence seemed so strong, she was tempted to reach out and grab him, hold on for all she was worth.

She knew only too well, though, that her fingers would clutch nothing but air.

Still, Johnny was beside her as she stepped into that chamber of horrors. The chill at her nape felt like the whisper of his breath; the gooseflesh that prickled along her arms was the brush of his ghostly fingers.

Whether she could see him or not, Johnny was there.

He was always there.

Inside the house, the techs were already hard at work. Two uniforms stood just inside the door talking to Tony Vincent, the coroner's investigator, and Evangeline acknowledged them with a brief nod before she quickly scanned the litter-strewn room.

A few years ago, the squalor would have appalled her because the house she grew up in had always been spotless. Now the filth barely registered as her gaze came to rest on the victim lying facedown on the floor.

She took note of his size—average height, average build, but the suit he wore looked expensive and she would bet a paycheck his loafers were Italian. This was no derelict. This was a guy who'd had access to money, and judging by the flash of the gold Rolex on his left wrist, plenty of it.

"Do we know who he is?"

"His name's Paul Courtland. We found his wallet," one of the officers explained when she raised a questioning brow. "Still had cash in it, too."

"Looks like we can eliminate robbery as a motive," Mitchell muttered.

"He has a Garden District address," another officer piped in. "One of the historic places on Prytania."

Mitchell whistled. "Old house, old money."

"Paul Courtland," Evangeline murmured. "Why does that name sound so familiar?"

"He was all over the news last fall," Mitchell said. "Sonny Betts's attorney?"

"Oh, right."

Sonny Betts. As slimy and vicious as they came and that was saying a lot for New Orleans.

Betts was one of the new breed of drug thugs that had flocked back to the city after Katrina. More ambitious and more brutal than their predecessors, guys like Betts no longer hid in the shadows to conduct their nefarious business practices because the city's corrupt legal system and lawlessness allowed them to operate with brazen impunity in broad daylight.

"The feds put a lot of resources into building a case against Betts, and then Mr. Big-Shot-Attorney here goes and gets him off without even a slap on the wrist," Mitchell said. "I think it's fair to say they were more than a little pissed."

"No kidding."

He nodded toward the victim. "You think Betts had a hand in this?"

Evangeline shrugged. "Seems a poor way to thank a guy for keeping your ass out of a federal pen, but I wouldn't put it past him."

Tony Vincent walked up just then and Mitchell clapped him on the back. "Anthony! How goes the morgue business these days?"

He grinned. "Clients ain't complaining."

His gaze drifted to Evangeline, and she pretended she didn't notice the lingering glance he gave her. She didn't like the way he'd started looking at her lately. He was an attractive guy and he had a lot going for him, but she wasn't ready to date. Not even close.

She couldn't imagine herself going out to a movie or to dinner with anyone but Johnny. She couldn't imagine another man's lips on her mouth, another man's hands on her body. She got lonely at times, sure, but never enough to betray the memory of her husband.

Which was not a very realistic or even sane way to spend the rest of her life, she freely acknowledged. But it was how she chose to live it at the moment.

Tony was still watching her. "Y'all ready to get this show on the road?"

Evangeline tried to ignore him, but, *damn,* the man really was something to look at. Almost too handsome in her book. She didn't go for the pretty-boy types.

Never in a million years would Johnny have been considered a pretty boy. Or even conventionally handsome. Not with his broken nose and crooked smile. But right up until the day he died, his boy-next-door looks had made Evangeline's heart pound.

"What have you got so far?" she asked crisply, snapping on a pair of latex gloves.

"Advanced putrefaction and seventeen-millimeter maggots. This guy's been here for a while."

She wrinkled her nose. "We can tell that from the smell. Can you be a little more specific?"

"Best guess, four to five days, but in this humidity…" Tony shrugged. "We'll know more when we get him on the slab."

"Cause of death?"

His eyes twinkled. "Oh, you're going to love this."

Yeah, I just bet I will.

They moved in unison to the body and squatted. With his gloved hands, Tony turned the corpse's head so they could see the right side of his face, which was severely swollen and discolored.

Extracting a pen from his pocket, he pointed to a spot near the jawline.

"What are we looking at?" Mitchell asked curiously.

"Puncture wounds. Skin necrosis is pretty severe so you have to look hard to spot them. See here?"

"What made them?" Forgetting about her previous wariness around Tony, Evangeline moved in closer to get a better look.

He gave her a sidelong glance when her shoulder brushed against his. "Would you believe, fangs?"

"What?"

He laughed at her reaction. "No need to sharpen the wooden stakes just yet. I don't think we're dealing with a vampire. See this dried crusty stuff on his skin? I'm pretty sure that's venom, probably mixed in with a little pus."

A thrill of foreboding raced up Evangeline's spine. She had a bad feeling she knew what was coming next. And for her, dealing with the undead would have been infinitely preferable.

"Holy shit." Mitchell stared at the body in awe. "You saying this guy died from a snakebite?"

"Bites," Tony clarified. "They're all over him."

"Jesus."

A wave of nausea rolled through Evangeline's stomach, and her skin started to crawl. She didn't like snakes. *At all.* It was an inconvenient aversion for someone who had lived in Louisiana all her life. Serpents in the South were almost as plentiful as mosquitoes.

Evangeline was pretty sure her almost pathological loathing could be traced back to a specific incident in her childhood, while she'd been visiting her grandmother in the country. They'd been fishing from the bank of a bayou, and Evangeline had been so intent on the bobble of her little cork floater among the lily pads, she hadn't noticed the huge cottonmouth that had crawled out from underneath the rotting log she'd perched on.

"Evie, honey, don't you move a muscle. You hear me?" her grandmother had said in a hushed tone.

Evangeline had started to ask why, but then she froze when she saw the look on her grandmother's face. She glanced down to find a thick, ropey body coiling around her ankle.

She'd seen snakes before, plenty of them. Her brother used to catch garter snakes in the yard and keep them in a cage in his bedroom.

But a cottonmouth was a far cry from a harmless garter snake.

The power of those sinewy muscles as they bunched around her leg both terrified and repulsed her. As she watched in horrified fascination, the snake lifted its black, leathery head and, tongue flicking, stared back at her.

For what seemed an eternity, Evangeline had sat there motionless, barely breathing. Finally, just as her grandmother arrived with a garden hoe, the snake unwound itself from her leg and glided to the water where it swam, head up, into a patch of cypress stumps.

But for the rest of the day, Evangeline couldn't get the image of that serpent out of her head. She imagined it crawling back up out of the swamp and following her home.

Even safely inside her grandmother's house, she

saw that thick, patterned body everywhere—draped over a chair, coiled in a doorway, slithering underneath the covers of her bed. The hallucinations had gone on for weeks.

She shuddered now as she stared down at the dead man.

"I found bites on both ankles," Tony said. "And two on his right hand. When we get him stripped, we may find even more. This guy was a veritable snake magnet."

"Boy howdy." Mitchell's tone was grim, but Evangeline could detect an undercurrent of excitement in his voice. This was something different from their normal caseload of stabbings and shootings.

She wished she could share his enthusiasm, but *snakes?* It could have been anything other than reptiles and she would have been fine. A disembowelment, no problem. Mutilation, all in a day's work. But not snakes. No way.

Mitchell shifted his weight, balancing himself on the balls of his feet. "Poor bastard must have died in agony."

"No doubt," Tony agreed. "Probably suffered heart failure."

"No chance this was an accident?"

Tony shook his head. "Not likely. Do you know how rare it is for someone to die of a snakebite in this country? There're only about a hundred and fifty cases a year."

"*Only?*" Evangeline tried to suppress another shudder. "That sounds like a lot to me."

Tony turned to her. "Relatively speaking, it's not. Most hospitals and clinics stock antivenom, although I read somewhere that the supply is running low because the company that made it isn't producing it anymore. I guess there isn't enough profit in it."

"He probably lost consciousness within a few seconds and the snake kept striking," Mitchell said. "If it was a moccasin, those bastards are vicious. Some people will try to tell you their aggression is a myth, but don't you believe it. I've got stories that would curl your hair."

"I've always heard a bite from a cottonmouth feels like a hammer strike," Tony said. "But I don't think one snake could have done this much damage to a grown man. Not even a pit viper. Even after the first couple of bites, he should have still been able to get away."

Unless he was restrained.

Gingerly, Evangeline lifted the cuff of the victim's shirt with a probe and peered at his right wrist. There was so much swelling and the skin was so discolored, she couldn't tell if he had ligature marks or not.

She moved to the left wrist, where she noticed faint bruising just below the edge of the Rolex.

"Could have been caused by the watch band when his arm puffed up," Mitchell said over her shoulder.

"Maybe," Evangeline said doubtfully. "But like Tony said, a grown man should have been able to get away, even after the first couple of bites. There must have been a reason why he couldn't. And how the hell did he end up in here?"

"I wish I could help you out," Tony said with a teasing smile. "But my job is just to bag 'em and tag 'em."

"And we'll need some time before you do that," Evangeline said.

"Sure thing. Just holler when you're finished." His eyes glinted with amusement as he added, "Have fun, Ghoul Girl."

Evangeline didn't bother getting irritated. What would be the point? Instead, she turned back to the dead man.

The swelling and discoloration around the wounds was a good indication that he hadn't died quickly. The venom had had time to spread, and what the poison had done to the body was ghastly.

"Looks like something from a horror movie," Mitchell muttered.

"Yeah. Or a nightmare."

Evangeline couldn't help wondering who the dead man had left behind. A wife? Kids?

She knew something about the anguish and loneliness that faced his loved ones in the coming weeks and months.

For the longest time, she'd tried her damnedest

not to let the victims and their families get inside her head, but no matter what she did, no matter how thick she built her defenses, they still found a way in.

They whispered to her in her dreams, screamed at her in her nightmares. And when their silent pleas tugged her from sleep, she obligingly rose in the middle of the night to go over and over the minutiae of their case files, hoping, always hoping, she would find something previously missed. She'd found that the young ones were especially tenacious.

This victim was no child, but what had been done to him was obscene and Evangeline knew it would haunt her.

It already did.

"What do you think?" she asked Mitchell.

"I think we've got ourselves an interesting case here."

"That's one way of looking at it."

Mitchell glanced over his shoulder, then lowered his voice. "Jesus, Evie. What the hell are we dealing with? Some kind of voodoo shit?"

"I don't know. Could be, I guess." But in spite of how the media tried to play up sensational cases, ritual murder was rare, even in New Orleans.

Evangeline moved to the victim's feet and examined the soles of his expensive shoes. "Take a look at this, Mitchell."

He came up beside her. "What'd you find?"

"The bottoms of his shoes are caked with mud, but I don't see any muddy footprints in here, do you?"

"Which means he didn't walk in here under his own steam."

"No big surprise there." Evangeline glanced around. "Whoever dumped him probably figured it'd be a while before he was found."

"Question is, was the poor bastard alive or dead when they left him?"

"There should be evidence of lividity somewhere on the body."

A movement in the corner of the room gave Evangeline a start, and it took all her willpower not to retreat from that filthy, ramshackle house as fast as she could. For all she knew, the serpents that had attacked the victim were still slithering around somewhere in the piles of rubble.

Great. Just great.

Coming face-to-face with a pit viper was all she needed to make her day complete.

All right, get a grip. It's not a snake. Probably just a rat. Or a big old cockroach.

But Evangeline had a sudden mental image of the victim, hands and feet bound, a gag in his mouth to stifle his screams as sinewy bodies crawled all over him, up his pant legs and down the collar of his shirt.

She imagined his agony as the razor-sharp fangs sank into his soft flesh and the poison spread through his bloodstream, making him weak and sick and maybe even blinding and paralyzing him.

She stood so abruptly, a wave of dizziness washed over her and she put out a hand to steady herself.

Mitchell rose and looked at her in surprise. "You okay?"

"Yeah, I just don't like snakes."

"Who the hell does?"

"No, I mean…I've got a real phobia about them," she admitted reluctantly.

A slow grin spread across Mitchell's face. "Well, I'll be damned. Detective Theroux has a weakness after all. Who would've thunk it?"

Evangeline's answering smile was forced. "Okay, so now you know my secret. Snakes are my kryptonite. No need to let that get around, is there?"

Mitchell kept right on smiling. He was definitely enjoying himself. "Oh, hell no. We wouldn't want anyone thinking you're human, now would we?"

"I'm serious, Mitchell. It's like you said earlier. It's different for a man. Different set of rules. But for someone like me…you know I'd never hear the end of it."

Plus, it wouldn't be above some of the guys to plant rubber snakes in her desk. Or even real ones, for that matter. She could just imagine the kick they'd get out of her reaction. Some of the more juvenile cops lived for that kind of crap.

"Now don't you worry, Evie girl. I've got your back on this one," Mitchell said, but he was still grinning from ear to ear and she had a bad feeling it was only a matter of time before word got out.

"So why don't I trust you?"

"Beats me." His amusement faded and his expression turned serious. "Hey, no joke, you don't look so hot."

She swatted a mosquito from her face. "I just need a little air. What do you say we get out of here and go knock on some doors?"

Three

As they stepped out on the porch, the humidity almost took Evangeline's breath away. There wasn't a lick of breeze, and the palm fronds and banana trees in the side yard stood motionless in the heat.

Her striped cotton blouse clung to her back as she stood in the warm shade of the porch, and her clammy black pants felt as if they weighed a ton. She thought of the shower she'd have when she got home. Cold at first, then hot enough to scrub away the dark, smelly nightmare inside that house.

Her gaze lit on an unmarked gray sedan parked across the street. Two men in dark suits and dark glasses leaned against the front fender as they watched the house.

Evangeline poked Mitchell's arm, her nod toward the newcomers almost imperceptible.

He followed her gaze and she felt him tense.

"Feds." His voice dripped scorn, the same oozing tone he might have used to designate a boil or a blister.

Evangeline swore under her breath. "What are *they* doing here? This is a homicide investigation."

NOPD rarely crossed paths with federal law enforcement because typically the big boys went after a different kind of prey. Plus, even though they tried to deny it, certain agents from a certain bureau had a nasty habit of looking down their noses at the locals, and their altruistic superiority bred a fair amount of antagonism among the rank and file.

"Not too hard to figure why they're gracing us with their presence," Mitchell said. "The victim is Sonny Betts's attorney. Looks to me like the Fibbies are still trying to nail his rusty hide."

Evangeline made a face. "I don't give a damn what they're trying to do. Our jurisdiction, our case. They try to muscle their way in, I say we go womp-womp on their smug asses."

"Mighty big words for such a little girl," Mitchell teased.

But Evangeline barely heard him. Her gaze was still on the men across the street. They were both tall with broad shoulders, polished loafers and closely clipped dark hair. She might have found their similar appearance comical if she hadn't been so annoyed by their presence.

One of them suddenly took off his sunglasses

and his gaze locked with hers. He said something to the man at his side, but his gaze never left Evangeline and she decided real fast that she would sooner pass out dead from heat stroke than break eye contact. No way would she let that arrogant so-and-so think he'd intimidated her.

His suit coat was unbuttoned and the whiteness of his shirt was almost blinding in the bright sunlight. Evangeline guessed him at six-one or -two, maybe one hundred seventy pounds. A little taller than Johnny and probably at least ten years older.

As he continued to stare at her, she was tempted to walk across the street and suggest a little come-to-Jesus meeting with him.

Instead, she folded her arms and stared back at him.

If he took her openly hostile demeanor as a challenge, so be it.

Special Agent Declan Nash had recognized her straightaway when she came out of the house.

Detective Evangeline Theroux looked much the way she did in the candid shot he had in his office. The blond hair and the pretty face—those things he'd expected, along with the wide blue eyes, which, even from across the street, he could tell were intense.

What he found surprising was her size.

From his vantage, she looked tiny. So slight, in

fact, he wondered if a strong puff of wind might give her a problem. He knew from her file that she was five feet four inches tall and weighed one hundred and twenty pounds, though he thought the latter was an exaggeration because she looked much smaller to him.

But in spite of her petite frame, there was an air of toughness about her—in the way she carried herself and in the way she interacted with her fellow cops.

And in the way she challenged him, Nash admitted. She exuded confidence and he admired that about her.

In fact, as he'd studied her file, he'd come to the conclusion that, under other circumstances, Detective Theroux was someone he would very much like to know.

Nash respected people who did their jobs well, and Theroux had one of the highest arrest records in the department. Her evaluations were stellar, her commendations glowing. From all accounts, she was a strong asset to the New Orleans Police Department.

But of her personal life, Nash knew very little, only that she was Johnny Theroux's widow.

And that was all he needed to know.

That was why he was here, after all.

Beside him his partner, Tom Draiden, made a wisecrack, but Nash ignored him. He didn't want to lose concentration or break eye contact because he suspected if he looked away first, Detective Theroux would view it as some sort of triumph on her end and a sign of weakness on his.

Considering her hostile stance, she seemed to labor under the misconception that she was in a position of power, and Nash didn't think fostering that impression would be advantageous to either of them.

"That her?" Tom asked.

"Yeah."

"Damn, that is one fine-ass Sarah Jane."

"Very professional observation," Nash said dryly.

"Well, yeah, but you might have at least warned me about the eye candy."

"I guess I didn't notice."

"What the hell? Check her out, man."

"Seems to me you're doing enough checking for the both of us," Nash said.

Tom smirked. "No harm in that, is there?"

"I don't know. Maybe you should ask Laura."

"You're a real buzz kill, Nash. You know that?"

"So I've been told."

"So what's our strategy?" Tom drawled.

He'd been born and raised in Macon, Georgia, and despite a stint in the navy and bureau assignments in Denver and Salt Lake City, he'd never lost his drawl. He had a knack for dealing with people, and he wasn't above pouring on the Southern charm when it suited his purposes. His laid-back charisma often came in handy when dealing with the local good ol' boys.

Tom's approach to their assignments was instinctive and organic while Nash tended to be more textbook and detail-oriented. He knew he could sometimes come off as arrogant and impatient, but he was neither.

What he was, was focused.

"Who owes us a favor at NOPD?"

Tom grinned. "You want me to make you a list?"

"A name or two will do."

"I take it you're down for a little arm-twisting," Tom said. "You want we should do it the nice way?"

Nash slipped on his sunglasses, turned and opened the car door. "I don't care. So long as it gets done."

He glanced over his shoulder one last time at Evangeline Theroux. He almost hated to do this to her. The murder of a prominent attorney would get a lot of media attention and a high-profile investigation could be a real feather in a young detective's cap.

But he had a job to do and the last thing Nash needed was Johnny Theroux's widow anywhere near Sonny Betts.

Four

With its lush gardens and gleaming white columns, Pinehurst Manor might have been a slightly care-worn cousin of the grand old dames situated along River Road, that fabled seventy-mile corridor of Southern plantation homes stretching on either side of the Mississippi between Baton Rouge and New Orleans.

But to the discerning eye, it soon became apparent that the house was merely a poor replica of its far grander predecessors. Built in 1945 as a personal residence for Dr. Bernard DeWitt, a noted psychiatrist and philanthropist from Baton Rouge, the original home was later expanded and converted into a private sanatorium.

Under Dr. DeWitt's stewardship, Pinehurst Manor became one of the most highly regarded psychiatric institutions in Louisiana. For over thirty years, the hospital treated patients from all over the state, suffering from all manner of mental disorders, but by the late eighties, the once pillared splendor of Pinehurst was but a distant memory.

Rocked by the twin scandals of misappropriation of funds and inappropriate behavior by some of the male orderlies, the hospital fell on hard times. By the end of the decade, only a handful of forgotten patients remained in treatment and those unfortunate few were eventually turned out when Pinehurst was forced to shut its doors for good.

The building remained boarded up for over a decade until the state bought the property and reopened it as a medium-security psychiatric facility, admitting only those patients who were not considered a serious threat to society.

But all that changed with Katrina.

Hospitals affected by the storm had to be evacuated quickly and even though every effort was made to relocate the more violent patients—those designated criminally insane—to maximum-security facilities in other parts of the state, the sheer number of beds lost to flooding forced low-to-medium-security hospitals like Pinehurst to take in the overflow.

One of the patients evacuated to Pinehurst was Mary Alice Lemay.

For over thirty years, Mary Alice had been incarcerated at a branch of the South Louisiana State

Hospital in Plaquemines Parish, a dingy, gloomy facility with cinder-block walls, chipped tile flooring and hallways that reeked of urine.

In that building, the worst of the worst were housed and treated—the serial killers, rapists and child molesters who had been remanded to a state psychiatric hospital rather than being sent to prison.

Mary Alice had spent the first few years of her custody under a suicide watch and in virtual solitary confinement. During that time, she received not a single outside visitor. Friends and relatives were so shocked by what she'd done, they couldn't bring themselves to meet her gaze in the courtroom, let alone visit her face-to-face in a mental institution—especially considering most thought she deserved the electric chair.

The weeks, months, years of her internment were passed alone and in complete silence until a new doctor assigned to her case decided one day that integration into the general population of the institution would be beneficial to her treatment.

So the door to her room came open, and Mary Alice Lemay stepped through into a world unlike any she could have previously imagined.

A nightmare world of confusion, misery and perpetual terror.

She was encouraged to mingle with the other patients, but she didn't like eating her meals in the cafeteria or socializing in the solarium or taking group walks around the grounds. Her ward was filled with all sorts of people suffering from all kinds of distress—addicts, schizophrenics, those with depression and bipolar disorder—and Mary Alice was afraid of them.

She'd been born and raised in a small town in Southern Louisiana. For the most part, she'd lived a very sheltered life, and what she saw inside the walls of that hospital shocked her.

Some of the patients were so violent, they were never allowed to leave their cells. Others were let out, but were kept restrained, and it was those patients that seemed to watch Mary Alice with more than a passing interest.

They were the ones with the dark stares and the knowing smiles, the ones who gave her a nod as she passed by in the hallway, as if to acknowledge a kindred spirit.

And then there were the sad cases, the distraught patients who tugged at Mary Alice's heart. The elderly woman who stood in a corner all day long pulling imaginary spiders from her tangled, gray hair. The young man who drew nothing but eyes, then cut them out and taped them to the back of his head.

Sometimes Mary Alice wondered what that young man had been like as a child. Had he been happy and carefree, or had the seeds of his sickness already been sewn?

Sometimes Mary Alice thought of her own children, but she'd learned early on that it was unwise to look back. No good could come of living in the past, of trying to remember a time when she, too, had been happy and carefree.

It had all been so long ago.

Before evil had invaded her life.

Before she had been forced to do the unthinkable. The unforgivable.

Mary Alice didn't want to look back, but the only thing she had to look forward to each day was art therapy where, instead of drawing eyes, she took up origami. Some of the doctors used the art of paper folding as a way to decrease anxiety and aggression in the patients, but for Mary Alice, it was an escape.

Her fingers were very nimble, her patience boundless, and she could lose herself for hours in the intricate folds. Soon her room overflowed with the tiny paper cranes, each one beautiful and unique and—to Mary Alice—each represented a very special wish.

She'd had to leave all her cranes behind when she was transferred to Pinehurst, but she didn't really mind. The new facility was so much better. The building was old, but it had a lot of character and there where windows everywhere. The green-gold light that filtered down through the trees outside her room each morning reminded her of the bayou, and when she stared out that window, she could easily ignore the bars and imagine that she was back in her own bedroom.

But she refused to dabble in the dangers of make-believe, nor would she allow herself the luxury of losing her mind. Every hour of every day, Mary Alice Lemay was cognizant of where she was and why she was here.

She knew what people thought of her, what they called her here and in the outside world. But they hadn't looked into the eyes of her children. They hadn't seen what she'd seen. They didn't know what she knew.

So, no, Mary Alice did not—*would not*—look back with regret.

Sorrow, yes, but not regret.

Whatever anyone else thought of her, she knew that she was neither a monster nor a martyr, but a mother who had willingly sacrificed her own soul in order to secure her children's eternal salvation.

She had done what any loving mother would do.

"Mama?"

Mary Alice was sitting in a rocking chair, staring through the bars of the window. When she heard that voice—the sound like the sweet tinkle of a bell—she thought at first she must have imagined it. But when she looked up, she saw a woman in the doorway of her room.

A woman with golden hair and beguiling blue eyes.

A woman with the face of an angel.

Her angel.

Her beautiful girl.

She put out a hand and the angel floated toward her, graceful and elegant. So loving and sweet.

It was only then that Mary Alice realized her visitor wasn't alone. A man had come into the room behind her. He was tall and dark and thin to the point of gauntness. His hair was swept back from his forehead and his dark eyes held a strange reddish hue. He had a terrible scar on the right side of his neck that looked as if he might have been burned years ago.

When his gaze met Mary Alice's, a shiver of dread crept up her spine.

She'd seen those eyes somewhere before, or what was behind them.

"Mama, this is Ellis Cooper. He's a very good friend of mine."

The man leaned down and tried to take Mary Alice's hand, but she pulled it away. For some reason, she didn't want him to touch her.

He picked up a paper crane from the floor and held it out in his palm.

"This yours?" he asked with a smile that chilled Mary Alice to her very core. "I always loved origami. Some guy once told me about a Japanese legend. Seems if you fold a thousand of these things, your wish will come true."

Mary Alice said nothing.

Ellis Cooper glanced around. "Looks like you've got a ways to go."

Mary Alice refused to look up. She would not meet the man's gaze. She would not stare into that dark abyss.

But she could feel his eyes on her.

"Your daughter's told me a lot about you," he said with a liquid smoothness. "I've sure been looking forward to coming to see you. If you don't mind my saying so, this is a pretty special day for me."

"Ellis," said the angel. "Would you leave us alone for a moment?"

"Oh, you bet. Take all the time you need. I'll just wait outside."

He bent suddenly and put his face very close to Mary Alice's so that she could no longer avoid his gaze.

And this time, he grabbed her hand before she could pull it away. He held it very tight between both of his. His skin was cold and dry, and there was something reptilian about those terrible, gleaming eyes.

"I expect we'll meet again very soon, Mary Alice. And I do so look forward to that encounter."

He released her hand then and straightened, and though Mary Alice still kept her gaze averted, she sensed something pass between the man and her daughter. A smile maybe. Or a brief, intimate touch.

A smaller, softer hand took hers once they were

alone. "Everything's going to be all right now. You'll see."

Mary Alice placed the angel's hand between both of hers and clung for dear life.

"It's okay, Mama. I know what I have to do. I've always known."

That soft hand came up to stroke Mary Alice's cheek.

"You taught me well. And now that I have Ellis helping me, it's going to be so much easier." The angel's blue eyes shimmered with excitement as she leaned forward and lowered her voice to a whisper. "Mama…he's one of us!"

No, Mary Alice thought in despair. *That man is not one of us.*

Ellis Cooper was one of *them.*

Ellis leaned a shoulder against the wall as he peered through the reinforced glass panel in the door, watching in fascination as the little drama unfolded inside.

Every so often, he would glance up the hallway in front of him and then over his shoulder behind him to make sure one of the patients or someone on the staff didn't sneak up and catch him unawares.

He was probably being a little paranoid, Ellis realized, but he knew only too well of the trickery and deception that went on in a place like this. You couldn't trust anyone.

Ellis had spent a couple of hitches in state mental wards, the first when he was only fifteen years old. Given his experience, he couldn't say he was exactly happy to be back in one. But at least today, he had the freedom to walk out whenever he chose. That was something.

Normally, he steered clear of any type of institution, be it a government office or even a regular hospital. He had a fundamental distrust of anything that smacked of authority, of any place in which he was not in complete control, but he'd found the prospect of a meeting with the infamous Mary Alice Lemay too irresistible to pass up.

So he'd temporarily disabled his aversion, if not his paranoia. Ellis knew from past experience that he could stand anything for a little while, even the worst kind of torture.

Now that he was here, though, all those old feelings were creeping up on him again. And dear God, the memories!

The slack jaws and vacant stares.

The unholy smells that drifted from the open doorways.

He glanced up at the surveillance camera at the end of the hallway. There was another one at the opposite end and probably a few hidden in places that were not readily discernable.

Oh, yes, Ellis knew all about those cameras.

The incessant winking of the red eyes had reminded him night and day that he was never alone. Not in his room, not in the cafeteria, not in the showers or on the toilet. As long as those red eyes were blinking, someone was watching. Always.

Even when he prayed.

Maybe especially when he prayed, seeing as how it had been his religion that had netted him his first trip to the psych ward in the first place.

Well, not *his* religion exactly. Not back then. That was before his awakening.

It was his father's interpretation of the gospel that had caught the attention of Child Protective Services in the backwoods Georgia town where he grew up.

His father, Nevil, had been a preacher and an avid follower of the teachings of George Went Hensley, one of the founders of the charismatic movement. Ellis's father, like Hensley, had believed in a strict interpretation of the Bible, including the "signs" passage from Mark:

> And these signs will accompany those who believe; in my name they will cast out demons;
> they will speak in new tongues; they will pick up serpents with their hands; and if they drink any deadly poison, it will not hurt them; they will lay their hands on the sick, and they will recover.

As a boy, Ellis had been enthralled by the serpent-handling spectacle that accompanied some of his father's sermons. Ellis hadn't been a true believer back then, but he'd loved watching the snakes. To him, they were among God's most glorious creatures. Even the thick, leathery water moccasins, with their white mouths and razorlike fangs, held a certain fascination.

Along with the rattlers and copperheads, the moccasins had been kept in cages behind the chicken coop at Ellis's home. Once his after-school chores were done, he would head out there and sit in the grass for hours, mesmerized by the sinewy movement of the reptiles as they climbed up the mesh wire of the cages and wrapped themselves around one another.

By this time, Ellis was quite adept at catching the creatures in their natural habitats—underneath rocks and rotting logs and in muddy sloughs—but once they were placed in the cages, he wasn't allowed to handle them. That privilege was reserved for his father and some of the elders of the church.

It was a common misconception that serpent-handlers believed the Holy Spirit would keep them safe. Every last one of them knew the dangers of what they did. Many had lost fingers and limbs as a result of the infection brought on by a bite. One or two had even lost their lives.

It wasn't a matter of faith, Ellis's father had once explained. It was about obeying the word of God.

Ellis's first snakebite had come just after his fifteenth birthday.

He'd found a copperhead sunning on the bank of the creek that ran behind their house. Holding the head so that the snake couldn't strike, he'd lifted the reptile close to his face, admiring the flicker of the serpent's tongue, the dark gleam in the slitted, catlike eyes.

Ellis had become so engrossed in watching the play of sunlight on the glistening scales that he hadn't realized the snake's head had slipped free of his grasp.

The fangs caught him in the side of his neck, and the copperhead hung there for a moment as Ellis's skin started to burn like wildfire.

Afterward, he hurried home, washed the bite with soap and water and kept his mouth shut. He didn't tell anyone about his carelessness or that he'd flown into a rage and killed the poor snake before it could slither away.

A few hours later, he began to feel achy and weak, like he was coming down with the flu. The bite area was swollen and tender, but he told himself he'd be fine. Copperhead venom wasn't nearly as dangerous as the poison from the other pit vipers. Sometimes the bites had no effect at all.

But within days, gangrene set in. His skin around

the afflicted area turned black and felt cold to the touch.

Still, he tried to keep the wound hidden by wearing his collars buttoned, but his science teacher noticed the swelling and discoloration one day and sent him to the school nurse. She took one look and rushed him to the hospital.

What followed was a nightmare scenario of painful surgeries and skin grafts where the dead flesh had to be cut away from the bone.

Convinced he had been bitten as the result of his father's dangerous religious practices, CPS removed Ellis from his home, but rather than placing him in foster care, they sent him to the state hospital for psychiatric evaluation.

It was there, in that place of misery and confusion, that he had finally experienced his religious awakening.

It was there, in a dark and reeking room, that Ellis Cooper had accepted his true calling.

A nurse passing him in the corridor gave him a curious glance. Ellis turned slightly so that she could see the "bad" side of his face. When she caught a glimpse of the scar tissue, she quickly looked away. Then her gaze came back to him, and she smiled in the tentative, flustered way that Ellis was used to.

He turned and watched as she hurried down the

hallway, and when she glanced over her shoulder, the smile he flashed seemed to momentarily stun her.

Ellis gave a low chuckle. That was the cool thing about his appearance. His scarred, pale countenance seemed to attract even as it repelled.

Today he had on a black suit that was perfectly tailored to his thin frame. He cut a striking figure and he knew it. He was only thirty-seven, but he'd started to go gray during his incarceration in the mental hospital. By the time he was released, his hair had been as white as snow, which he took as an outward sign of his spiritual metamorphosis.

He'd worn his hair natural for a long time, but these days, he'd taken to dyeing it black, and he liked to slick back the glossy strands from his high forehead in the manner of an old-timey preacher.

But his hair and even the scar played second fiddle to his eyes. They were by far his most prominent feature. So dark a brown they were almost black, but in the center radiated the heat and fury of a fire-and-brimstone zealot.

Ellis didn't think of himself that way, though. He considered himself a soldier and sometimes a prophet.

Turning his attention back to the glass panel, he lifted the origami crane he'd found in Mary Alice's room and watched her over the graceful curve of the paper head.

She stared back without blinking. Her eyes were clear and blue and mesmerizing in their intensity.

And Ellis thought, almost in awe, *She knows*.

It was almost as if Mary Alice Lemay could peer straight down into his soul.

Five

The day was still, hot and hazy as Evangeline and Mitchell drove into the Garden District.

The streets in this glorious old neighborhood were lined with the gnarled branches of live oaks, and the lush, vivid yards—heavily painted with crepe myrtle, oleander and flaming hibiscus—provided a striking contrast to the gleaming white houses.

Underneath second-story verandas, ceiling fans rotated in the sluggish heat. Children played in the lawn sprinklers while gardeners dripping with sweat clipped hedges and weeded flower beds thick with petunias and geraniums.

This was a neighborhood steeped in history and quiet refinement; a lifestyle of summer garden parties, servants and drinks by the pool.

A world very different from the one Evangeline knew.

After leaving the crime scene earlier, she'd showered and changed her clothes, but the scent of Paul Courtland's rotting flesh still clogged her nostrils as she pulled the car to the curb in front of his house.

She leaned her arms against the steering wheel and stared out the window at the house, dreading the moment when she would have to climb out of the car, walk up to the house and ring the bell.

Mrs. Courtland? I'm afraid I have some bad news for you.

Evie? I hate like hell to be the one to have to tell you this.

"Evie?"

For a moment, Mitchell's voice seemed so much a part of her memory, Evangeline forgot he was in the car with her. She turned and glanced at him. "Yeah?"

"You ready to do this?"

"Can I just go have a root canal instead? Or maybe get some surgery done without anesthesia?"

"'Fraid not. Comes with the territory. Could be worse, though," he added, and Evangeline knew that he was thinking about the night Johnny died, too.

Silently, they got out of the car and started up the walkway together.

The Courtland home was a three-story Greek revival with wide Doric columns in the front and a walled garden in the back. Baskets of trailing ferns hung from the balconies, and the carefully tended flower beds exploded with color.

The sound of splashing water and laughter drifted over the garden walls, and as Evangeline walked up the front steps, she heard a child singing in the back, a happy, inane tune that tugged at her heart and made her wish she was anywhere in the world but where she was—standing at a dead man's front door.

A middle-aged woman with short gray hair answered the door straightaway. She wore brown slacks and a blue, nondescript top that she tugged down over her rounded hips. "Yes?"

"We're NOPD," Mitchell said as he hauled out his wallet and showed her his ID. "Are you Mrs. Courtland? Mrs. Paul Courtland?"

"No, I'm the Courtlands' nanny." Her hazel eyes flickered with uncertainty. "Is there some trouble, Officer?"

"It's Detective. And, yes, I'm afraid there's been some trouble. Is Mrs. Courtland home?"

"She's out by the pool with her daughter. Hold on a second and I'll get her for you."

Instead of inviting them in, she closed the door in their faces.

Mitchell gave a nonchalant shrug. "Lots of riffraff in the city these days. Can't be too careful."

"You do look a bit dodgy. Where'd you get that shirt?"

"Salvation Army," he said. "A buck twenty-five."

They waited in silence until the door was drawn back again a few minutes later. The woman who stood on the other side this time was a thirtysomething blonde wearing a green-and-gold bikini top with a matching sarong fastened at the top of one hip. She was tan and lean with the kind of soft beauty and quiet elegance women of her social station seemed to acquire naturally.

Her full lips glinted with pale peach lip gloss and when she propped a hand on the door, Evangeline saw the same shade of shimmer on her nails. *Fine-tuned* was the first description that came to mind. *Pampered* was the second.

"I'm Meredith Courtland," she said as her cool gaze skipped from Evangeline to Mitchell and then darted past them to the unmarked car at the curb. "How may I help you?"

"I'm Detective Hebert, this is my partner, Detective Theroux." They both presented their IDs. "Ma'am, I'm afraid we have some bad news for you."

"Bad news?" She stared at them blankly, as if such a concept were unheard of in her comfortable, insulated world. "Is this about the accident?"

Mitchell glanced at Evangeline. "What accident would that be, ma'am?"

"The fender bender I had in the Quarter yesterday. I left all my information with the other driver, and I've already contacted my insurance company. I don't know why he felt the need to get the police involved." She looked mildly annoyed as she ran her manicured nails through the precisely clipped strands of her blond bob.

"We're not here about a car accident," Evangeline said. "This is regarding your husband."

"Paul? What about him?" She must have glimpsed something in their faces then because her annoyance vanished, and for a moment, her blue eyes looked as if they were drowning. "Is he…" She drew a quick breath and seemed to dismiss the possibility of any real unpleasantness. "He's all right, isn't he?"

"No, ma'am, he's not." Evangeline tried to keep her voice neutral, without letting the pity she felt for the woman creep in. "If it's okay, we'd like to come in and talk to you for a few minutes."

For the longest time, Meredith Courtland didn't say a word, just stood there clutching the door while, in spite of her best efforts to cling to denial, her world started to crumble around her.

Evangeline's heart ached for her. She knew only too well what it was like to be on the other side of that door. To feel so overwhelmed by the news that you forgot how to breathe. You could hear someone talking to you. You could even make out their words. But what they said made no sense. Nothing made sense. How could the husband you'd kissed goodbye that morning, the man you loved more than life itself, be dead?

How, all of a sudden, could the life you'd shared with him be nothing more than a memory?

Evangeline could feel the burn in her eyes of a thousand unshed tears and she had to glance away for a moment. Sometimes even now a future without Johnny seemed too much to bear.

Meredith Courtland stepped back from the door. "Please come in," she said shakily.

They stepped into a cool, terrazzo entryway with gilded mirrors and tall vases of pink and white roses. Sunshine spilled in from a domed skylight and dazzled the crystals of a huge chandelier. A floating staircase swept gracefully up to a second-story gallery, where a black maid temporarily appeared at the railing before vanishing back into the shadows.

Meredith Courtland's gold sandals clicked against the marble floor as she led them down a wide hallway that opened into a large living area decorated with an eclectic mix of modern and antique furnishings.

A wall of French doors opened into the garden, a sun-dappled paradise of banana trees, palms and scarlet bougainvillea cascading over the stucco walls. Just beyond a white gazebo, Evangeline could see the sparkle of turquoise water in a kidney-shaped pool.

Indeed, a world very different from her own.

A little girl in a blue polka-dot swimsuit sat on

the floor in front of the windows. She had a feather duster in one hand that she used to tease a tiny black-and-white kitten. When the adults entered the room, the child tossed aside the duster and got to her feet.

"Hello," she said, with a smile that showcased a perfectly matched set of dimples. She looked to be about four, with gold ringlets and tanned, chubby little legs. "Do you want to see my kitten?" She picked up the tiny cat and clutched it to her chest. "His name is Domino."

"That's a good name for a black-and-white kitten," Evangeline said, captivated by the little girl's charm.

"Daddy wanted me to name him Bandit, on account of his mask. See?" She held up the kitten so they could admire the black markings on his face. "I like Domino better. Daddy's just an old silly billy anyway. Right, Mama?"

Meredith Courtland stared at her daughter in stricken silence. When the nanny appeared in the doorway, she said on a quivering breath, "Colette, would you please take Maisie back out to the pool? I'll join you in a few minutes."

"Can Domino come, too, Mama? Please? Pretty please with sugar on top," the little girl pleaded.

Meredith Courtland pressed a hand to her breast. "No, sweetie, cats don't like the water. Domino can stay in the kitchen while you swim."

"Can I give him a treat?"

"Just one."

The child grinned impishly at Evangeline as she skipped out of the room behind the nanny.

"Please, have a seat," Meredith said, indicating a white sofa behind a mahogany coffee table inlaid with chips of colored glass. As she sat down in a chair opposite the sofa, the gossamer fabric of the sarong floated gracefully around her slim legs.

Her posture was very straight, the lines of her face carefully composed. Except for the tears glistening on her lashes, Meredith Courtland looked rigid and emotionless.

She doesn't dare let herself feel anything, Evangeline thought. Not yet. Not until she's alone. And then the pleasant ennui of her once-cosseted existence would pass into memory with the dawning of a stark, cold reality.

She would awaken in the morning, mind swept clean by sleep, and turn, see the empty side of the bed and it would hit her again, that terrible sense of loss. That bottomless pit of despair.

"Paul's dead, isn't he?" Her voice was flat with acceptance, but there was a glimmer of something that might have been hope in her eyes.

Evangeline dashed that hope with one word. "Yes."

Her eyes fluttered closed. "When?"

"His body was found this morning in an abandoned house in the Lower Ninth Ward. We think he'd been dead for a few days."

"*A few days?* Dear God…" Meredith Courtland's neck muscles jumped convulsively as she swallowed. "How did it happen?"

"We won't know the exact cause of death until after the autopsy. But we have reason to believe your husband was the victim of foul play."

She gave a visible start. "You're saying…he was *murdered?*"

"I'm very sorry," Evangeline said softly.

"But…" Her expression went blank again. "That's not possible. It's just not."

Murder happened to other people.

"Is there someone you'd like us to call? Family or friends you'd like to have come and stay with you right now?" Evangeline asked.

"Stay with me? I don't know…." She couldn't seem to form a clear thought. She skimmed her fingers down one arm. "Colette and my daughter are here…." She closed her eyes briefly. "Oh, God. How am I going to tell Maisie? She adores Paul…."

Her voice cracked and her bottom lip trembled as she lost the struggle for self-control. "God," she whispered on a sob and put her hands to her face as if she could somehow forcibly stem the tide of raw emotion that bubbled up her throat and spilled over from her eyes.

Evangeline fumbled for a tissue in her purse and handed it across the coffee table to the crying woman. Meredith Courtland took it gratefully and after a moment, she dabbed at her eyes as she turned to look out the French doors at her daughter.

In the ensuing silence, every sound in the house seemed magnified. The ticking of the grandfather clock in the foyer. The soft humming of the maid upstairs.

And into that awful silence came the high-pitched laughter of Paul Courtland's little girl as she splashed happily in the shallow end of the pool.

Meredith drew a deep, shuddering breath and folded the tissue into a neat little square on one thigh. But her eyes never left her child.

"I wondered if something was wrong when he didn't come by for Maisie on Sunday," she finally said. "They always spend the afternoon together, and he never missed a single Sunday. *Never.* He loved being with her. He was a wonderful father." She paused to unfold the tissue as painstakingly as she had creased it. "A lousy husband, but a great father."

Evangeline and Mitchell shared a look.

"You and Mr. Courtland were divorced, then?" Mitchell asked carefully.

"Separated. He moved out a few months ago. He has a place in the Warehouse District. A *loft*." Her head was still turned away, but there was no mistaking the bitter, derisive edge to her tone. She may as well have informed them he'd moved into a whorehouse for all the scorn that dripped from her voice.

"I guess the Garden District just wasn't a cool or hip enough address for him anymore."

Evangeline and Mitchell exchanged another glance. Mitchell's nod was almost imperceptible.

"Do you have his current address?" Evangeline asked.

"No, I'm sorry, I don't. It's just off Notre Dame, I think. I don't know the street number. I've never been over there. When I needed to get in touch with him, I called his cell phone or the office."

She was still watching her daughter, and Evangeline studied her profile. There was a lot of anger beneath that cool surface. Was Meredith Courtland the kind of woman who would retaliate against a husband who had rejected her and her lifestyle?

It was hard to imagine, especially considering the way Paul Courtland had died. But then, Evangeline had seen a lot of things that were hard to imagine.

"When was the last time you talked to him?"

"Sunday before last. He came over early so that he could take Maisie to a movie she'd been begging to see. They had dinner afterward and then he brought her home."

"You had no contact with him after that? Not even a phone conversation?"

She shook her head. "We rarely talked on the phone once he moved out. And we only saw each other when he came by for Maisie. But as I said, I did think it strange when he didn't show up for her on

Sunday last. I called his office the next day, but Lisa, his assistant, said he'd taken a few days off. I just assumed he'd gone out of town and forgotten to tell me. That wasn't like him, but then…a lot of things he'd done in the past several months weren't like him."

"Such as?"

She gestured helplessly. "Moving out. Leaving his family. A year ago, I could never have imagined we'd be separated. Let alone…" She shook her head. "This all just seems like a bad dream."

Evangeline gave her a moment. "How did he seem the last time you saw him?"

She turned with a frown. "What do you mean?"

"His demeanor. His mood. Did you notice anything about him that was out of the ordinary? Did he seem worried or anxious? Anything at all that you can remember?"

"Not really. He may have been a little preoccupied, but that wasn't unusual for Paul. He had a case that was about to go to trial, and he always got a little strung out before going into court." Her gaze dropped to her hands. Her nails had completely shredded the tissue. "I just don't understand," she whispered. "Who would want to kill him?"

"That's what we're trying to find out."

"I've been sitting here going over it in my mind. None of what you've told me makes any sense. You said his body was found in the Lower Ninth Ward.

Why would Paul go there? Everyone knows how dangerous that area is. I can't imagine that he would have a client in that part of town. Maybe... Is it possible this could be just some terrible mistake?" she asked in a hopeful voice, but her hands were balled into fists, and when she looked up, the pain in her eyes struck Evangeline anew.

My God, she thought. *Is that how I looked?*

Evangeline didn't have to try to put herself in the distraught woman's place. She'd been there herself. She knew exactly how Meredith Courtland felt.

Except she and Johnny had still been together at the time of his death. He had remained, until the very end, the love of her life.

"Identification was found on the body," she said. "It's highly unlikely there's been a mistake."

"But..." Meredith's voice trailed off, as if she finally realized the futility of false hope.

"I know this has been a terrible shock for you, and I'm so sorry we have to burden you with all these questions at a time like this," Evangeline said. "But the sooner we get them out of the way, the sooner we'll be able to figure out what happened."

Meredith nodded. Her blue eyes were brimming again. "Of course. I'll do whatever I can to help. Paul and I had our differences, but he was... I still cared about him." The latter she said with a catch in her throat. "I want you to find who did this. I want you to make them pay," she said fiercely.

Outside the French doors, Maisie Courtland began to sing again, off-key and at the top of her lungs. She was a beautiful, happy child whose life, from this day forward, would never be the same.

J.D. had been born after Johnny's death. Evangeline's son had never even seen his father, never had the chance to know him, but maybe it was better that way.

Maybe you can't miss what you've never had.

"Mrs. Courtland…" Mitchell leaned forward, his gaze searching the woman's face. "Did your husband ever receive any threats?"

"What kind of threats?"

"Guys in prison have a tendency to blame their lawyers," he explained. "Did your husband ever have any problems with disgruntled clients?"

"Not that I know of. But…even if he did, he probably wouldn't have mentioned them to me. Paul was… He used to be very protective." She swallowed and glanced away.

"What about his coworkers? Did he get along with the other attorneys at his firm?"

"Paul was the rainmaker. Everyone loved him."

Now it was Evangeline who leaned forward, her gaze scouring Meredith Courtland's smooth, tanned face. "Do you have any idea who might have wanted your husband dead?"

She blinked, as if confused by the directness of the question, and then her expression hardened. "That's why you're here, isn't it? You think I had something to do with this. The spouse is always the prime suspect. Especially when there's an impending divorce."

"Right now, all we're trying to do is come up with a lead. If you can think of anything, anything at all that might give us something to go on, we would certainly be grateful for your cooperation."

"My God, if I knew anything, don't you think I would tell you? He was my *husband*. My child's father!"

Her anger was so quick, the flash of fire in her eyes so genuine, that her reaction told Evangeline more about the woman than an hour's worth of questions would have yielded. Despite the bitter separation, Meredith Courtland had still been very much in love with her husband.

Her eyes shifted away, as if she were embarrassed by how much her outburst had revealed.

"What can you tell us about Paul's relationship with Sonny Betts?"

Meredith jerked up her head and she looked at Evangeline with a mixture of fear and revulsion. "They certainly weren't friends. It was a professional relationship only. Paul believed everyone was entitled to the best defense possible. Even slime like Sonny Betts."

"Did you ever meet Betts?"

"Once at Paul's office." She shuddered. "He was not someone I would ever have in my home. I can't tell you how relieved I was when he and Paul parted ways."

"When was this?"

"Right after the trial."

"Did they have a falling-out?"

"All Paul ever said about it was that his services were no longer required."

"The split was amicable, then."

"I guess so...." She looked doubtful all of a sudden.

"What is it?"

She bit her lip as she glanced out the window, collecting her thoughts. "I don't know if it means anything... I'd forgotten all about it until now...."

"That's okay. The more you can tell us, the better chance we'll have of finding who did this," Evangeline persisted.

"It was a few days after the verdict came back." Meredith placed the shredded tissue on her thigh and absently smoothed out the wrinkles. "Paul had scheduled some time off from work so that we could go to a friend's place in the Bahamas. Then all of a sudden, he said he couldn't get away. Something had come up at work, but he wanted Maisie and me to go on without him. I didn't really want to...we hadn't had a family vacation in ages. But he was so insistent, almost as if he were trying to get us out of town." She paused. "Which I suppose he was and I was just too naive to see the signs."

"So you decided to go on the trip without him?" Evangeline prompted.

"Yes, after some arguing. The night before we were to leave, I finished packing and went to bed early. I'd just dozed off when I heard voices downstairs. Loud voices. I thought Paul must have fallen asleep in front of the television, but when I came downstairs, I saw two men with him in his study. Which struck me as odd because it was after midnight. We never had visitors that late."

"Did you recognize the men?"

"I'd never seen them before in my life."

"You said you heard loud voices. Were these men arguing with Paul?"

"It appeared so. Paul was clearly angry. He kept telling them that he'd done what they asked, and now that the trial was over, he wanted out."

"Did you know what he was talking about?"

"I didn't have a clue. But the way he kept pacing back and forth…the look in his eyes…" She took another breath. "He wasn't just angry. He looked scared. I remember he said something about a cop. 'I don't want to end up like that dead cop.' Or words to that effect."

A wave of shock rolled through Evangeline. Her face felt frozen, and for the longest moment, she didn't trust herself to speak.

Beside her, Mitchell shifted forward on the sofa. "Do you know who he was talking about?"

"No idea."

"Did you ask him about the conversation?"

"Of course I did. As soon as the men left. The way he was behaving…it frightened me. I don't know why, but I had a feeling that those two men were also some kind of cops or agents, and they were trying to get Paul to do something he didn't want to do. Something dangerous. When I confronted him, he said it was nothing to worry about. Just a misunderstanding about a case."

"You believed him?"

She sighed. "I didn't have any reason not to. Then."

Evangeline hesitated for a split second to make sure nothing in her voice betrayed her agitation. "Did you ask him specifically about the dead cop?"

"Yes, but he said he was just being melodramatic. Trying to make a point. Paul could be very theatrical when he needed to be. That's why he was such an effective trial lawyer."

"He didn't mention the cop's name?"

Something in Evangeline's voice caught Meredith's attention. She gave her a thoughtful look. "Not that I remember."

"What about the two men? Did he call either of them by name? Or a title? Detective So-and-So, for instance. Or maybe Agent So-and-So?"

"I don't believe so, no. But as I said, I'd forgotten about the incident until now. Maisie and I left for the Bahamas the next day, and when we got back, Paul had already moved out. He told me the marriage hadn't been working for him for a very long time." She shook her head, as if she still couldn't believe it. "Just like that, our marriage was over. And I thought everything was so good between us. We had arguments, of course, like every married couple, but for the most part…" Her voice thickened. "I guess that's why they say the wife is always the last to know." Her tears spilled over and Evangeline handed her another tissue. "I'm sorry. This is bringing back a lot of painful memories."

"Don't worry about it." Evangeline fished a card from her purse and laid it on the coffee table. "Here's my number if you think of anything else. My cell number is on the back. Call anytime, day or night."

"In the meantime, we'll need someone to come to the morgue to ID the body," Mitchell informed her.

"But…you said identification was found on the body."

Hope springs eternal, Evangeline thought wearily. "A positive ID is just routine procedure. If you're not up to it, we can talk to another family member."

Meredith winced at the suggestion. "Oh, no, please don't call his mother. Not until I've had a chance to break it to her first. This is going to kill her."

"I understand."

"It's just…it hasn't even been a year since she lost her other son. Paul's younger brother."

"I'm so sorry," Evangeline said.

"It was such a horrible accident and poor Leona… she's never gotten over it. None of us have. I still have nightmares about it."

"What kind of accident was it?" Mitchell asked.

"Paul's family has a fishing cabin on the bayou near Houma. David took the boat out alone one day last summer and he must have hit something in the water. The boat overturned and he was…" She trailed off on a violent shudder.

"He drowned?"

She shook her head and put a hand to her throat. "It was like one of those terrible things you hear about but don't really believe. An urban legend or something. The water where David fell in was infested with water moccasins. He was bitten over a dozen times before he could swim to the bank."

Six

A few moments later, Mitchell put voice to his skepticism as they pulled away from the Courtland home.

"I'm telling you, Evie, this case is starting to give me the creeps."

"No kidding."

"What are the chances that two brothers dying of snakebites within months of each other could turn out to be just some bizarre coincidence?"

"In my professional opinion? Slim to none."

Mitchell was driving this time and Evangeline turned to glance back at the house. She couldn't get Meredith Courtland out of her mind. Now that her husband was dead, their separation would haunt her even more. She'd find herself constantly wondering about the what-ifs and the what-might-have-beens if they'd stayed together.

Evangeline knew all about those games and how they could creep up on you in the middle of the night. How they could undermine your memories, make you think of all the stupid little things you should have done differently, all the petty arguments you wished you could take back. She knew firsthand how all that blame could wear you down night after night, month after month, until you had nothing left but regrets.

Mitchell looked at her. "I'm wondering if someone's been playing around with the goofer dust."

"The what?"

"You know, graveyard dirt. Zombie powder. The Brothers Courtland may have crossed someone dabbling in something a little heavier than the practice of law."

"Like voodoo?"

"Voodoo. Hoodoo. Conjure." He scowled at the road. "A lot of names for the same crazy-ass mumbo jumbo."

"Yeah, I admit the snake angle is freaky. And pretty damn messed-up. But my money is still on Sonny Betts. He's involved in this somehow, we just have to find the link. I say we pay him a visit, rattle his cage a little. See what falls out."

Mitchell rubbed the side of his nose with his index finger. "You know, a lot of guys like Betts are into Santería. Especially the ones with connections to the Mexican drug cartels."

"Oh yeah?" Evangeline peeled her sticky pony-tail from the back of her neck.

"I saw a show about it on the Discovery Channel."

She turned to stare at him.

"What?"

"You watch the Discovery Channel? Somehow I figured the Cartoon Network was more your speed."

"I'm a man of many tastes," he said. "You should know that about me by now."

"So you were watching the Discovery Channel…"

"Yeah, and like I said, it was about these drug dealers using Santería to impress their enemies and keep their underlings in line. Only they called it *La Regla de Lukumi.* Or some shit like that." He rolled down his window and a breath of hot air rushed in. "This car smells like a friggin' ashtray." Like a lot of ex-smokers, Mitchell had a low tolerance for cigarette odor.

"I've never even heard of…what did you call it?"

"*La Regla de Lukumi.* I'd never heard of it, either, until I saw it on this show. Anyway, there's a group that operates along the border called the Zetas. They're militia and ex-military officers from south of the border with some Guatemalan Special Forces thrown in to boot."

"In other words, a bunch of real badasses."

"Badasses with a capital *B*. The drug cartels re-cruit these guys to act as enforcers. And now they're deepening their networks into cities like Houston and Dallas. From what I saw, they're about as nasty a gang as you're ever likely to meet up with, and get this—they even have their own witch doctor, shaman, big kahuna…whatever you want to call it…that advises them."

"You think these Zetas have made it all the way into New Orleans? That's who Betts is trying to impress?"

"Not the Zetas, per se, but their employer. You gotta understand how these people operate, Evie. They don't just believe in taking out the enemy. They think if he dies screaming, they'll still have power over him in the afterlife. Hence, their affinity for torture. I'm willing to bet Paul Courtland and his brother did some heavy-duty screaming before they died."

"I don't doubt it, but it all sounds a little too spiritual for a guy like Betts."

"I'm not saying he *believes* it. He's just not above using it to make a point."

Evangeline reached over and adjusted the air conditioner vent so that it would blow directly on her face. Mitchell took the hint and rolled up his window.

He shot her a quick glance. "So what do you think?"

"I'm not sure I buy the whole Zeta thing, but I guess I wouldn't put much of anything past Betts."

"Exactly. That's all I'm saying."

"I've been thinking about those two men Meredith Courtland saw in her husband's study that night. From the way she described that meeting, it sounds like they were putting the screws to Courtland. She heard arguing and she could tell her husband was angry. The trial was over, he'd done his part…yada, yada, yada. If those guys were federal agents, isn't it possible Courtland was playing both ends against the middle?"

"Working for the feds, you mean?"

"Let's say, cooperating with the feds."

"Aren't you forgetting something? It was Courtland who got Betts off."

"So?"

"If Courtland was 'cooperating' with the feds—" Mitchell put the word in finger quotes "—why would he work so damn hard to get Betts acquitted?"

"Maybe they had bigger fish to fry. The middleman, for instance, between Betts and the cartel. What better way of finding out who his supplier was than by putting someone inside his operation that he trusted? His lawyer, no less."

"So Betts's acquittal, according to your theory, was all some master plan by the men in black?" Mitchell thought about that for a moment. "What about Courtland's brother? Where does his death fit into this whole grand scheme of yours?"

"His death was a warning. Or an insurance policy. Betts didn't go to trial until the fall, but Courtland would have already been prepping the case in the summer when his brother was killed. Betts ordered the hit, then threatened the rest of Courtland's family if things didn't go in his favor. That could be when Courtland started cooperating with the feds."

"And the snakes?"

Evangeline suppressed a shudder as she turned to stare out the window. The gardens along St. Charles flashed by the window in a colorful blur. "Maybe they wanted to make it look like an accident to anyone but Paul Courtland."

"Or maybe, like I said, Betts wanted to impress the head honchos."

"Yeah, maybe so."

Mitchell was still frowning at the road, deepening the creases in his forehead and around his eyes. He never wore sunglasses and probably didn't even own a bottle of sunscreen. The skin on his face and arms was like old leather. "So a few days after Meredith Courtland overhears the conversation in the study, her husband moves out and tells her the marriage is over. What do you make of that?"

"It sounds to me like Paul Courtland was trying to put some distance between himself and his family."

"Yep. That's what it sounds like to me, too. Or maybe, like she said, she just missed the signals. The trouble between them could have been brewing for a long time. Meredith Courtland wouldn't be the first person to lie to herself about the condition of her marriage."

They fell silent for a few minutes while Mitchell negotiated the heavy traffic in the Quarter. As they drove by the liquor stores and souvenir shops on the lower end of Decatur, Evangeline could tell something was on his mind. He was still watching her out of the corner of his eye.

"Okay, spit it out," she said.

He suddenly looked uneasy. "How long are we going to ignore the elephant in the backseat?"

She pretended not to know what he meant. "What elephant?"

"'I don't want to end up like that dead cop.' That's what she said her husband told those guys that night, right?"

"I guess."

Mitchell turned and dropped his chin, as if he were peering at her over the top of invisible glasses. "You guess?"

"All right, yeah, that's supposedly what Courtland said."

"So let's talk about it," Mitchell said impatiently. "Because I know damn well you're thinking about it."

Evangeline closed her eyes as she let her head fall against the back of the seat. It was a relief to finally say it. "What if he was talking about Johnny?"

"You know that's a long shot, right?"

"Why?"

"Why?" He ticked off the reasons on one hand. "One, Johnny's not the only cop who's been killed in this city. Two, we don't even know that he was talking about an NOPD cop. Three, there's not a shred of evidence that connects Johnny to Sonny Betts or Paul Courtland."

"That we know of."

"Four…*four*," he insisted when she tried to talk over him. "Johnny's death was a random act of violence. Tragic and senseless, but that's all it was. He was at the wrong place at the wrong time."

"I don't believe that."

"I know you don't, but it happens, Evie. New Orleans is a dangerous place. We don't call tourists 'walking ATM machines' for nothing."

He eased his way around a stalled car, and from Evangeline's perspective, they seemed to squeeze by with only a hair to spare.

"George Mason was the lead on Johnny's case. He's a determined guy. If there was something to find, he would have found it."

"Not if the crime scene was swept before he got there," she said.

"Well, hell. Why didn't I think of that?"

She responded with an irritated glower.

Mitchell sighed. "Okay, humor me, here. Swept by who? Elvis?" He shook his head. "Do you hear what you're saying? Do you know how you sound?"

She knew exactly how she sounded, but she wasn't backing down. This had been eating at her for months. "You were the one who brought it up."

"I was hoping if we talked it through, you'd get how ridiculous this all sounds. If you keep going on like this…" His mouth tightened.

"What?"

He hesitated. "Okay, I didn't want to get into this, but maybe it needs to be said. You want to know why some of the other cops have a hard time looking you in the eye these days? Why they're not so crazy to work with you anymore?"

"Uh, because they're a bunch of macho asstards?"

He ignored that. "It's because ever since the shooting, you've made it clear you think something about the investigation wasn't kosher. You've been letting some none-too-subtle insinuations slip out about a cover-up. Hell, for all I know, you think I'm in on it, too. Whatever *it* is."

"You know I don't think that."

"The God's honest truth? I don't know what to think anymore. I don't have the slightest idea where your head is these days. Kathy said you'd called the house at least a dozen times last week looking for Nathan."

"That's an exaggeration. I called twice."

Nathan Mallet had worked cases with Johnny in the year before his death. They weren't officially partners, but Nathan would know better than anyone if Johnny had been involved in something dangerous.

But the shooting had shaken him up. He'd been a mess at the funeral and afterward he wouldn't return Evangeline's phone calls. Now it seemed he'd dropped off the face of the earth. His wife, Kathy, claimed she hadn't seen him in weeks.

"I just don't understand why he won't talk to me," Evangeline said.

"No big mystery there. From what I hear, he's down in New Iberia working on one of his old man's shrimp boats. I talked to his sister not too long ago, and she said the last time she saw him, he looked terrible. She thinks he may be on dope. Crystal meth, most likely. That shit is everywhere these days."

"And you don't find that kind of behavior at all suspect? He hasn't been the same since Johnny died, and you know it."

"You try losing a partner and see how it affects you."

"He and Johnny weren't partners."

"Neither are we," Mitchell said. "Not officially anyway. But I'd hate like hell for something to happen to you. Even if you do exasperate the crap out of me at times."

"Thanks," she said dryly. "What I can't get over is how Nathan left. He didn't even resign. He just dropped out of sight."

"Like that's unusual around here. We're the Big Easy, remember?"

She shrugged.

"Besides, Nathan's always been a flake. Comes from being raised by a drunk. His old man was always half-stoned, even at work. I'm not surprised Nathan has some of the same reliability issues. They say addiction runs in families, don't they?"

"Yeah, that's what they say."

Evangeline decided to let the matter drop, but she still had her own theory regarding Nathan Mallet. His behavior sounded to her like the manifestation of a guilty conscience. Why else would he go to such pains to avoid her?

"I wish you'd just let this go," Mitchell grumbled.

"I will. Just as soon as I find some answers."

"And if you don't find the kind of answers you want?" His worry for her seemed to settle in all the deep grooves and crevices of his careworn face. "You think Johnny would want you obsessing about his death like this?"

Evangeline didn't answer.

"Hell, no, he wouldn't. He'd want you to get right back out there and build a life without him."

She drew a breath and said quietly, "If the situation were reversed, he'd be doing the same thing I am."

"You sure about that? The Johnny Theroux I knew would make sure his kid was his main priority."

"You think I'm neglecting J.D.?" Her voice sounded more hurt than she wanted it to.

"I never said that. But one of these days, that boy is going to need a daddy, Evie."

She stared at him in outrage. "I can't believe you just said that."

His shrug was anything but apologetic. "Call me old-fashioned, but I happen to think a boy needs a male role model. And no offense, but you're not—"

"Not what?" she demanded. "Getting any younger?"

He grinned. "I was going to say, you're not taking care of yourself. Look at you. You're as skinny as a fence rail."

"So? I'm also as healthy as a horse."

"Physically, maybe," he muttered.

"I heard that."

His grin broadened. "It'd do you good to get out more. Have some fun, is all I'm sayin'." His tone turned sly. "A blind man could see that Tony Vincent's got a thing for you. Would it kill you to throw the man a bone? Maybe have dinner with him or something?"

"What are you, his pimp?"

Mitchell chuckled. "You could do a lot worse."

"I don't even know why I'm having this conversation with you. It's ridiculous. We should be talking to Sonny Betts right now."

"That's going to be tricky. The feds consider him their territory."

Evangeline shrugged. "He's a person of interest in a homicide investigation. He's our territory now."

"Okay, but if we're taking a ride out there today, I need some fortification first. How about lunch? I'm in the mood for catfish. Let's go to Dessie's."

Mitchell let her out in front of the restaurant while he drove around the block to find a parking place.

As Evangeline stood in the shade of the colonnade, she spotted a dark gray sedan in the traffic on Decatur. She wondered for a moment if it was the same gray car they'd seen at the crime scene that morning, if they were being tailed by the feds.

But when Mitchell came whistling around the corner, she decided not to mention it to him. He'd probably think she was starting to obsess about that, too.

"Hey," he said. "Give me a day or two and I'll see if I can find out where Nathan is staying. The old lady's pretty tight with his sister."

Evangeline smiled gratefully, her previous irritation evaporating. "I owe you one."

"Damn straight you do. Which is why I'm gonna let you buy me lunch today."

"Gee, thanks."

As they walked up to the restaurant, she turned and glanced at the street. The gray car was nowhere in sight.

Seven

The high brick wall that surrounded Sonny Betts's sprawling stucco mansion was all but hidden by twenty-foot-tall crepe myrtle trees that also concealed surveillance cameras. The wind was blowing off the lake, and as Mitchell pulled the car up to the scrolled iron gates, the scent of oleander drifted through the open window.

A guard with a clipboard came over to the car and leaned down so that he could see into the window. He was tall and swarthy with the forearms and neck of a former linebacker.

"Can I help you folks?"

Mitchell and Evangeline hauled out their IDs. "I'm Detective Hebert and this is my partner, Detective Theroux. We need to talk to Betts."

"Is he expecting you?"

"Just tell him we're here," Mitchell said. "He'll

want to see us. Unless, of course, there's a reason he wouldn't want to cooperate with a homicide investigation."

The man smirked. "Homicide, eh? Who died?"

"Open the gate, asshole. Or else the first call I make will be to the *Times-Picayune*. I've got a buddy over there who's just itching to put your boss back on the front page. Unless he likes the publicity, nosy reporters poking through his trash and all that, he'll talk to us."

With an angry glare, the guard lifted the cell phone to his ear and walked away from the car. A moment later, the gates slid open and Mitchell drove through.

"Nice bluff," Evangeline said as they pulled up to the house.

Mitchell shot her a glance. "What bluff? My buddy writes the obituaries at the *Times-Picayune*. Like I said, he's just itching to do a real nice write-up on Sonny Boy."

Betts was out by the pool watching a blonde in a turquoise bikini swim laps. When he saw Mitchell and Evangeline, he walked over to the edge and waited for the young woman to hitch herself out of the water. Then he wrapped a fluffy white towel around her shoulders and gave her a pat on the ass.

As she sauntered toward the pool house, she gave Evangeline a sideways scrutiny, sizing her up with one disdainful glance.

Betts was dressed in white trousers, sandals and a dark blue shirt left unbuttoned to expose a smooth, muscular chest. He was just shy of middle age, with brown hair, brown eyes and a mouth that tilted at the corners in a perpetual sneer. A silver medallion hung from a chain around his neck and glistened in the sun as he turned and watched their approach.

"Miguel tells me you're homicide detectives. Hebert and Theroux, right?" His gaze moved from one to the other, his eyes narrowing in the sunlight. "Which is which?"

Evangeline could smell the cologne that emanated from his heated skin. It was something expensive and cloying.

His gaze vectored in on her. "Let me guess. Detective Theroux, right?" He held out his hand. "This is an unexpected pleasure."

Evangeline ignored the proffered hand. "We need to ask you some questions about your relationship with Paul Courtland."

He cocked his head, his insolent gaze raking over her.

Betts wasn't exactly what Evangeline expected. Since he'd slithered up from the New Orleans gutters after Katrina, he'd acquired a pseudosophistication that did little to disguise the puckered knife scar under his right cheekbone or the gleam of cruelty in his cold, dark eyes.

The way those eyes lingered on Evangeline's body made her skin crawl.

"Let's go talk in the shade, get out of this heat." He walked over to a table covered by an umbrella and sat down. Evangeline and Mitchell followed him over, but neither took seats. "Let me get you something cold to drink," he said. "Or maybe you'd like to take a swim. I'm sure Monique could rustle up a swimsuit that would fit."

"I'll pass," she said.

He shrugged and turned to Mitchell. "What about you, Detective Hebert?"

"I'm afraid of sharks," Mitchell said and Betts laughed.

"So you want to ask me some questions about Paul Courtland. Once upon a time, he was my attorney. Was, as in the past tense. I haven't seen or talked to him in months. Why? Is he in some sort of trouble?"

"He's dead," Mitchell said.

One brow rose slightly. "Is that so? I assume since you're here, someone must have whacked him."

"Someone whacked him, all right. Someone whacked him good," Mitchell said. "But you wouldn't know anything about that."

"That's right, I wouldn't. I've got a dozen people right inside the house that will swear to my whereabouts."

"On what day?"

"On whatever day he died." He took out a pocketknife and ran the blade underneath his manicured fingernails.

An old habit, Evangeline thought. "Why did the two of you part ways?"

"After the trial I didn't need him anymore."

"A guy like you is always in need of an attorney," Mitchell said.

"I'm a law-abiding citizen. Why would I need to throw my money away on a high-priced lawyer like Courtland?" His gaze was still on Evangeline and she saw recognition kick in. "Now I know who you are. You're Johnny Theroux's widow."

"Yes, I am," Evangeline said, returning the man's stare. She suddenly had an urgent, unreasonable need to put her hands around the man's throat and squeeze. The notion that he might have been involved in Johnny's death filled her with rage, but despite his claim that he didn't employ lawyers, she knew better than to lay a finger on a guy like Sonny Betts.

"Damn shame what happened to him." He leaned in. "I heard a hollow point messed up his face so bad, a DNA test was needed for a positive ID. Can't help wondering if there's any truth in that."

Before Evangeline could answer, Mitchell planted his hands on the table and bent toward Betts. "You know what I'm wondering about? I've been noticing all the goons you got patrolling this place.

If you're such a law-abiding citizen these days, what's got you so worried?"

"It's a dangerous world out there," Betts said. "Just ask Detective Theroux."

"What are they, Guatemalan? Colombian? You ever hear of an outfit called the Zetas?" Mitchell asked.

"Sounds like a college fraternity," Betts said as he continued to clean his nails with the knife. His hands were rock-steady.

"They're a fraternity of slime and cutthroats," Mitchell said. "What you might call south-of-the-border enforcers. They do the dirty work for guys like you. I hear they like to get a little creative with their victims."

"Maybe you've been watching too much TV. Sounds like an episode of *Law & Order.*"

Mitchell reached over and tapped the silver medallion around Betts's neck. "I've seen one of these before. A Haitian I once knew kept it tied around his ankle. He was the real superstitious type. 'Course, he had reason to be superstitious. He used to work for Aristide, so he had plenty of demons preying on his conscience. They caught up with him one night down on Canal Street. Doused him with a can of gasoline and lit him on fire. Now tell me something, Betts." Mitchell jerked the necklace and the silver chain snapped. He dangled the medallion in front of Betts's face. "You wouldn't be worried about a little karma, would you? That why you wear this thing?"

Betts just laughed. "Leave it to a cop to get everything ass-backward. You shitheads seem to have a knack for asking the wrong questions. I've got a theory about that."

"Is that so?"

"Yep." He reared back in his chair. "See, I don't think it's stupidity so much as self-preservation. You ask the *right* questions, you might have to deal with the answers," he said, his dark gaze burning into Evangeline's. "Isn't that so, Detective Theroux?"

By the time Evangeline got home that night, she was worn-out. It had been a long and trying day.

After they left Betts, she and Mitchell had gone their separate ways. He'd headed off to track down some of Paul Courtland's neighbors while she'd dropped by the law firm in Canal Place to question his coworkers.

The interviews had not gone well. Courtland's assistant had become hysterical at the news of her boss's death. Evangeline had finally given up trying to question her.

And then the senior partner sent in to "handle" the situation had made it clear that under no circumstances would the police be allowed to go through Courtland's office. With or without a search warrant. And he had flat-out refused to answer any questions about the firm's relationship with Sonny Betts, neither confirming nor denying that Betts was still a client.

Evangeline had expected no less. She'd dealt with enough law firms to know how they closed ranks in times of crisis, all under the useful umbrella of attorney-client privilege. But she always suspected the defensive posturing had as much to do with CYOA—*covering your own ass*—as any high-minded code of ethics. She'd yet to meet the lawyer whose survival instinct didn't run pretty damn deep.

Wearily, she climbed the porch steps and let herself into the house. Despite the shower, clean clothes and the hours that had passed since she'd left the crime scene that morning, the smell of death still clung to her nostrils, and she wondered if J.D. could smell it, too.

He began to fret the moment she picked him up, which in and of itself wasn't so unusual. She and her son were still wary of each other, and after a day with the sitter or at his grandmother's, he often seemed uneasy around her.

But rarely did he use his little hands to push himself away from her as he was doing at the moment.

"Don't take it personally," her sitter, Jessie Orillon, said with a shrug. "He's been kind of crabby all day."

Jessie was only nineteen, but she was really great with J.D. and he adored her. If money were no object, Evangeline would have tried to get the girl to move in and be a full-time nanny to the baby, but apart from the financial issues, Jessie had her own ideas about her future. She only babysat to help put herself through school. On the days when she had class—Tuesdays and Thursdays—Evangeline drove the baby to her mother's house in Metairie.

If J.D. adored Jessie, he absolutely worshipped his nana, and he demonstrated his devotion, much to his grandmother's delight, by protesting at the top of his lungs each and every afternoon when Evangeline came to pick him up. He sometimes fussed when Jessie left for the day, too, but not as loudly. The only time he didn't carry on was when Evangeline left for work in the mornings.

She tried not to take that personally, either.

"He's drooling like crazy," Jessie told her. "I bet he's cutting a tooth." She pulled back her blond hair and fastened it into a high ponytail. Even after a day with a cranky baby, she looked lovely and fresh. Her crisp white shorts made her tanned legs look about a mile long.

Evangeline couldn't remember the last time she'd put on a pair of shorts, or the last time she'd bought anything as cute and flattering as the apricot top Jessie had on. Since Johnny's death, she hadn't paid much attention to her appearance, but lately her dismal wardrobe was starting to depress even her.

Jessie reached for her backpack as she slipped her feet into a pair of white flip-flops. "My grandmother says you should make a clove paste and rub it on his little gums. She swears that'll do the trick."

Evangeline shifted the baby to her other arm. "Good to know."

Of course, the advice would have been even more helpful if she actually knew what a clove paste was, but for some reason, she couldn't bring herself to ask. Her ignorance in the teething department was yet another way she felt totally incompetent as a mother.

Absently, she ran her finger along the baby's smooth cheek. His little face always amazed her. He looked so sweet and innocent and yet somehow wizened, as if that tiny body harbored an old soul.

And those eyes. Like bottomless pools.

His eyes were so much like Johnny's that sometimes Evangeline had to look away from him.

It was at those times that her son would grow very quiet, almost pensive it seemed to Evangeline, and she wondered if he could sense her despair. She'd read somewhere that babies were very intuitive and their keen instincts made them hyperaware of even the most subtle change in emotions or their environment.

She also wondered if he would one day hold all of this against her.

"What did you guys do today?" she asked as Jessie gathered up her iPod.

"We went to the park this afternoon. We had a good time, didn't we, J.D.? There was a squirrel that kept trying to steal my sandwich. It was pretty hysterical. Oh…I almost forgot." She pointed toward the dining room. "A package came while we were out. I put it on the table."

"Thanks."

Jessie swung her backpack over one shoulder. "So I'll see you guys on Wednesday, then."

"How're you getting home?" Evangeline asked as she walked Jessie to the door. "I didn't see your car out front."

"Yeah, my mom came by and got it this afternoon. Hers is in the shop."

"Do you need a lift?"

"It's not that far. I don't mind walking."

Evangeline glanced out the window. "It's getting pretty late."

Jessie laughed. "It's not *that* late. It's still daylight out."

"And this is still New Orleans."

"Hey, you're a cop. You should know you can't believe everything you hear on the news about the crime rate here."

Evangeline didn't point out that there was plenty of crime that didn't even get reported, let alone make the evening news.

Jessie cocked her head. "You okay? You seem a little stressed."

"I'm just tired. And I guess I am being a little too soccer momish. Sorry."

Jessie grinned. "It's nice to have someone worry about me once in a while."

Even though she lived only a few blocks over, Evangeline didn't know that much about Jessie's home life. She had the impression, though, that things between Jessie and her mother had been tense lately.

She also had a feeling it had something to do with a boyfriend, but Evangeline wasn't about to pry. She remembered all too well how hurt and angry she'd been by her father's disapproval of Johnny.

Besides, whatever the problems in her personal life, Jessie was a conscientious and caring sitter, and J.D. loved her. That was really all that mattered to Evangeline.

Jessie came over to drop a kiss on the top of the baby's head before she left, and he grabbed the necklace that dangled from her throat. It reminded Evangeline of the medallion that Sonny Betts wore. "Be a good boy for Mama, J.D. Let her get some rest tonight, okay?"

"That'd be a nice change."

"You ever want me to come over and stay while you take a nap or something, just call. I could always use the extra cash."

"I may take you up on that."

Evangeline carried the baby out to the porch and watched as Jessie ran down the steps. She waited until the girl was out of sight before she turned to go back inside.

Despite the baby clutter all over the place and J.D. fussing in her arms, the house seemed empty and quiet as she closed the door.

An image of Meredith Courtland came to her

suddenly, and Evangeline wondered if the woman felt all alone tonight in that great big house of hers. She had everything that money could buy, but her wealth wouldn't inoculate her from loneliness. It wouldn't spare her the despair that would set in as soon as she lay down to sleep.

Evangeline walked across the room to the windows that looked out on the tiny backyard. As she stared out at the deepening shadows, J.D. dropped his little head to her shoulder and gave a deep, troubled sigh.

"It's all right," she whispered. "I'm here."

But even as she held her son close, Evangeline's mind refused to shut down. Snippets of the day's conversations kept rolling around inside her head.

I don't want to end up like that dead cop.

There's not one shred of evidence linking Johnny to Paul Courtland or Sonny Betts. Not one shred.

You're grasping at straws, Evie.

Maybe she was. Maybe the reason she clung so hard to her obsession was because when she finally let it go, she would have to let Johnny slip away, too.

And Evangeline wasn't ready to say goodbye. She wasn't sure she ever would be.

After the baby was fed and bathed, Evangeline put him in his swing while she examined the box Jessie had left on the table.

The package had been sent via UPS by a local company she'd never heard of and the return address was a post office box rather than a physical address.

Being a cop and naturally cautious to boot, a strange package would normally have given her pause, but her mother had recently developed a mean shopping addiction, which, Evangeline suspected, was in retaliation for her father's perceived neglect.

In the past few months, Lynette Jennings had entered the world of home shopping networks with a vengeance—cubic zirconia jewelry being her favorite indulgence—and lately she'd also discovered the Internet.

To conceal her expensive obsession, she'd started having some of the packages shipped to Evangeline's house. Although Evangeline had long ago concluded that if her father were home as rarely as her mother let on, he probably wouldn't even notice all the deliveries anyway.

But that little contradiction didn't seem to faze her mother, who seemed to get a perverse pleasure from thinking that she could still pull the wool over her husband's eyes.

So Evangeline kept her observations to herself. The last thing she wanted to do was get caught in the middle of her parents' squabbling. She tried her best to stay neutral, but if everything her mother told her was true, she could only deduce that her sixty-year-old father had slowly but surely lost his mind.

But she was too tired to worry about all that tonight.

As she tidied up the living room, she started to place the box by the door so she'd remember to take it to her mother's the next morning. Then she changed her mind, and thought, what the heck? Her name was on the label so she might as well take a peek inside. A diversion would do her good, and besides, sometimes her mother actually did order things for her and the baby.

Removing the packing tape, Evangeline unfolded the flaps and removed a layer of bubble wrap. Nested inside sheets of pale blue tissue paper was a mobile made out of origami cranes. Each was done in a different color and pattern, but the shape and size were identical.

Lifting the mobile from the box, Evangeline carefully untangled the gold cords from which the paper cranes were suspended.

"See the pretty birds, J.D.?" She held them up so that her son would notice them.

There wasn't a card, but Evangeline knew the mobile had come from her mother. Who else would spend good money for a bunch of paper birds?

"That Nana. I'd hate to be the one paying her American Express bill these days. But that's not our problem, is it, J.D.?" Evangeline placed the mobile back in the box and got to her feet. "Let's go put this on your bed."

She laid the baby in the crib while she fastened the mobile to the rail. J.D.'s arms and legs flailed excitedly as she wound the music box. But once the melody started to play and the cranes took flight, he grew very still, almost as if the sound had a hypnotic effect on him.

The tune was something lovely and haunting, and it seemed familiar to Evangeline, but she couldn't place it. The soft tinkle was like a memory that flittered just out of her reach.

As soon as the mechanism wound down, J.D. started to fuss, so Evangeline turned the key a few more times.

The same thing happened when the music stopped.

He grew very agitated only to fall silent the moment the melody started up again. After five or six turns, his little eyes started to droop and finally he drifted off.

For the longest time, Evangeline stood beside the crib, watching her son sleep.

When will it happen? she wondered. *When will it finally seem as if he's really mine?*

She loved him, of course, but she'd never felt that overwhelming rush of emotion that new mothers were supposed to experience when they looked at their babies. J.D. still seemed like a tiny stranger to Evangeline, and more often than not, she felt completely out of her depth.

She did everything a mother was supposed to do for her child. She fed him, bathed him, walked the floor at night when he couldn't sleep. She even made time to cuddle. But it wasn't enough, and Evangeline knew there was something lacking in her.

The baby whimpered in his sleep as if even then he could pick up on her mood.

He was so sweet and so innocent and so totally at her mercy. The notion that she and she alone was responsible for his well-being overwhelmed Evangeline, and she'd never in her life felt so inadequate.

"I'm doing the best I can," she whispered.

Not good enough, said a voice inside her head. Johnny's voice.

He's our son, Evangeline. Why can't you love him the way he deserves to be loved?

It was a question she'd asked herself a million times since the rainy Tuesday night her baby had been born.

Turning out the light, she tiptoed from the nursery and headed for the kitchen, where she poured herself a glass of wine. Grabbing the baby monitor, she went outside to sit on the front stoop for a while.

With twilight came a cooling breeze from the gulf that stirred the banana trees and the night-blooming jasmine climbing up a neighbor's trellis.

This was the time of day, with the sky still glowing from the sunset and the air soft and perfumed, that Evangeline missed Johnny the most. At times like this, her loneliness seemed bone-deep and boundless.

Down the street, several cars were parked in front of a house blazing with lights. Music and laughter drifted through the open windows, and melancholy tightened like a fist around Evangeline's heart.

She wondered if they were celebrating an anniversary or a birthday, or if a casual get-together had blossomed into a full-blown party.

That was the way it used to happen at their place. Not this house, but the home she and Johnny had shared. Almost all of their parties had begun with a few friends dropping by. Then calls would be made, food and drink would be brought in. Before Evangeline knew it, their tiny house would be brimming with cops and the spouses of cops.

People who worked in law enforcement were an insular bunch, and as with any other group, there were those who fit in and those who didn't. Most of the cops Evangeline worked with had always viewed her as something of an odd duck, but once she and Johnny became a couple, they'd at least made an effort to accept her. If doubts lingered, it was shelved for Johnny's sake because everyone loved him.

But since his death, Evangeline was once again the odd man out. Not that she cared about a social life. Even growing up in the midst of a loving family, she'd always been a loner.

But Johnny was the opposite. He'd loved being surrounded by people.

Evangeline supposed his need for company came from being so alone as a child. His mother had abandoned him when he was a baby, leaving him to be raised by an aging grandmother who lived in the country. When she passed, he'd been shuffled through a series of foster homes until he was old enough to strike out on his own.

So, yeah, it was easy to understand why family and friends had meant so much to him.

Which made it all the more poignant that he'd died alone, in a deserted parking garage, crawling toward the exit.

Evangeline drew a shaky breath as memories of that night flooded through her.

Mitchell had come to the house to break the news to her. She'd been so stunned and distraught, she hadn't asked for many of the details that first night. It was only later that she'd found out Johnny had been shot three times.

According to the coroner, the first bullet had only maimed him. He'd tried to get away from his assailant, but the second shot to the heart had killed him. The third shot had hit him in the face and obliterated his appearance so that even a forensic dental exam had been useless.

"Evangeline? That you up there, hon?"

She'd been so engrossed in dark memories, she hadn't noticed her elderly neighbor approach the walkway in front of her house. The woman stood at the edge of the yard, peering through the falling dusk.

"You're out kind of late, aren't you, Miss Violet? Is everything okay?"

"I'm looking for Smokey. That blame cat got out again. You haven't seen him, have you?"

"No, but if I do, I'll grab him and bring him home."

"Thanks, hon. I'd be much obliged. Ornery ol' coot ain't worth much, but he's all I got. I'd hate to lose him."

"Try not to worry. I'll keep my eyes peeled," Evangeline promised.

She watched as Violet shuffled back across the street. The woman stood in the yard for a few minutes, calling loudly for her cat before she finally gave up and went inside.

The night fell silent, except for the occasional burst of laughter from down the street. A moth flitted past Evangeline's cheek, and as she swatted it away, she caught a movement off to the side of the porch.

She froze, trying not to react, but her heart thudded against her chest, and she suddenly wished she'd brought her gun outside with her. She, of all people, knew how dangerous the city had become, with roving gangs of thugs terrorizing neighbor-hoods that had once been considered safe havens.

As Evangeline searched the darkness, she thought about her son, all alone in the house. If someone were hiding in the shadows, it would be up to her to protect him.

She waited, breathless, but nothing happened.

After a few moments, she got up and went inside. Locking the door, she turned out the light and went straight for her weapon. Then she moved back to the front door and parted the curtain.

Nothing moved outside. Maybe it had been her imagination.

But for the longest time, Evangeline watched the darkness. She felt restless and uneasy, and she couldn't shake the notion that someone had been at the corner of the porch, watching her. That he might still be out there now, waiting for her to go to bed.

She left the window and headed for the nursery. She could see the glow of the night-light from down the hallway, and as she pushed open the door, her gaze went immediately to the crib, where she could see her son sleeping.

Nothing was out of place, so there was no reason to worry. No reason at all for the chill that slid up her spine as she stepped into the room or for the hammer of her heart as her gaze fastened on the baby.

He was lying just as she'd left him earlier, and yet...

Something was...not right.

Evangeline could feel it. It was as if the very air had been disturbed by…what?

Her breath came a little too fast as she reached for the light switch. The sudden brilliance caused her to blink and J.D. fretted in his sleep. Quickly, she moved to the side of the crib as her gaze darted around the room.

The space was furnished with only the baby's bed, a changing table and a rocking chair by the window. Evangeline could see the whole room in one glance, and she knew, without a doubt, that she and her son were alone.

So why was the hair at the back of her neck standing on end?

Why was she suddenly so uneasy in her own home?

She walked over to the window and parted the curtains to glance out. It was still early and she could see a light shining in the window of the house next door. But the fact that her neighbors were up and about did little to assuage her disquiet.

As she turned from the window, she saw something on the floor. She thought at first it was a piece of transparent paper that had fallen off the mobile or out of the box that it had been packed in. But when she stooped to pick it up, she jerked her hand back in revulsion.

It wasn't paper, she realized with a shiver.

It was a bit of molted snakeskin.

Eight

By the time Evangeline dropped the baby off at her mother's house the next morning, listened to the latest tirade about her father and fought rush-hour traffic back into the city, she felt as if she'd already put in a full day.

Waking up tired was getting to be an annoying habit with her, but she supposed it was the same with any new mother. This time, though, she couldn't blame her exhaustion on the baby. He'd slept soundly through most of the night, but even with the house so quiet, Evangeline had slept fitfully. Paul Courtland's grisly murder had mingled with that piece of molted snakeskin to create some very disturbing nightmares.

She was convinced the skin had fallen out of the box the mobile had come in or else she or Jessie had carried it inside on the bottom of a shoe. Just in case it had come from the crime scene, Evangeline had used tweezers to bag the skin, and then she'd put it in her purse to drop off at the lab.

With her heart in her throat, she'd gone through the house checking in cabinets and underneath furniture, although she didn't see how a snake could get inside. For all she knew, the skin could be an old one. The reptile that had shed it was probably long gone.

Still, the very thought of a snake lurking somewhere in her house gave her uncontrollable shivers, and before she'd left that morning, she'd arranged to have a professional exterminator come and search every square inch of the house, including the tiny attic. She'd left a key with her neighbor, who had promised to come over and supervise the search.

The fact that the skin had been in J.D.'s room made Evangeline all the more nervous. She was glad he would be spending the day with her mother in Metairie.

As soon as she got to the station, she went straight for coffee, but she barely had time to stir in a packet of sweetener before the captain called her and Mitchell in for a briefing. The Courtland homicide was shaping up to be a high-profile investigation, and that was exactly the kind of case that Angelette Lapierre liked to micromanage.

She was seated behind her desk reading the *Times-Picayune* when they entered her office. Motioning for them to take seats across from her, she held up the paper. "Either of you see this?"

"Not yet," Mitchell said as he settled into his chair. Like Evangeline, he'd carried in a cup of coffee, which he placed on the corner of Lapierre's desk. "What's going on?"

"Paul Courtland's murder made the front page. You two should be happy they got your names right."

"You hear that, Evie? We're famous. Think we can parlay our fifteen minutes into a book deal?"

"I'd rather you parlay it into an arrest," Lapierre said dryly. She was a gorgeous woman, the kind that generated controversy and gossip everywhere she went. But she wasn't exactly known for her sense of humor.

"Goes without saying," Mitchell muttered.

She gave him a withering look. "The murder of a wealthy white attorney puts a different face on the violence down here, so you better believe the media will milk it for all it's worth. And once they get wind of how Courtland died, they'll go ape-shit crazy. That's why I want to keep a lid on this thing until we know what we're dealing with. Don't go talking to reporters, either of you. Let me handle the press."

Evangeline resisted the urge to shoot Mitchell a knowing glance. "Fine by me."

"Yeah, me, too," he agreed.

Lapierre folded the paper and tossed it aside. "Where are we on the investigation?"

"I've located Courtland's loft in the Warehouse District," Mitchell said. "I'm meeting his landlady over there this morning."

"And I'm looking into the brother's death," Evangeline added. "No way can that be a coincidence."

"What about the wife?" Lapierre's gaze went from one to the other, giving them each a turn on the hot seat. "How do you like her as a suspect?"

"I don't think she had anything to do with it," Evangeline said. "Her shock seemed genuine to me, but I know we've all come across some pretty good actresses in our time."

Lapierre turned to Mitchell. "Hebert?"

"I agree with Evie. I think the brother's death pretty much puts the kibosh on the Widow Courtland as a suspect, but if we find out she and the brother were engaged in a little horizontal mambo, I reserve the right to change my mind. Likewise if we turn up a mistress at Courtland's loft."

"I think we need to lean a little harder on Sonny Betts," Evangeline said.

Lapierre sat back in her chair and studied her for a moment. Her eyes were dark and hooded. She couldn't seem to turn off her sensuality even when talking to another woman. "As soon as you open up that can of worms, you'll have feds crawling all over the place. Betts is their boy."

"Somebody's already opened it," Evangeline said. "I seriously doubt those guys just happened upon the crime scene yesterday morning."

"You think someone here tipped them off?"

Evangeline shrugged. "They found out somehow. And they were there for a reason."

"And you think that reason has something to do with Sonny Betts."

"It's worth looking into. Courtland was his attorney, although according to both Mrs. Courtland and Betts, the two parted ways after he was acquitted." She paused, then said, "From everything Mrs. Courtland said, it sounds as though the feds might have been leaning on Courtland pretty hard. If they convinced him to drop a dime on his client, that'd be a pretty good motive for murder."

"Mrs. Courtland also mentioned something about a dead cop," Mitchell offered. When Evangeline blasted him a warning glance, he barely shrugged.

"What about a dead cop?" Lapierre's tone sharpened.

"As in, Courtland said he didn't want to end up like that dead cop."

The captain's gaze lit on Evangeline and her attitude subtly shifted. "I see."

Damn you, Mitchell.

"Theroux?"

"Yeah, Captain?"

"You have anything more to add?"

"It would sure be helpful if we knew who those two agents were yesterday and what they're up to."

"I've got a contact or two in the federal building." Lapierre absently tapped a manicured nail on the desk, as if her mind were suddenly somewhere else. "I'll make a call, see what I can find out."

"What do you want us to do about Sonny Betts?"

"We need to be careful how we handle that situation so we don't step on any toes. And right now we don't have anything but a hunch tying him to Courtland's murder." She reached for her phone, indicating their meeting was over. "One more thing," she said as they stood and headed for the door.

They turned in unison.

"This whole thing leaves a real bad taste in my mouth. This isn't just murder. There's something dark going on here, and I don't much like where this case seems to be headed. I'll like it even less if somebody starts leaking to the press. You get me?"

They both indicated that they did.

"Then go find me the killer before somebody else turns up dead on my watch. And, Theroux?"

"Captain?"

"Don't make this personal. It's not about you and it's not about a dead cop. It's about finding Paul Courtland's killer. Understood?"

"Understood." Evangeline resisted the temptation to add *but what I do on my own time is my business.*

* * *

As it turned out, she had another chance to make that argument a little while later when Lapierre called her back into the office, this time alone.

"I'm taking you off the Courtland case," Lapierre said without preface.

Evangeline had not expected that. She stared at her superior in speechless outrage.

"Mitchell will take the lead. Turn over all your notes to him."

"Am I allowed to ask why?" Evangeline said through clenched teeth. She was furious, but she also knew losing her temper would do far more harm than good with Angelette Lapierre.

"I saw the way you looked when Mitchell brought up that conversation about a dead cop. You've already fixated on the notion that Johnny's death is somehow tied to Paul Courtland and Sonny Betts. Fixated, I might add, without a shred of evidence."

"That's not true," Evangeline protested. "I've done nothing but work this case by the book."

Lapierre gave her a cool appraisal. "That may be true at the moment, but I see the potential for conflict of interest and I'm nipping it in the bud before we have a compromised investigation."

Evangeline glared back at her. "What brought this on so suddenly? You weren't concerned this morning. Someone must have said something."

Lapierre folded her hands on the desk and leaned forward. "Actually, your behavior since Johnny's death has caused me concern for quite some time now. You're obsessed with finding his killer, so much so that you're in danger of losing your objectivity. And a detective with tunnel vision is no good to me or anyone else."

"So that's it."

"That's it for the Courtland investigation, but there's no shortage of misery in this city. You've got a shitload of other cases to work on. Do us both a favor and let this one go without a fight. There's no way you'll win it."

Wordlessly, Evangeline stood and started toward the door.

"Evangeline?"

She glanced over her shoulder. It was the first time the captain had ever addressed her by her first name.

"Contrary to what you may think, I like you. You've got the potential to be a damn good investigator. Don't do something stupid to derail a promising career before it ever gets traction."

"With all due respect, Captain…"

Lapierre lifted a brow, but her expression made it clear she didn't want to hear further argument.

Evangeline decided to let it go. You had to pick your battles and all that. "With all due respect, *I'm* the one who could have found Paul Courtland's killer for you."

"You'll get your chance on another case. In the meantime…I have a question for you. Ever cross paths with an FBI agent named Declan Nash?"

Evangeline thought for a moment, then shook her head.

"Never even heard the name?" Lapierre asked.

"Not that I remember. Why?"

Lapierre's expression turned pensive as she observed Evangeline from across the room. "He sure as hell seems to know a lot about you."

Nine

❧❧❧

As fleecy white clouds scuttled across the bright blue sky, temporarily blocking the sun, Lynette Jennings cast a wary eye heavenward. Despite the cloud coverage, the day was hot and humid, with only the barest hint of a breeze blowing in from the lake.

But a storm was headed their way.

Lynette could feel it in her bones.

She'd lived all her life on the Louisiana Gulf Coast, and even as a kid, she'd always been highly attuned to a sudden shift in weather patterns and wind direction, the slightest drop of barometric pressure. The atmospheric changes seemed to creep along her skin, giving her aches and pains in her joints and chilling her all the way down to her core.

A storm was brewing, all right. She could smell the rain already.

The wind shifted ever so slightly, and she thought

to herself that it was time for her and J.D. to make tracks. She'd taken him out for a stroll along the shady side of the sidewalk, and as she turned back toward the house, it seemed to Lynette that the edges of the low-hanging cumulus clouds had already begun to darken.

She stopped for a moment to adjust the top on the stroller. J.D. had fallen asleep, and as Lynette fiddled with the canopy, she paused to graze her finger along his soft cheek.

You sweet little thing. You're just the spitting image of your poor daddy.

But there was something of Evangeline in the beguiling curve of his lips, in the way his brow puckered when he got upset.

And those eyes.

So dark a blue, they were almost violet, and so deep, a body could easily drown in them.

Lynette had never seen a baby with such intense, knowing eyes.

He had quite the temper at times, too, but in sleep, he looked so vulnerable and innocent.

A precious little angel.

A shadow passed across the baby's face, and Lynette looked up, expecting to find that the sky had darkened even more. But instead, a man stood just behind her, gazing down at her sleeping grandchild.

His sudden appearance caught Lynette by surprise, and for a moment, she didn't even notice the terrible scar on the side of his face.

What she did notice, though, were his eyes.

Black as coal and focused on the baby.

Abruptly, she stood, putting herself between the man and the stroller. "Can I help you?"

His smile was oddly charming, considering his grotesque appearance, but with the black hair and dark clothes, he seemed too much like a manifestation of the coming storm.

He held up a pale hand, and Lynette couldn't help but notice how long and bony his fingers were. The gesture was graceful, but those skeletal fingers were creepy.

"Sorry. So sorry. I didn't mean to startle you. I'm trying to find a friend's house, and I've been driving in circles for the better part of an hour. I saw you out here with the baby and I thought...*hoped* you could help me find my way."

"What's the address?" Lynette said with a frown, although his deep voice was surprisingly pleasant. But she didn't like how silently he'd come up behind her. She also didn't like the way he kept glancing down at her sleeping grandson.

"Twelve-fourteen Sabine Way."

"I've never heard of that street. I think you must have the wrong neighborhood."

"Cypress Valley?"

"No, this is Cypress Grove."

"Ah. That explains why I can't find his house, then."

He moved to the side of the walkway so that he had a better view of J.D. Lynette fought the urge to once again step in front of the stroller.

He smiled then, as if he'd picked up on her trepidation, and that was when Lynette began to truly fear him.

There was something diabolical in that smile. Something evil lurking in those dark, dark eyes.

He inclined his head toward the stroller. "Yours?"

"My grandbaby. Now if you'll excuse me," she said coldly, "I have to get home. It's about to rain."

"So it is." His eyes trapped her again, and it was as if one of those skeletal fingers had traced an icy trail up her spine. "You can feel it, can't you? Something bad is coming this way."

Without answering, Lynette moved behind the stroller and gripped the handle tightly so that he wouldn't see the sudden tremble of her hands.

She wondered what she would do if he stepped in front of the stroller and barred her way. Her cell phone was in the diaper bag stowed on the rack beneath the seat. If he made a move toward her or the baby, she'd never be able to reach it in time.

But the only way he'd ever touch her grandchild was over her dead body. Somehow Lynette didn't think that obstacle would unduly concern him.

Two houses up, Peggy Ann Grainger came out her front door and headed down the walkway to check her mailbox. Lynette lifted a hand and called out to her. "Hey, there! Yoo-hoo! Peggy Ann!"

The woman looked up and around, and then waved back when she spotted Lynette. "Hey, Lynette! Long time no see."

"You enjoy your trip to Florida?" Lynette shot a wary glance at the stranger. He was staring down at her in amusement. It was all she could do to suppress a shudder.

"Sure did. Ate too much, though. What else is new?" To Lynette's relief, Peggy Ann started toward them. "That your grandbaby you got there with you?"

"Come see how much he's grown!"

The man continued to smile down at Lynette, but something shifted in his eyes. When he turned to glance at Peggy Ann, Lynette could have sworn she saw a flash of red near his pupils.

"Excuse me," she said again as she wheeled the stroller around him. "Good luck finding your friend's house."

She didn't look back until she met up with Peggy Ann on the sidewalk, and then she glanced over her shoulder as the other woman bent to admire the sleeping baby.

The man strode across the street where he climbed into an old black Cadillac Eldorado. After a moment, he started the engine and pulled away from the curb, and it was only then that Lynette glimpsed the passenger in the front seat.

A beautiful blond woman stared out the window as they drove by. Her gaze was fixed, not on Lynette or Peggy Ann, but on the stroller that carried the sleeping baby.

Ten

Nash was having a late breakfast in his favorite dive when he saw Evangeline Theroux walk in. He wanted to believe it was just one of those odd occurrences, but he knew better than to discount her investigative skills.

He dropped his gaze to the newspaper in front of him and didn't look up again until she stopped beside his booth.

Today she had on a gray suit with black shoes, and her badge was clipped to a leather messenger bag strapped across her slim torso. Her blond hair looked windblown, as if she'd been riding in a convertible, but he suspected she'd been running her fingers through it in agitation.

"Special Agent Nash?" She plopped down on the red vinyl bench without waiting for an invitation. "I'm Evangeline Theroux. But then…you already know who I am, don't you?"

His gaze moved over her in a curious sweep. The lashes that rimmed her blue eyes were coated with mascara, but she wore no other makeup, and beneath her tan, he could see a shower of freckles on her nose and across her cheekbones.

From a distance, the ill-fitting drab suit coupled with the blond ponytail and the plain shoes had given her the appearance of a kid playing dress-up, but now Nash noticed the tiny lines around her eyes. He knew from her file that she was thirty-three, and up close, she looked every year of her age and then some.

"What can I do for you, Detective Theroux?"

She smiled at the use of her title. "So you do know who I am."

He held up the *Times-Picayune*. "I was just reading about you in the paper."

"Now that's what I call synchronicity." She cocked her head, her expression benign, but he could see the glitter of anger in her electric blue eyes. "What I find really strange, though, is that you don't seem all that surprised to see me. Why is that?"

"I've been in this business for a long time. Nothing surprises me anymore."

"That whole jaded G-man shtick…" She waved a hand. "It's a little tired, don't you think?"

Her drawl was exaggerated, her tone openly goading. Nash was amused. He tossed aside the paper and picked up his coffee cup. "How did you know where to find me?"

"I heard you like to come here. Seems you're a creature of habit." She smiled at his expression. "Now you do look surprised. You federal boys aren't the only ones with the resources and know-how to track someone down, you know."

"Well, we do have a pretty good record," he said.

"Right. And how's that whole Jimmy Hoffa search coming along?"

"We're still pursuing leads," he said without cracking a smile. "We don't like to rush in impulsively and make a lot of mistakes."

She missed his subtle jab. Or ignored it. "If that's what passes for a sense of humor down at the federal building these days, I think you guys should seriously rethink having those sticks removed from your butts."

"Now that's funny," he said.

"Really? Because I was dead serious." She waved off an approaching waitress, then glanced at his empty cup. "Oh, did you want more coffee?"

"That's okay. One cup's my limit."

"The old Hoover Discipline, huh?"

Nash shoved the empty cup aside and sat back against the padded bench. "So now that you've found me, what is it I can do for you, Detective Theroux?"

"I'd like to ask you some questions, if you don't mind." *Or even if you do mind,* her eyes told him.

"Am I to consider this an official NOPD visit?"

"Official?" She threaded her fingers together and popped her knuckles. "Not hardly, considering I've been taken off the Courtland case. But then, I expect you already knew about that, too, didn't you?"

"What makes you think so?"

She cut her eyes to the ceiling as if considering the answer. "Oh, let's see, maybe because less than twenty-four hours after I spot you at a crime scene, I'm removed from the case for reasons that don't make a whole helluva lot of sense. And at the same time, my captain just happens to let your name drop. Call me paranoid, but I can't help wondering if there's a connection."

So much for Draiden's subtlety. "I think you must be laboring under a gross misapprehension, Detective. The FBI doesn't make a habit of meddling in the operation of local police departments."

"You don't make a habit of getting your hands dirty with plain old everyday murder, either, but there you were at my crime scene yesterday. Are you telling me that was a coincidence? You just happened to be in the neighborhood?"

When he said nothing, she smiled. "I'll take your lack of response as a no."

"All right," he finally said. "Let's just say, for the sake of argument, we currently have an ongoing situation that's eaten up a lot of manpower, resources and taxpayer money over the past couple of years. We wouldn't like it much if some clueless detective blundered in over her head and we had to risk the whole operation just to wade in and pull her out."

Temper flared in her eyes, but she managed to give him a sly smile. "For someone so clueless, I seem to have gotten your attention pretty fast."

"Clueless only in regard to our current situation. Goes without saying you're an intelligent detective with a reputation for being tenacious and thorough in your investigations. In fact, it's your tenacity that worries us the most. Obviously, in law enforcement, resolve and determination are admirable qualities, but in this case, an obstinate disposition could be a detriment to everyone involved."

"I like all those big words," she said. "A clueless bumpkin like me gets all tingly at anything over two syllables. But maybe, just so I can keep up, you could dial it back a notch and explain to me again how doing my job is such a bad thing."

"It's simple. Inadvertently stirring up a hornet's nest could get a lot of people killed. Yourself included."

"The hornet's nest being Sonny Betts?"

"He has a lot of fingers in a lot of pies these days, and a cop asking questions would be of less concern to him and his people than a speed bump. After all, you have to drive around a speed bump, but a nosy detective could just be made to go away. Is that blunt enough for you?"

"That's pretty blunt, all right."

"Good." He threw some bills on the table and stood. "Why don't we take a walk?"

Outside, a bank of low-lying clouds temporarily obscured the sun, dropping the temperature to the low nineties, and the breeze that blew off the river felt cool in the shade along Decatur. The doors to some of the souvenir shops were open and the scent of jasmine and frangipani drifted through, mingling with the less appealing aroma of the gutter.

As they neared Jackson Square, the carriages were already lined up along the curb, and the bored horses swished away flies and gnats with their tails as they watched the passersby with dark, liquid eyes.

Nash and Evangeline walked into the square and sat down on a bench near Pirates' Alley, where the sidewalk artists were busily setting up their paints and easels beneath striped umbrellas. The air here smelled old and damp, the timeless perfume of crumbling brick, stagnant fountains and creeping ivy.

"I've always liked coming here," Nash said. "It was one of the things I missed most about New Orleans when I lived in Washington."

She turned in surprise, as if his casual comment had caught her off guard. "What does that have to do with the price of tea in China?"

He shrugged. "Just making an observation."

She looked as if she didn't quite know what to make of him at that moment. A part of her wanted to demand they go back to their previous conversation, while another part cautioned she might learn something useful if she just sat back and let him do the talking.

He smiled to himself. He had no doubt Evangeline Theroux was a complicated woman, but in some respects, he could read her quite easily.

"What's with that shit-eating grin?" she asked suspiciously.

"Nothing. Like I said, I enjoy coming to the Quarter."

She settled back against the warm wrought-iron bench. "You must have been gone a long time. You've lost your accent."

That's not the only thing I've lost, he thought as he glanced at her profile.

She sat near him on the bench, her shoulder not quite touching his, but Nash could feel the warmth from her body. He found something strangely comforting about her nearness. Something softly reminiscent about the sound of her voice and the scent of lavender that drifted up from her hair. He recognized the feeling for what it was, of course—the first faint stirring of attraction.

And it seemed to Nash at that moment that her appeal was in keeping with the nostalgic tug of the Quarter. Detective Theroux and her drawl seemed very much a part of the New Orleans that had called out to him when he was away.

"A lot of people are afraid to come here these days," he said. "They consider it a haven for all sorts of deviants and miscreants. And they're right. You'll see all kinds in the Quarter. But the past is here, too. You can smell it in the air. History lingers on every street corner, along with the hustlers and the hookers and the burnt-out dopers."

"How poetic."

He smiled. "For all its decadence, the enduring spirit of the Quarter is actually what gives me the most hope for this city."

She was still looking at him strangely, not able to figure him out. "It's a nice thought," she said. "But I'm not so sure I agree. Sometimes I think our inability to let go of the past is our biggest problem. It keeps us tethered to incompetence and corruption. Why do you think the same crooked politicians get elected year after year? We don't much cotton to change down here."

"I don't know that New Orleans is so different from the rest of the country in that respect. I lived in Washington for a long time. I know firsthand about incompetence and corruption."

"How long have you been back?"

"A couple of years. I was like a lot of people who felt the need to get back here after the flood. Do whatever I could to help rebuild the city. But I also wanted to be near my daughter. So when a spot opened up in the field office, I put in for a transfer."

"Your daughter is here in New Orleans?"

"No, but she's close enough I can visit her on weekends."

She looked as if she wanted to ask more questions about that, but Nash headed her off before she had the chance. "How about you?" he said. "Have you always lived here?"

"Born and raised." She turned back to the square to watch the parade of tourists among the panhandlers and the street vendors. In spite of the breeze, he could see a thin sheen of sweat on her brow.

"Never thought about getting out?"

"It's funny you should ask that. My partner is considering a move to Houston to help run his uncle's security firm. He keeps telling me there'll be a place for me, too, if I want it. He thinks Houston would be a good place for me and my son to start over."

"And what do you think?"

"My son is only five months old. He doesn't care where we live."

"And you?"

She shrugged. "It's hotter than hell in Houston. If I move, it'll be to someplace where there's snow."

"You say that now. Just wait until you've had to shovel your driveway a few times."

"Some people might think shoveling your driveway pales in comparison to watching your house float away." The breeze loosened her ponytail and she reached up to tighten the band.

The sun came out from behind a cloud for a moment, and the square seemed to explode with color—pink and purple impatiens spilling over clay pots; orange flames of hibiscus licking at the narrow walkways; yellow roses tangling around the rusted pikes of an iron fence.

Behind the bench where they sat, palm fronds waved in the breeze, the sound like the rustle of an old silk skirt.

"Anyway, enough with the yammering," she said. "I don't know what any of this has to do with Paul Courtland's murder or why you feel my clueless blundering is such a threat to your operation. Surely, it's occurred to you the investigation will move forward with or without me."

"Not with—shall we say?—the same amount of zeal."

She gave him a cool appraisal. "I think you seriously underestimate the NOPD. Particularly, Mitchell Hebert. He's a thorough investigator, too. If he finds a lead that points him in the direction of Sonny Betts, that's where he'll go."

"We don't think that's where the leads will take him, though."

"Why not?"

"Because we don't think Sonny Betts had anything to do with Paul Courtland's murder."

"And you base this on…?"

"Simple logic. Courtland was his attorney. Why would Betts kill him?"

"I can think of at least one good reason. Maybe Betts found out Courtland was working for you guys."

Nash frowned. "Why would you think that?"

"Something his wife told us. Sounds like you were leaning on the poor chump pretty hard, and he was afraid he'd end up like some dead cop. You wouldn't know anything about that, either, I don't suppose."

"No, I don't."

He couldn't tell if she believed him or not. She looked like she wanted to call him out on it, but instead she took another tack.

"How did Betts find out about Courtland? Someone talked?"

"You're barking up the wrong tree, Detective. Betts had nothing to do with Courtland's murder."

"And I ask you again, how do you know this?"

He hesitated, wondering how much he would have to tell her to get her to back off. "A few days before he was last seen, Courtland was overheard expressing a concern that he was being followed. On several different occasions, he'd spotted a strange car parked outside his apartment and his office building, and a blond woman appeared to be tailing him once when he took his daughter to the movies. She later turned up at the same restaurant."

"Could she have been working for Betts?"

"Highly unlikely."

She turned to face him. "You say that so definitively. Like there's not much room for error."

"We don't think there is."

"Who overheard Courtland 'express' this concern of his? You?"

"Not me personally."

"Who, then?" When he didn't answer, she folded her arms. "You had him under electronic surveillance, didn't you? His phone was tapped. You guys really are Big Brother."

"The point is, there's a very high probability the person or persons who were following Courtland know something about his murder. If you find this blonde, you may just find his killer."

She remained silent for a moment, as if carefully digesting everything he'd told her. When her gaze finally met his, he could see the wheels turning and he knew, with a sinking feeling in his gut, that she was going to be trouble. And he was already wondering what more he would have to do to keep her in line.

"Why didn't you just tell us about this woman yesterday? Why pull strings to get me removed from the case?"

"Would you have listened? Or would you have dug in your heels?"

She frowned. "Don't presume you know me well

enough to predict my behavior in any given situation. And don't think this is over. You guys have gone and meddled in my life, and now I'm going to have to spend some time figuring out why."

A few moments later, Nash watched her weave her way through the square, heading for Decatur. For a moment, he considered going after her, maybe even asking her out to dinner. A little damage control might be in order because he was certain they hadn't heard the last of Detective Theroux.

Then common sense prevailed and he realized that was about the worst idea he'd had in years. The less time he spent with Johnny Theroux's widow, the better.

If he wanted a woman's company, all he had to do was make a phone call or two. Not that he had the proverbial black book full of numbers, but he'd never wanted for female companionship.

Since the breakup of his first marriage, Nash had crossed paths with any number of women who had sent interested signals. Sometimes he acted on those invitations; other times he ignored them. What he never did was mix business with pleasure. He was smarter than that, although he'd made his share of mistakes, especially in the months following the divorce.

Looking back now, his reckless behavior during that time puzzled him. It was out of character for him to take so many risks, and it sure as hell wasn't like him to fall for a beautiful, soulless woman with whom he had so little in common and about whom he knew next to nothing. Rushing into marriage was something a love-struck kid would do, not a grown man with a troubled daughter to look after.

Nash's second marriage had lasted all of six months. When he came home on that last night to find Sophia packing her bags, all he'd felt was relief. All he could think was *thank God it's over.*

A few months later, the marriage was nothing but a bad memory. A tear in the whole fabric of his stable, conservative life.

The one good thing to come from the brief union was the return of his common sense, and for that Nash was grateful. Ever since Sophia, he'd been a lot more careful. Temptations these days were few and far between, and that was the way he liked it. He was finally at a comfortable place in his life. He neither looked forward with anticipation nor back with regret. Instead he'd learned to take each moment as it came. He liked his job, he liked New Orleans and he liked living alone.

On the rare occasions when he allowed himself time to reflect, his thoughts more often turned to his daughter rather than to his two failed marriages.

Jamie was his real failure, but that was a door he couldn't afford to open too often and never while on the job. The guilt and anger, even after all these years, still had the power to overwhelm him. To creep up and steal his composure if he wasn't careful.

Luckily, Nash was an expert at keeping his professional life separate from his personal. That was one of the reasons his first wife had left him. That…and because she didn't want to deal with her own guilt. Better just to run away. Start over. Find someone who could give her what she wanted and needed. A new life, a new husband, a new family.

Nash wondered if Deb ever even thought of Jamie these days. All that social climbing probably kept her pretty busy.

Not that he had any room to cast such bitter stones. How long had it been since he'd driven to St. Gabriel to see Jamie? Hadn't that been his reason for transferring back to New Orleans? So he could spend more time with her?

He tore his thoughts from his beautiful, tormented daughter and concentrated instead on Evangeline Theroux. He told himself his preoccupation with the detective was necessary in order to determine the best way to handle what could still turn out to be a sticky situation.

Of course, he knew better.

The truth was, he liked thinking about her. He liked being with her, too. There was something sensual about the way she carried herself. Something earthy and elemental about his response to her.

Hidden underneath that tough veneer was a very appealing woman.

His phone rang and he hauled it out to check the caller ID. It was Tom Draiden.

"Yeah?"

"I just heard something that's going to give you a real tingle. Nathan Mallet's back in town."

Nash swore. "How reliable is the intel?"

"I'd say about ninety-nine-point-nine percent. What do you think brought him back?"

"He still has family in town. Could be he just got homesick."

"Should we pick him up?"

"Not yet. Let's cut him a little slack and see what he does with it."

Tom chuckled. "Careful, Nash. Your sadistic side is showing."

Nash ended the call as he hurried out of the square. He'd hoped Nathan Mallet was out of their hair for good, but he should have known better. Mallet had too many ties to New Orleans. Like a bad penny, he was bound to keep turning up, but the former cop still had plenty of secrets. It was those secrets that made him so controllable.

Besides, even if he did decide to renew old acquaintances, it wasn't too late to come up with a more permanent solution.

Evangeline Theroux was the real loose cannon here. If she began to put it all together, a two-year operation could easily explode in their faces because hell had no fury like a scorned woman.

But even now, Nash had a hard time reconciling the threat she constituted with her appearance. No doubt people underestimated her all the time, but that was a mistake he couldn't afford to make.

Eleven

⟳∽⟲

That afternoon, Evangeline met Mitchell for lunch at a little takeout joint on Magazine Street. They carried their trays to the picnic tables around back and sat down in the shade of a pistachio tree. Despite a brief rainstorm earlier, the heat was thick and oppressive, and Evangeline pressed an icy can of Dr Pepper to her cheek.

"You said on the phone you needed to talk to me about something," Mitchell said as he tucked into his fried oyster po'boy. It was dressed and messy, and the look on his face was pure rapture. "Mmm, mmm, *mmm.*"

"Good?"

"You know it." He took another bite. "So let's have it."

"Have you talked to Lapierre today?"

"Not since this morning. What's going on?"

"She took me off the Courtland case."

Mitchell continued to munch, but his eyes grew sober. "What happened?"

"She thinks I'm in danger of losing my objectivity."

"Really? That's what she said?"

Evangeline tore a piece of French bread from her sandwich and nibbled. "Go ahead."

"What?"

"Go ahead and say 'I told you so.' I know that's what you're thinking."

"Okay. I told you so." He went back to eating.

"That's it? No lecture? No gloating?"

His tone turned reproachful. "Now, Evie, when have you ever known me to gloat?"

That was true. Mitchell wasn't the type to revel in other people's misery or mistakes, but still, considering their conversation the day before, Evangeline thought he was letting her off the hook a little too easily. "This is the curious part, Mitchell. In spite of what Lapierre said, I got the distinct impression that wasn't the real reason. I think the feds are pulling some strings on this case."

"Why? What'd she tell you?"

"It wasn't so much what she said. More the way she let a name drop. Declan Nash. It was like she was letting me know he was behind it without letting me know. So I paid him a little visit."

Mitchell shook his head. "Why am I not surprised? How'd you manage to track him down so fast?"

"I've got my ways."

"As in…"

She grinned. "As in my neighbor's granddaughter works at the federal building. She helped me out."

"She did, huh?" Mitchell wiped sauce piquant from his chin with a paper napkin. "Well, were we right? Does all this have something to do with Sonny Betts?"

Too late, Evangeline realized that to recount the whole conversation with Declan Nash would be to imply the FBI didn't regard Mitchell's detective skills at the same level with which they viewed hers. Not that she'd bought most of that crap anyway.

She skirted the issue as best she could while giving him the lowdown on the rest of her conversation with Nash. While she talked, Mitchell listened silently as he wolfed down his food, and when she finished, he got up without comment and went back inside to order another beer.

Evangeline ate as much as she could of her sandwich, then wrapped it back up and threw away their trash. A coffee can of begonias sat on the table, and while she waited for Mitchell, she idly plucked off the dead flowers.

It was nice outside. The street traffic was muted by the banana trees and crepe myrtles, and the scent of the plumeria blossoms made Evangeline think of an island oasis. She picked a bloom from one of the thick stalks and held it to her nose.

Mitchell sat down across from her and handed her another drink. "Here. Don't say I never gave you anything."

"I'll be running to the bathroom every fifteen minutes if I drink another soda," she complained, but she took a long, thirsty sip anyway.

"So let's talk about this blond woman for a minute," Mitchell said. "You think there's anything to it?"

"Honestly? I have no idea. It's pretty obvious the feds want to keep us away from Betts. For all I know, this whole thing about Courtland being followed is just some bullshit diversion." She toyed with the straw in her drink. "Does this jibe with anything Courtland's neighbors told you?"

"No, but now that I've got something specific, I'll have another go at them. Your buddy Nash didn't happen to say what kind of car Courtland saw, did he?"

"Conveniently, no. But that could be because Courtland didn't mention it in the overheard conversation."

"Maybe his wife put a P.I. on his tail. She seemed pretty bitter about the breakup."

"Yeah, she did. And that would explain why he thought he was being followed. But what it doesn't explain is how his brother's death ties into all this. I still say Sonny Betts has to be the key." She paused when she saw Mitchell's look. "What? Am I getting fixated again?"

"Maybe just a tad."

"And none of this is my business anyway, right? Not my case, not my headache."

"You okay with that?"

"I don't have much of a choice, do I? Let's just drop it for now. Talk about something else."

"Okay, then, speaking of diversions…I've got a trip planned for weekend after next," Mitchell said. "I thought you and J.D. might like to come along for the ride."

"Where are you going?"

"Houston."

"You want to make a six-hour drive with a five-month-old baby?" Evangeline asked incredulously. "You're crazy. You'd be tearing your hair out. What's left of it, anyway."

He ignored the hair comment. "You forget I helped raise four girls. When we used to go on vacation, the squabbling from the backseat was epic. Not to mention all the potty breaks. Took us nearly twenty hours to drive to Orlando one summer. Compared to that, a five-month-old is a piece of cake. Besides, a change of scenery might do you both some good."

"What about Lorraine?"

"What about her?"

"Doesn't she want to go?"

"Nope."

Evangeline lifted a brow. "Weekend after next or ever?"

"I didn't ask for clarification."

"Don't you think you should? Assuming your aim is to talk to your uncle about that job." Evangeline's tone was mildly scolding.

Mitchell picked up his beer and took a long swallow. When he set the bottle back down, an uncharacteristic defiance gleamed in his eyes. "Lorraine's mind is all made up, and that's all well and good. More power to her. But why should I let her make up mine for me?"

"Because you're married? Because you're the one talking about uprooting the family to move to another state?"

"Uprooting what family? It's just me and her. The girls are scattered to the four corners."

"You know what I mean."

"Yeah, I know." He gave her a look that was almost apologetic. "Look, I hear what you're saying, Evie, but this is something I need to do. I'm not saying it's a done deal or anything close, but I'm sure as hell going to consider it. I've been married for nearly thirty years, a cop for twenty. Maybe I need a change of scenery, too."

She swallowed her protest and nodded. "Okay."

He nodded back. "Okay."

"Here," he said, tossing a five-dollar bill on the table. "How about picking us up some pralines for the road while I hit the can?"

After Evangeline bought the candy, she went outside to wait for Mitchell. Standing in the shade of the awning, she searched through the steady flow of traffic for a dark gray sedan even though she told herself she was probably just being paranoid. It seemed the FBI—or more specifically, Declan Nash—had easier ways to keep tabs her.

But when her phone rang, she kept her eyes on the street as she fished it out of her bag.

"Theroux," she said.

"Detective Evangeline Theroux?"

"Speaking."

"My name is Lena Saunders," a feminine voice drawled. "You don't know me, but I'm calling about the murder of that lawyer…Paul Courtland. I read about it in the paper this morning. I also saw your name mentioned."

"What can I do for you?" Evangeline wondered how the woman had gotten her cell phone number and why her name sounded vaguely familiar.

"It's what I can do for you, Detective Theroux. I think I can help you find Paul Courtland's killer."

"I'm listening," Evangeline said, though she refused to get too excited. Phone calls like this were a dime a dozen, especially in high-profile cases.

The publicity brought the crackpots out of the woodwork.

"I'd rather not get into it over the phone," Lena Saunders said. Her voice was soft and cultured. It reminded Evangeline of Meredith Courtland's. "Could we meet in person?"

"That's a bit of a problem for me. I'm no longer working that case. You'll need to talk to Detective Hebert or Captain Lapierre…." Evangeline trailed off when she realized she was talking to a dead phone.

"What's going on?" Mitchell asked as he came around the corner.

"Does the name Lena Saunders ring a bell for you?"

"Can't say that it does. Why?"

"She claims she can help us find Courtland's killer. When I tried to give her your name and number, she hung up."

He grinned as he shifted the toothpick in his mouth to the other side. "Obviously a crank if she didn't want to talk to me."

"Yeah, that's what I thought, too, but she didn't sound like the typical nut-job. I can't say why, exactly, but I think I know her. Her voice sounded kind of familiar."

"Maybe she'll call back, then."

"Yeah, maybe."

"Oh, say, I almost forgot to tell you. Lorraine

talked to Nathan's sister last night. She said he's driving up here sometime today."

"Did she happen to say where he'll be staying?"

"No, but it seems there's a place he always visits when he comes to town. I don't think you're going to like it, though." He took the toothpick out of his mouth and flicked it toward a nearby trash can.

"What is it, a strip joint?"

"It's a cemetery. Mount Olive."

"But that's where—"

"Yeah, I know. It's also where his first wife was laid to rest."

A shiver prickled along Evangeline's spine. She hadn't been out to Mount Olive since the day of Johnny's funeral. Somehow she just couldn't bring herself to visit his vault. Seeing his name engraved in the plaque would make his death all too real and all too final.

"I hear anything else, I'll let you know."

"Thanks, Mitchell."

"You bet." Giving her a little salute, he turned and disappeared down the street.

Evangeline stood in the shade for a moment as a feeling of being watched came over her. Instead of glancing around, though, she closed her eyes.

Her husband's presence was so strong at that moment, he might have been standing on the sidewalk beside her.

The breeze picked up a strand of her hair and

lifted it up off her neck. But Evangeline told herself the touch of ghostly lips against her skin was probably nothing more than her imagination.

Twelve

⸻❦⸻

Late that same afternoon, Lynette was in the kitchen rolling out pie dough when she experienced a strange feeling that something was wrong in the house.

She couldn't put her finger on the trouble. It was nothing concrete. No rhyme or reason for it. She hadn't heard a noise or seen movement out of the corner of her eye. Nothing like that at all.

It was more the sixth-sense type of sensation she got about the weather, although those premonitions were also rooted in science.

This feeling was just plain weird.

She tried to ignore it, but the impression grew so strong, she dreaded looking over her shoulder for fear of what she would see in the doorway.

She turned anyway, and of course, nothing was behind her.

J.D. was in his high chair at the table, banging a wooden block against the plastic tray. He seemed oblivious to whatever had raised his grandmother's hackles.

Drying her hands on her apron, Lynette walked calmly to the back door and checked the lock. Then grabbing the rolling pin, she marched through the house to the front door and checked that lock, too. Naturally both doors were secured. She'd always been cautious about that sort of thing, but especially since Katrina.

Moving over to the window, she looked out on the street. After a brief rainstorm earlier, the sun was back out, but Lynette wondered if another front might be brewing over the gulf. Maybe that was why she felt so uneasy.

She spotted Peggy Ann Grainger across the street sitting on Janet Tilson's front porch steps. The two women were having drinks, and she saw Peggy Ann gesture toward Lynette's house with her glass. At first, Lynette thought Peggy Ann was waving at her, but then she realized that the woman wasn't even looking her way.

They were probably talking about her, Lynette thought peevishly. For all she knew, her marital problems were already fodder for the neighborhood gossips, Janet being one of the biggest motormouths on the block. Her son, Ronnie, worked at the auto parts warehouse that Lynette's husband owned, and God only knew what Don might have let slip.

At the thought of her husband, a wave of rage washed over Lynette. How dare he treat her like this? After she'd given him the best years of her life. She knew that sentiment was a cliché, but in her case it was true! She had done *everything* for that man. Good God, the sacrifices she'd made, and for what? To suddenly be cast aside like an old coat when she was no longer needed or wanted?

Even when Don was home—which was rare enough these days—it was as if…he didn't even see her. And that was the worst insult of all. To look at her and not see her. He sat across from her at the dinner table and made small talk just as they had for years. Sometimes they even watched television together afterward. But something had changed. *He'd* changed.

Lynette didn't even know him anymore and that seemed to her like the worst betrayal of all. He'd changed while she'd stayed the same. He'd moved on while she remained embedded in their old way of life. How unfair was that? Here he'd gone and turned everything upside-down, and she hadn't even had a say in it. Yet she was just supposed to accept whatever he dished out without a squabble.

Across the street, the two women were still chatting up a storm, and as Lynette backed away from the window so they wouldn't see her, she saw an old black Cadillac parked at the curb a few houses down. A Cadillac exactly like the one the stranger had driven away in earlier.

From this distance, Lynette couldn't tell if anyone was inside, but she still got uneasy just looking at it. She didn't like the idea of that weirdo lurking around the neighborhood. Why had he come back? If he'd truly been looking for his friend, he should have been long gone by now.

But that was the same car. Lynette was sure of it.

And with that certainty, the premonition of danger swooped down on her again. She gave a little gasp of panic as she turned and rushed back to the kitchen.

The baby was still playing in his high chair, but when Lynette came bursting through the door, the noise startled him and he began to cry. She went over and picked him up, cradling him against her bosom.

"It's all right, Boo. Nana's here."

She held him close until he quieted and then she reached for the phone. "Let's give your granddad a call, what do you say? See if we can get him to come home early today."

Maybe she was overreacting, but seeing that car parked at the curb, along with her earlier premonition, had left her shaken. She didn't have grounds for calling the police, though, and besides, she didn't want to worry Evangeline. Don could just get his ass on home for a change and take a look around the neighborhood himself.

She was facing the glass slider to the patio, and as she punched in the number, she saw what she thought was a tree branch on the brick pavers. When she realized what it really was, she stifled a scream so as not to scare the baby again.

Lynette saw snakes all the time when she gardened. The garters didn't particularly bother her, but the snake on her patio now was at least six feet long and as thick as a man's arm. She was pretty sure it was a water moccasin and big enough that she wasn't about to go out there and try to kill the thing by herself.

"Jennings Auto Parts," said a feminine voice on the other end of the phone.

Lynette had been so fascinated by the snake, she'd forgotten she had the phone to her ear.

The woman who answered was Don's new secretary. *New* being a relative term. She'd been there for several months, but compared to Adele, her predecessor, who had worked for Don for nearly thirty years, Deanne Hendrix was still a novice.

Though you couldn't tell that by her attitude.

The woman grated on Lynette's nerves something fierce.

"This is Lynette. I need to talk to Don."

There was a slight hesitation on the other end. "I'm sorry, Mrs. Jennings, but he's out in the warehouse right now. May I take a message?"

"Last time I checked, there was a phone in the warehouse. Can't you transfer my call out there?"

"It would be easier if I just took a message. That way he can call you back whenever he has a free minute."

"Now, look," Lynette said testily, "I need to talk to my husband and I need to talk to him *right now*. You get him on the line. I don't care if you have to carry the phone out to the warehouse yourself."

"Hold, please," the woman said coolly.

Snotty-ass bitch.

It was times like this that Lynette really missed Adele. The older woman had her faults, but she'd also had the good sense and the gracious manners not to try and make the boss's wife jump through hoops every time she called the office.

Lynette kept her eye on the snake while she waited for Don to pick up. As far as she could tell, it hadn't moved so much as an inch. Maybe it wasn't even alive, but who in the world would put a dead snake on her patio?

"Lynette? What's going on? Deanne said you sounded upset about something."

"I am upset and I need you to come home."

"What's wrong?"

"Come home and I'll tell you."

He gave a frustrated sigh. "I can't just leave work. We've still got a lot of orders to get out."

"Even if your grandbaby's in danger?"

That stopped him cold. "What are you talking about? What's happened to J.D.?"

"Nothing yet. But there's something strange going on around here, and I need you to come home and help out." Quickly, she told him about her unsettling encounter earlier with the scarred man, the car she'd spotted down the street a little while ago and the snake that was still stretched across the back patio.

"Lynette, for God's sakes, you've seen snakes before. They were all over the place after Katrina. If you're that worried about it, just don't take the baby outside."

"And what about that strange man?" she demanded. "What if he tries to break in?"

"He's not going to try and break in. Not in broad daylight. He was probably lost, just like he said."

"But what if he wasn't? What if something happens to me or the baby? How are you going to like having that on your conscience?"

"Come on, Lynette."

"No, *you* come on. If you cared a whit about either one of us, you'd already be on your way home. Just forget it. I'll call Vaughn. Or Evangeline. Although you know how she feels about snakes."

"All right, all right. Jesus. I'll get away as soon as I can."

"How soon?"

"It'll take me a few minutes to wrap things up here. Is that soon enough for you?"

"I guess it'll have to be, won't it?" Lynette grumbled. She hung up and walked over to the window with the baby. She peered around the edge of the slider until she could see the snake's head and she caught sight of the flicking tongue. Definitely not dead.

Then she saw now what she hadn't noticed before. There were two of them. The second snake was coiled at the edge of the patio, head lifted, tail quivering as if ready to strike.

Heart hammering, Lynette backed away from the glass. Two snakes on her patio. What were the chances of that?

Don took his time clearing off his desk. In spite of Lynette's call, he was in no hurry to get home. It was obvious she was trying to manipulate him and he refused to rise to the bait. If she hadn't dragged his grandson into the conversation, he would have told her flat out he wouldn't come home until he was damn good and ready.

Well, maybe he would have couched it a little more diplomatically than that, but still, Lynette's behavior was getting tiresome. After forty years, Don had had enough.

Forty years of marriage and only the first five had been good. It was a wonder he'd stuck it out for as long as he had.

But for a time there, right after Vaughn's birth, life had seemed pretty damn great. Lynette had been so beautiful back then, so sweet and flirty, and she'd devoted herself to being the kind of wife and mother any man would be proud to call his.

But then a string of miscarriages had plunged the woman Don had married into a black abyss of despair, disappointment and bitterness. Even after Evangeline came along, Lynette had never fully recovered. It was like a part of her had withered and died with each lost pregnancy.

After a time, she'd learned to put up a good front. Sometimes everything would seem so normal that Don would be fooled into thinking his old Lynette had finally found her way back to him. But then he'd look into her eyes and realize all over again that the woman he'd married was gone forever.

To be fair, much of their life together hadn't been as bleak as he now made it out to be when he looked back. Lynette had always kept herself fit and attractive, and he'd always been proud to be seen with her. Their home was immaculate, their children well-cared for, and she had never denied him in bed. Things could have been worse.

But things could also be a whole lot better as Don had recently discovered.

He glanced out the glass partition that divided his office from the reception area. Deanne sat in front of the computer, her brow furrowed as she concentrated on her work. Her dark hair fell like a curtain across her smooth cheek, and she unconsciously lifted a hand to tuck it behind her ear.

With his eyes, Don traced the contour of her jawline, the graceful curve of her neck, the sensuous mounds of her breasts beneath the light blue blouse she wore. For a moment, he imagined himself undoing the pearl buttons, slipping the silky fabric over her shoulders and down her arms, planting his lips on one of her dusky nipples as she moaned softly into the darkness.

Jesus.

He took no small measure of delight in the stirring of his body as he watched her. What a kick it had been to find out that he could still pleasure a woman like Deanne. That even at his age, he still had a few good miles left in him.

But guilt punched a hole in his happiness, and his newly found swagger deflated like a pinpricked balloon.

He didn't know what he was going to do about Lynette.

Don hadn't set out to hurt her. She was still his wife, the mother of his grown children, and he would always care about her. But he was sick and tired of the pretense. Maybe if Deanne hadn't come along, he could have muddled through the rest of his life without thinking too much about what he was missing. But now he didn't see how he could ever go back.

Shoving some paperwork aside, he got up and walked out to Deanne's desk. She looked up with a ready smile, the same one she had for everyone, but there was a little knowing glitter in her eyes that she reserved just for Don.

How had he gotten so damn lucky?

"Hey," she said softly.

"Hey." He could see just the barest hint of cleavage from where he stood. Deanne was a curvaceous woman, and even the conservative clothes she wore couldn't disguise the lush body beneath. Lynette was thinner and firmer and a much better dresser, but there was something so…earthy and maternal about Deanne's softness.

"Is everything okay at home? Lynette sounded pretty upset."

"I don't know. I need to drive out there and see what's going on."

"Of course. If there's anything I can do…" She slid her hand over his and squeezed.

Don waited a moment, then slipped his hand away. They'd been careful to keep their relationship private. He didn't want word to get out until he'd had a chance to talk to Lynette.

Coward, a little voice in the back of his head goaded him.

He'd had plenty of chances to talk to his wife. It wasn't like it would come as a total shock or anything. Lynette had to know things weren't right between them. It might even come as a relief.

Of course, Evangeline wouldn't take the news well. Not that it was any of her business. He'd had reservations about her marriage to Johnny, but she hadn't been of a mind to listen so now she could just damn well sit back and bite her tongue the way he'd had to do for so long.

Vaughn would be okay. He was a lot less judgmental than his sister. He might not be thrilled by the news, but at least he'd be supportive.

"I don't know how long this will take. I might not make it back in time to have dinner with you," he warned.

A little frown puckered Deanne's brow as she pouted her full lips. "I'll miss you."

"I'll miss you, too."

Her voice lowered and her eyes deepened. "What about…later?"

"I'll get away if I can. You know that."

"Don?"

He'd started toward the door, but now he turned back. "Yes?"

She glanced around as if making sure they were all alone. "Come back to me," she whispered.

His heart melted and he nodded.

He thought about Deanne all the way home, and it was only when he pulled into his driveway that his conscience started to act up again.

What was he doing? What the *hell* was he doing?

Men his age didn't have affairs. This was just crazy. Men his age gardened and golfed and took fishing trips with their buddies.

Men like him didn't cheat on their wives or turn their backs on a forty-year marriage. They didn't attract the attention and the affection of a woman almost half their age.

Except…miracle of miracles, he had.

And as he sat in his car and stared at the one-story ranch he and Lynette had shared for nearly as long as they'd been married, it hit him suddenly that this house was no longer his home. He didn't belong here anymore.

The only place he felt truly at peace was in Deanne's soft, warm embrace.

He was so preoccupied with getting back there, he didn't even notice the blond woman who watched the house from across the street.

Thirteen

❧❧❧

Evangeline was driving back from the lab late that afternoon when she got a call from Lapierre. As usual, the captain got right to the point.

"Did you hear from a woman named Lena Saunders today?"

"Yeah, I did," Evangeline said. "She called you, too?"

"A little while ago. What did she tell you?"

"She said she had information that might help catch Paul Courtland's killer and she wanted to meet in person to talk about it. I told her I was no longer working that case. When I tried to redirect her to Mitchell, she hung up. I figured she was just some crackpot having a little fun."

"She's not a crackpot," Lapierre said. "At least, not the kind that we usually hear from on investigations of this nature."

"Who is she, then?"

"She's a writer."

"You mean like a reporter?"

"No, she writes books about true crime, mostly sensational murder cases in Louisiana. Turns out she's published several books over the past ten years or so."

"So she's working on a book about the Courtland case already?" Evangeline's tone was skeptical.

"I don't know about that," Lapierre said. "All I know is that she dropped some pretty big names during our phone conversation. By the sound of it, she's cultivated an impressive roster of sources in local law enforcement, including an NOPD deputy chief."

"Which one?"

"Doesn't matter. What does matter is that the woman is well-connected."

"Okay. So she's well-connected." Evangeline was puzzled by the phone call. Why was Lapierre telling her all this? "Is she coming in to give a statement?"

"She claims she suffers from a mild form of agoraphobia. According to her, she's prone to panic attacks anytime she leaves her house. So I'm sending someone to her place in the morning to hear what she has to say."

"If you don't mind my asking, why are you telling me about her?" Evangeline said. "I'm off the case, remember?"

"Oh, I remember all right. But Lena Saunders is refusing to talk to anyone but you, Theroux."

"*Me?* Why? I don't even know her."

"She says she knew Johnny."

Evangeline was stunned into momentary silence. Her heart started to pound as she clutched her cell phone. "How?"

"Evidently, he was one of her NOPD contacts."

"On which case?"

"She didn't say."

Even though the name had sounded familiar to Evangeline earlier, she was almost certain she hadn't heard about Lena Saunders from Johnny. She would have remembered. And yet if he really had been one of the woman's contacts, why hadn't he mentioned her? He surely would have brought it up if he had talked with a writer.

"I still don't understand why she wants to see me."

"You can ask her yourself tomorrow," Lapierre said.

"Does this mean I'm back on the case?"

"Nice try, but this is a one-time-only situation. The woman claims to know something about the Courtland murder case and we need to know what that something is. And since she has some influential friends up the food chain, I'm inclined to accommodate her just this once. The last thing I want is a deputy chief breathing down my neck."

Lapierre's voice lowered conspiratorially. "Look,

Theroux. I can't tell you what to expect when you go over there in the morning, but just watch yourself, okay? This woman may not be the kind of tinfoil-hat whacko we're used to dealing with, but if you ask me, she sounds like a real kook. This could be nothing more than a figment of her imagination, but we've got to hear her out anyway. When you leave her place, you come straight back to the station and see me. Don't talk to anyone else about this, not even Hebert. You got me?"

"Yes, ma'am," Evangeline said, resisting the urge to gloat. The unintended consequence of Lena Saunders's request was that now Evangeline had more leverage than she'd had ten minutes ago. Not much more maybe, but if she played her cards right, she might just persuade Lapierre to put her back on the case.

"Where and when do I meet her?" she asked.

"Nine o'clock tomorrow morning at her house." She gave Evangeline the Garden District address, then hung up.

A few minutes later, Mitchell called. "Thought you'd like to know, I just heard from Lorraine. She was over at Linda's house when Nathan called. Sounds like he's on his way to the cemetery. If you hurry, you can probably still catch him."

"Hey, thanks for the heads-up."

"No problem. You want me to meet you over there?"

"I'm only ten minutes away. He'd probably be gone by the time you could get there."

"Yeah, you're probably right about that. Traffic's a bitch today. Anything else going on I should know about?"

Evangeline hated keeping things from Mitchell, but she also knew better than to get on Lapierre's bad side. "Same old, same old," she muttered.

They chatted for a few more minutes, and then she called her mother to warn her she'd be late picking up J.D.

It wasn't until she'd hung up that Evangeline remembered she'd yet to thank her mother for the mobile.

The sun was just setting when Evangeline pulled her car to the curb near the cemetery gates. Killing the engine, she watched as a tour guide shepherded a group of tourists to a waiting bus.

That's good, she thought. *Get them all out of there before dark.*

Although popular destinations for tourists, New Orleans cemeteries were extremely dangerous at night. Common sense dictated that the narrow paths between the rows of vaults and tombs could effectively conceal a mugger, and yet every year people fell prey to vicious assaults, especially in the old cemeteries near the Quarter.

Before she climbed out of the car, Evangeline slid

her gun into the back pouch of her bag. Then she slipped the strap over her shoulder and across her body for easy access. As she walked across the street, she stayed alert for any untoward movement.

And for Nathan Mallet.

She'd already spotted his red Mustang across the street. The 1967 classic stood out among the SUVs and minivans of the tourists, and Evangeline remembered how much Johnny had always coveted that car.

But to her eyes, the Mustang looked worse for the wear since the last time she'd seen it, and she wondered again what Nathan had been up to since Johnny's shooting. Why he had felt the need to leave town so quickly.

Several people still milled about inside the brick walls even though the sun was already setting. By New Orleans standards, Mount Olive was relatively new, but it had many of the same characteristics as the older cemeteries. The rusty iron gates opened into an eerie necropolis of sun-bleached tombs and contrasting shadows cast by the crosses and statues.

If she had come to visit Johnny's vault, Evangeline would need to turn right inside the gates, but that wasn't why she was here. Her plan was to ambush Nathan on his way out.

But after a moment, she found herself threading through the ornate tombs and mausoleums to the row of vaults at the back of the cemetery.

Someone had placed fresh flowers and a votive

candle in front of Johnny's marker, and Evangeline wondered uneasily who had been visiting here while she'd been estranged.

She touched the bronze plaque, still warm from the day's heat, but she felt no connection to her husband's remains. It was strange, but here, where his body had been laid to rest, Evangeline couldn't feel his presence at all.

The sun dipped below the treetops and the promise of twilight settled over the vault. But she knew it wasn't a sign or a message from Johnny. Not this time. It was just the end of another day without him.

Turning to leave, Evangeline noticed a man coming toward her on the path. He was tall and thin with a pale, emaciated face that was badly scarred on one side. He was dressed all in black and his hair gleamed like India ink.

As he came closer, Evangeline could see that his lips were moving, and she thought at first he was speaking to her. Then she realized that he must be talking to himself.

An icy awareness slid down her neck. She wanted to look away, but there was something oddly compelling about the strange man. She was intrigued by the scar on his face, by the pallid gauntness of his features.

But what held her enthralled were his eyes. They were as black as night, and yet they seemed to burn with an inner fire that chilled her to the bone.

His disturbing gaze was still on her when he drew even with Johnny's tomb. He said something aloud, which Evangeline didn't understand.

"Excuse me?"

He kept on walking, cutting her a sideways glance as he went by.

When he was all the way to the end of the row, he looked over his shoulder. He said something else, and this time Evangeline could have sworn he mouthed her name.

She started toward him, but by the time she got to the end of the vaults, he'd disappeared behind a large mausoleum.

Slipping her hand into her bag, Evangeline closed her fingers around the handle of her weapon. Wary of a trap, she gave the mausoleum a wide birth as she circled around to the front.

The man was nowhere to be seen.

Light from the fading sun sparked off the crypt's stained-glass windows and a cross on the top cast a long shadow across the eerie landscape.

Something had fallen to the grass on the path in front of her, and as Evangeline drew closer, she saw that it was an origami crane.

She thought instantly of the mobile on her son's crib, and she had the strangest feeling that the dark-haired man had dropped it there for her to find. But why? She didn't even know who he was.

Searching the path ahead of her, she caught a

glimpse of him again. He was looking over his shoulder, smiling at her in a way that made her heart pound in trepidation. Who the hell was this joker and what did he want with her?

Evangeline started after him again, but he was adept at using the maze of crypts and vaults to conceal himself. She followed him for several minutes, catching enough quick glimpses to lead her back to the gates. But when she emerged onto the street, he was nowhere to be found.

Completely unsettled by the odd chase, Evangeline crossed the street and waited beside the red Mustang for Nathan Mallet. She kept an eye out for the scarred stranger, but he didn't show himself again.

Nathan came through the gates a little while later, but he didn't see Evangeline until he was almost in front of her. He looked up in astonishment, as if suddenly catching sight of a ghost.

"Evangeline? What are you doing here?" He was a lot thinner than the last time she'd seen him, and like his car, he looked a lot worse for the wear. His clothes were ragged, his hair unkempt and he seemed to have a hard time looking her in the eyes.

"I came to see you, Nathan."

He glanced around nervously. "How did you know I'd be here? Never mind." He lifted a hand and rubbed the scruff on his chin. "My sister's always had a big mouth."

"Why haven't you returned any of my phone calls?" Evangeline asked.

Even in the disintegrating light, his eyes looked glassy and unfocused. "You know how it is. You never know what to say in a situation like that. Plus, I've got a lot of personal problems I've been dealing with lately."

"We've all got personal problems."

"Yeah, I know."

"Could we go somewhere and talk?"

"About what?"

His darting gaze made Evangeline uneasy. He was on something, which could also make him volatile.

"I've still got a lot of questions about the night Johnny died," she said.

"What makes you think I know the answers?"

"You were working cases with him at the time of his death."

"Yeah, but we didn't work every case together." He shoved his hands in his pockets and stood looking out over the street. "You really shouldn't have come looking for me," he said softly. "I'm not going to be able to help you."

"Because you can't or you won't?"

"You need to just go on home to your baby."

His tone deepened Evangeline's disquiet. "That almost sounds like a threat, Nathan."

He shrugged. "You don't need to be afraid of me."

"Is there someone else I should be afraid of?"

He paused. "Can't you just leave it alone? Johnny's gone. Nothing I can say will bring him back."

"I know that. But I still want to talk to you. Can we sit in your car for a few minutes? I don't like standing out here in the open like this. I feel too exposed."

He gave her a strange look, but he unlocked his car and they both climbed in. The interior smelled of reefer.

Nathan's head dropped to the back of the seat as he ran a hand across his eyes. "I don't know what you think I can tell you. I wasn't with Johnny that night."

"But you must have some idea of what he was doing in that parking garage. Why did he go there?"

He stared straight ahead. "I don't know."

"I don't believe you."

It was getting dark fast, but there was still enough ambient light coming through the windshield that Evangeline could see the harsh angles of Nathan's face when he turned toward her. She could even see the regret in his eyes as he stared at her for the longest moment.

Then he shook his head. "You don't want to ask me any more questions about that night, Evangeline."

Her heart skipped a beat at the look on his face.

"I have to know," she whispered. "What was Johnny doing in that parking garage?"

He drew a long breath and released it. "He went there to see a woman."

Fourteen

To humor Lynette, Don spent several minutes driving around the neighborhood, looking for the old Cadillac Eldorado she'd spotted earlier, but apparently the car was long gone and so were the two snakes that had been on the patio.

Lynette had watched them slither away just before Don got home, but to his credit, he'd grabbed an old machete from the garage that he used for hacking down bamboo and went outside to tramp around in the yard and flower beds.

While he was out there, he decided the grass needed cutting, so he hauled out the lawn mower and got to work.

Lynette stood at the kitchen window and watched him make pass after pass through the grass. The light was almost gone, but he didn't let up until the whole backyard was trimmed. Somewhere along the way, he'd discarded his shirt, and Lynette was surprised by the flutter of awareness in the pit of her stomach.

How long had it been since she'd noticed how attractive her husband still was? How long since she'd paid him a real compliment?

Despair settled around her heart. She was still so mad at him she could spit, but her anger did nothing to fill the hole left by his indifference.

Lynette wanted to turn away from the window, pretend that nothing was wrong. Pretend their lives would go on just as they always had. But she had the strangest notion that if she looked away, or even blinked, she might never see him again.

Mistakenly, she'd believed that the glue of a forty-year marriage was strong enough to bind them together forever. But while she'd remained rooted to the past, entrenched in their settled ways, Don had moved on. And she'd let it happen without lifting a finger to stop it.

Lynette's eyes burned dryly as she watched him wheel the lawn mower toward the back gate. She didn't take her eyes off him until he'd disappeared on the other side of the fence, and then finally she turned back to the stove.

He came inside a few minutes later and she heard him go into the bathroom to get cleaned up. She wondered if he would even notice the scrubbed tile in the shower, the stack of clean towels in the linen closet, the cake of fresh soap in the porcelain dish. Had he ever noticed any of those things, or did he just take her labors for granted?

When he came back into the kitchen, he was dressed in pressed khakis and a pullover shirt in the color of blue that Lynette had always loved on him.

His hair still damp from the shower, he stood in the doorway and propped one hand against the frame. "Something smells good."

She glanced over her shoulder as she continued to work. "It's nothing special. Just gumbo and cornbread. Peach pie for dessert."

"Your gumbo's always special," he said.

Lynette turned in surprise and she felt a catch in her chest as their gazes met briefly. But when he saw her hopeful smile, he glanced away.

She tried not to let it bother her as she bustled around the kitchen, cleaning the counters and loading the dishwasher.

"I should get back to the office," he finally said. "I've still got work to do tonight."

Lynette tried to mask her disappointment as she shrugged. "That's too bad. Evangeline will be here to pick up the baby soon. I was hoping we could all have dinner together tonight. It's been a while since you've seen her, hasn't it?"

Don glanced at his watch. "How much longer before she gets here?"

"She had an errand to run first, but she should be here any time now."

"I guess I can stick around for a little while." He folded his arms and leaned a shoulder against the door frame. "Listen, Lynette, when she gets here, I don't think we should mention any of this to her. She's got enough on her plate these days as it is."

"Mention what?" Evangeline asked. She'd let herself in the front door and had come up behind Don without either of them seeing her.

It was likely no one else would have noticed her pinched mouth or the feverish gleam in her blue eyes, but Lynette knew her daughter too well.

Something had happened to badly upset her, but Lynette had learned a long time ago that Evangeline didn't like to talk about her work. Not the bad cases, anyway. Nor did she talk much about her personal problems, even when Johnny had died. She kept so much bottled up inside her.

Maybe that's my fault.

Lynette had never been one to talk about her feelings, either. Maybe if she'd been a little more open with Don, their marriage wouldn't be on the brink of disaster.

Her first instinct still was to wrap her arms around her daughter, hold her close, protect her as best she could from the ugliness out there in the world. Shield her from any more pain that might be headed her way.

God knows, she's suffered enough.

Lynette had always been protective of both her children, but especially Evangeline, in large part because of her gender and size. But she needn't have played favorites because Evangeline was stronger than Vaughn, stronger than all of them. Her daughter had grown into a remarkable young woman.

Maybe in trying to shelter Evangeline, she'd really been trying to protect herself, Lynette thought. Maybe it was high time she faced some hard truths about her own life.

"What were you two talking about?" Evangeline asked as she came into the kitchen.

Lynette took a deep breath and spoke before Don had a chance to. "Your dad is moving out."

She couldn't believe she'd actually said it, and now that she had, she couldn't bear to witness the look on Evangeline's face.

So Lynette turned instead to her husband. She could tell he was shocked that she'd beat him to the punch, but the relief she'd expected to find in his eyes was slow to form.

Instead, the emotion that flickered across his face looked a little like panic.

Well, Lynette thought. *Well.*

Evangeline sat at the kitchen table, bouncing J.D. on her knee. Her father had left before dinner, mumbling something about getting back to the office, and now she and her mother sat across from one another, avoiding each other's eyes.

J.D. crammed a blue plastic rattle in his mouth, then offered it to Evangeline. "Hmm, slobbers," she said, and he gave her a toothless grin as she pretended to lick the toy.

Her mother had given him a bath earlier, and now he smelled of baby powder and the apple sauce he'd had for dinner. The red-and-white-striped sleeper he wore looked so soft and adorable, Evangeline just wanted to cuddle him, but at the moment, J.D. had other ideas. He was wide-awake and raring to go. Flinging the rattle to the floor, he squealed in delight when it landed with a loud *clack* against the tile. Then he started to fuss until the toy was retrieved so that he could do it all over again.

"Dinner was great, Mom," Evangeline finally said. "Let me put J.D. in his high chair and I'll do the dishes real quick."

Her mother gave an absent wave. "Don't bother with the dishes. It'll give me something to do after you and the baby leave." She looked tearless and stoic, but Evangeline knew it was just a facade.

"Are you sure you're okay?"

"I'm fine. This has been building for a while now. Your father…" She trailed off as her gaze darted away. "After all these years, you think you know someone," she murmured.

Evangeline thought about Nathan's revelation earlier. Of all the things she'd imagined him telling her about the night Johnny died, another woman had never once crossed her mind.

"It's not how it sounds," he'd rushed to assure her. *"He was just visiting a friend."*

"Is that what he told you?"

Nathan glanced away without answering.

"Who is she?"

"I don't know her name. I don't think Johnny ever mentioned it."

"You're lying."

He sighed and scrubbed a trembling hand down his face. "She was a material witness on one of his cases, okay? That's how they met. She was having a hard time getting by, like a lot of people are these days. He felt sorry for her and tried to give her a hand now and then until she got back on her feet. They were just friends. Johnny swore that's all it was."

"Then why did he never tell me about her?"

"Maybe he was afraid you'd get the wrong idea."

No kidding, Evangeline thought now as she gazed down at her son.

But she'd never given Johnny a reason for worrying she'd jump to the wrong conclusion. She wasn't clingy and emotional, nor had she ever been the jealous type. She was not the kind of wife who harbored unwarranted distrust for any woman who came into contact with her husband. Evangeline had no problem with Johnny having female friends. After all, she had Mitchell.

So there was no reason for him to keep things from her, even a friendship with a female witness. Evangeline had always believed their relationship was open and honest and mutually trusting. There was nothing they couldn't tell one another.

Apparently, she'd been wrong.

Not only had Johnny kept that friendship from her, he'd never mentioned Lena Saunders, either.

Now Evangeline couldn't help wondering what else she might discover about her dead husband. Something Meredith Courtland said about her own marriage came back to her.

I guess that's why they say the wife is the last to know.

Maybe the cracks had been there in their marriage all along, but also like Meredith Courtland, Evangeline had chosen not to see them.

Impulsively, she reached across the table and took her mother's hand. "I'm sorry you're having to go through this. But all marriages have problems. Maybe Dad will come to his senses and it'll all blow over."

"Maybe he will," Lynette said with a wan smile.

"Can I ask you something, Mom?"

"What is it?"

"What was Dad's problem with Johnny?"

Lynette looked up in surprise. "What do you mean?"

"It was so obvious he didn't like him, and I never understood why."

"Fathers are always protective of their daughters. It's only natural."

"Are you sure that's all it was. Dad didn't…he didn't suspect something about Johnny?"

"Like what, honey?"

At her mother's tender tone, Evangeline felt an unexpected flood of tears. She lifted J.D. to her chest and rested her cheek against the top of his head. He tolerated the affection for a moment before he pulled away.

What if Johnny really had been involved with another woman? What if everything she thought about him, about their life together, was nothing but a lie?

What if he had never really loved her?

"What's wrong, Evangeline?"

She squeezed her eyes closed. "I still miss him, Mama. Sometimes I don't think I can bear it, I miss him so bad."

"I know, honey."

"At least with Dad, you've still got a chance to make things right. But with Johnny…I just keep thinking about all the things I wished I'd said to him before it was too late. I lie in bed at night and all the arguments we ever had go round and round in my head. I remember every petty little thing I ever said to him, the way I used to nag at him for leaving his clothes on the bathroom floor or dishes in the sink. And I wish I could take it all back. I wish…even now…I wish…" She wiped a hand across her wet cheek. "I just want him back. I don't care what he did…I just want him back."

Later that night, Evangeline awakened to the strangest feeling. She'd been so certain when she opened her eyes that she'd find Johnny standing over her, she was actually startled when no one was there. Something lingered, though. She thought at first it was his cologne, but it was really just a memory.

Even so, she got up out of bed and checked in the bathroom. Then she padded down the hallway to the baby's room. She checked every inch of the house before crawling back into bed and huddling under the covers.

Johnny was gone. He wasn't coming back. Ever.

She rolled to his side of the bed and buried her face in his pillow. But the linens had been laundered too many times and his scent had long ago faded.

And Evangeline knew that no matter how hard she tried, eventually some of her memories would slip away, too.

Fifteen

❧❧❧

Hours after Nathan Mallet left Mount Olive, he drove to a bar a few blocks from the cemetery and parked on the street so that anyone tailing him would be sure to spot his car.

Taking his time, he locked the door, pocketed the key, then went inside and found a table at the back where he could watch the whole room, including the front door.

When the bored waitress came over to take his order, he discreetly showed her his badge—after all, she wouldn't know that he'd walked off the job months ago—and asked if there was a back way out of the place.

She pointed to the restroom area. "Go through that door, past the men's room and it's at the end of the hall." Nervously, she glanced around the empty bar. "Is there going to be trouble?"

"Nothing for you to worry about," he told her. "I just need to get someone off my tail."

She didn't look at all reassured. Mallet saw her talking to the bartender a few minutes later, and they both kept glancing in his direction. He just hoped they didn't decide to call the cops, at least not before he could get out of there.

When the waitress returned with his drink, Mallet downed the whiskey, slid the empty glass to the edge of the table and motioned for another. He discreetly dropped some bills on the table, then got up and headed toward the restrooms, bypassing the men's room for the rear exit at the end of the hall.

He opened the door and slipped outside. Pressing himself into the shadows, he peered down the alley toward the street. When the coast seemed clear, he hurried to the back where he climbed a chain-link fence and jumped down on the other side.

A few minutes later, he was back at the cemetery.

The gates were closed and locked by this time, but he scaled the brick wall easy enough and soon he was making his way through the crypts and mausoleums to his first wife's vault, where he'd been earlier.

Dropping to the ground, he leaned back against the still-warm concrete as he removed his gun from his pocket and tucked it beneath his leg. Then he pulled a fifth of whiskey from his other pocket, uncapped the bottle and took a long swig before letting his head fall back against the vault.

OFFICIAL OPINION POLL

Dear Reader,

Since you are a book enthusiast, we would like to know what you think.

Inside you will find a short Opinion Poll. Please participate in our poll by sharing your opinion on 3 subjects that are very important to all of us.

To thank you for your participation, we would like to send you your choice of **2 FREE BOOKS** and **2 FREE GIFTS**!

Please enjoy them with our compliments.

Sincerely,

Pam Powers

Editor

P.S. Don't forget to indicate which books you prefer so we can send your FREE gifts today!

YOUR OPINION POLL
THANK-YOU FREE GIFTS INCLUDE

▶ **2 ROMANCE OR 2 SUSPENSE BOOKS**

▶ **2 LOVELY SURPRISE GIFTS**

DETACH AND MAIL CARD TODAY!

OFFICIAL OPINION POLL

YOUR OPINION COUNTS!
Please check TRUE or FALSE below to express your opinion about the following statements:

Q1 Do you believe in "true love"?

"TRUE LOVE HAPPENS ONLY ONCE IN A LIFETIME."
○ TRUE
○ FALSE

Q2 Do you think marriage has any value in today's world?

"YOU CAN BE TOTALLY COMMITTED TO SOMEONE WITHOUT BEING MARRIED."
○ TRUE
○ FALSE

Q3 What kind of books do you enjoy?

"A GREAT NOVEL MUST HAVE A HAPPY ENDING."
○ TRUE
○ FALSE

Place the sticker next to one of the selections below to receive your 2 **FREE BOOKS** and 2 **FREE GIFTS**. I understand that I am under no obligation to purchase anything as explained on the back of this card.

Romance

193 MDL EVKZ

393 MDL EVMZ

Suspense

192 MDL EVKD

392 MDL EVLZ

0074823   FREE GIFT CLAIM # **3622**

FIRST NAME	LAST NAME

ADDRESS

APT.#	CITY

STATE/PROV.	ZIP/POSTAL CODE

(TF-RS-09)

The Reader Service — Here's How It Works:

After a while, it started to mist and he turned his face skyward, letting the moisture cool his over-heated skin. He was nervous and punchy, but being back here with Teri helped calm him. It always did.

Man, he still missed that girl.

She'd only been eighteen when they married, fresh from her high school graduation when they ran off to Biloxi. He'd just celebrated his twenty-first birthday. Young, stupid, crazy in love.

Back then he'd wanted nothing more than to be with her day and night. Even now, he could re-member feeling that he would never be able to get enough of her.

A year later, she was dead. Killed by a drunk driver when his car hit hers head-on.

Nathan had quit drinking after the accident. He felt he owed her that much. For years, he never so much as touched a drop, but then his life had taken one bad turn after another. His mistakes had started to catch up with him, and he'd sometimes have a drink or two just to get through the day. Before he knew it, he couldn't crawl out of bed without the sauce. He went to sleep loaded and he woke up reaching for his next drink.

His second wife, Kathy, was a good woman and God knows she deserved a lot better than what he'd put her through over the years. But after all this time—well over a decade—he'd never been able to forget about Teri. He'd never been able to stop thinking about what might have been. If only he'd been with her that day. If only she'd taken another route home.

Nathan's visits to the cemetery had become both easier and harder over the years. Easier because it was the only place where he ever felt any real peace. Harder because it always hit him anew how much he'd lost when Teri died.

"Hello, Nathan."

With an effort, he opened his eyes. He hadn't even realized he'd drifted off, but when he saw the man standing over him, he came fully awake and a warning shivered down his spine.

He couldn't see the man's face, but he knew that voice.

"Long time no see," Nathan said as he dropped his hand to the ground beside his leg. "I was about to give up. Thought no one was coming. I'd have been mighty pissed, too, after driving all the way up here to see you."

"Have you ever known Sonny to go back on his word?"

Nathan shrugged. "Like I said, it's been a long time. People change."

"You sure have." The man kicked Nathan's foot with the toe of his boot. "You look like shit."

"Thanks a lot." He lifted the bottle and took a long swig.

"You need to take better care of yourself. Maybe try a steady diet of something besides Jim Beam."

"I'll make you a deal. You live your life, I'll live mine."

The man laughed softly and turned to glance around. "I didn't see your car on the street. How'd you get over here?"

"Walked."

"From where?"

"From where I left my car," Nathan said, evading the question.

The man turned back to him. "The feds are bound to know you're back in town by now. You sure you weren't followed?"

Nathan snorted. "None of those fuckers know New Orleans like I do."

"Don't get too confident."

"I'm not," he said. "Matter of fact, I ran into a little unexpected trouble when I was here earlier."

"Yeah, we know about that."

Nathan looked up in surprise. "You know? What, you guys spying on me?"

"Just keeping an eye on things," the man said. "Big difference."

Right.

"What did Evangeline Theroux want?" he asked.

Nathan scowled. "What do you think she wanted?"

The man hesitated. "Let me rephrase that. What did you tell her?"

"Nothing, man."

"She sure seemed upset when she left. So I repeat…what did you tell her?"

Nathan wiped a shaky hand across his mouth. "She kept asking about that night. I had to tell her something to get her off my back."

"And?"

"I told her about the woman."

Another long pause. "I see."

"At least now she'll stop asking questions," Nathan said hopefully.

"You think?"

"Yeah, man, we're chill." He handed up the bottle to his companion. "Have a drink and relax."

"No, thanks, but you go ahead and knock yourself out."

"Don't mind if I do." Nathan took another swallow and recapped the bottle.

"What else are you on?" the man asked conversationally.

"What do you mean?"

"I'm talking about drugs, Nathan. Narcotics. Chemicals. What gets you baked these days?"

"Hey, I'm clean."

"Sure you are. That's why you look like a walking corpse. Hooch didn't do that kind of damage. If I was a betting man, I'd put my money on meth. The nirvana of the Southern redneck."

Nathan's hand was still beside him on the ground. Just a fingertip away from his gun. "Something tells me you didn't come here just to insult me. Why'd you want to see me anyway?"

"We've got some loose ends that need tying up."

"Such as?"

"You've got an addiction, Nathan. That makes you dangerous to Sonny. Especially with the feds breathing down his neck."

"Nah, man. What are you talking about?" Nathan's fingers inched closer to his weapon. He didn't like where this conversation was headed.

"When you run out of money, you might be tempted to start selling secrets. We can't have that, now can we?"

Nathan reached for his gun, but he was too late. He barely caught a glimpse of the silenced weapon before a bullet caught him square between the eyes. His head flew back, spraying blood and membrane all over his dead wife's tomb.

He was dead instantly, but the killer pumped two more rounds into his chest for good measure. Then he squatted beside Nathan's body and rummaged through his jacket until he found a wallet and car keys.

Standing, he pocketed the booty, then turned and made his way to the back of the cemetery, where he slowly walked down the row of vaults, reading the plaques.

Johnny Theroux. *Rest in peace, asshole.* Scaling the brick wall, he dropped like a cat to the other side.

A moment later, he disappeared into the night.

Sixteen

⟨ornament⟩

The next morning, Evangeline pulled to the curb in front of the address Lapierre had given her the day before. It was a little before nine, and she was glad to have a few minutes to herself before interviewing the mysterious Lena Saunders.

Evangeline hauled out the notes she'd scribbled earlier at the station, but she found it impossible to focus her thoughts. Her eyes burned from fatigue, and she squeezed them closed for a moment against the blinding sunlight that bounced off the windshield of a parked car.

She hadn't slept much the night before. Too much on her mind.

On the heels of Nathan's disclosure had come the news of her parents' impending separation. She supposed the trouble in that marriage had been brewing for a long time, too, but she'd managed to convince herself they'd work things out. If their relationship had survived the hell her brother, Vaughn, had put them through back in his youth, she would have thought they could weather any storm.

Apparently, she'd been wrong about that, too.

Was there such a thing as a healthy marriage these days? she wondered.

Her parents. Mitchell and Lorraine. And now the memory of her and Johnny's marriage was tarnished with doubt.

Glancing at her watch, Evangeline saw that it was almost nine. She climbed out of the car and took a moment to gaze around the neighborhood. Lena Saunders lived only a few blocks over from Meredith Courtland in the Garden District. The houses along this street were slightly smaller, but the yards and gardens were just as well kept, the white facades of the homes just as sparkling in the summer heat.

Out on the street, two boys rode by on bicycles, ball gloves swinging from their handlebars. They laughed and clowned as they sped through the lawn sprinklers, and Evangeline wondered for a moment what her life would be like when J.D. reached that age.

She watched the boys until they were out of sight, and then she turned and started up the walkway. The bushes were still dripping from the sprinklers, and the air smelled of wet grass and honeysuckle.

The door was opened by a young man in linen pants, leather sandals and a thin cotton shirt. His light brown hair was stylishly cut, and behind the thick black frames of his glasses, green eyes twinkled with good humor.

"You must be Detective Theroux," he said, stepping back from the door so that she could enter. "Come on in. Lena is expecting you."

He led her from the light-flooded foyer into a large room decorated in gray and black with punches of red. The layout of the house reminded Evangeline of the Courtland home, but the clean, minimalist furnishings were a far cry from Meredith Courtland's lush, eclectic style.

But the view from the French doors was exactly the same—a sun-drenched courtyard and sparkling pool.

"I'm Josh, by the way." He waved toward a spectacular leather sofa in silver. "Make yourself at home. I'll go tell Lena you're here."

After he left the room, Evangeline wandered over to the French doors and stood admiring the garden. She and Johnny had always talked about landscaping the tiny backyard of their home, but there'd never been enough time or money and neither of them had much of a green thumb anyway.

Johnny.

She closed her eyes.

How she hated this. Hated having doubts about

a man she'd once trusted more than anyone. Hated having her memories of their time together now stained with a terrible suspicion.

"You must be Evangeline."

She glimpsed the woman's reflection in the glass a split second before she spoke.

Evangeline turned.

"I'm sorry," the woman said. "I should call you Detective Theroux. It's just…you look so young!"

Thin, blond and elegant, Lena Saunders was dressed in snug black pants and a sleeveless black sweater that gave her a chic, artsy flair. Evangeline put her age at somewhere around forty, though she wasn't sure why. The woman's face was still smooth and taut and as pale as alabaster.

When she took Evangeline's hand, her skin was cold, as if she'd just come indoors from a brisk, wintry day.

"Let's sit," she said and, leading the way, she perched on the silver sofa while Evangeline took the matching chair to her right. As they settled in, Josh appeared quietly in the doorway.

"Can I get you ladies something to drink? Coffee, tea?"

"Nothing for me, thanks," Evangeline said.

"I'll have coffee, black," Lena told him.

He cocked a brow. "Decaffeinated, I assume. Otherwise, you'll be climbing the walls by noon and that won't be pleasant for either of us."

She waved a dismissive hand. "Stop fussing. You're getting on my last nerve."

"What else is new?" he said with a grin before vanishing down the hallway.

Lena turned back to Evangeline. "Josh is my assistant, but sometimes he acts as if he's my guardian."

"I heard that!" he yelled from down the hallway.

Lena ignored him. "You must be curious as to why I was so insistent on speaking only with you today."

"I am," Evangeline said. "Captain Lapierre mentioned that you knew my late husband."

"Johnny, yes." She smiled faintly. "A lovely man. Such wonderful manners. A true Southern gentleman."

"He had his moments," Evangeline murmured, feeling an all-too-familiar pang of loneliness.

"He was very helpful and so patient. Never acted as though my calls were an inconvenience, although I'm sure my questions got to be tedious for him after a while."

"When was the last time you talked to him?" Evangeline asked curiously.

"Oh, it's been a few years. I was so sorry to hear about what happened. You must have been devastated."

"It's been a rough time," Evangeline admitted.

"I can imagine. He always spoke so highly of you. I could tell he was very much in love."

Evangeline's heart gave a painful thud as she glanced down at her hands.

"I'm sorry," Lena said. "I don't mean to bring up painful memories."

"No, it's fine."

They both fell silent for a moment as Lena busied herself with the coffee service Josh had brought in.

"Are you sure you wouldn't like some coffee?"

"No, I'm good." Evangeline was fascinated by the woman's hands. They were smooth and pale with the long, elegant fingers of a pianist.

"How did you know Paul Courtland?" she asked when Lena had settled back against the leather sofa with her coffee.

"I didn't know him. In fact, I never met the man, although I spoke with him once on the phone. I tried to explain why I thought his life might be in danger, but unfortunately, he didn't believe me. You may not, either," she warned.

"I'm here to listen to whatever you want to tell me," Evangeline said. "But if you know who killed Paul Courtland, we can just skip to the chase as far as I'm concerned."

"I can give you a name," Lena said slowly, "but it won't mean much unless I give you a bit of background information. Without context, nothing I say will sound the least bit credible."

"Fine. Start wherever you like."

Lena leaned forward and placed her cup and

saucer on the coffee table. "Are you familiar with the concept of an evil gene?"

Evangeline frowned. "I've read some research about the criminal brain. Is that what you mean?"

"No, not really. The criminal brain refers to the correlation between serious crime and brain abnormalities in the perpetrator. The cause of the anomalies can be any number of reasons—head trauma, chemical ingestion, birth defects. But the concept of the evil gene suggests that the propensity for violence—for evil, if you will—can be passed down genetically from family member to family member. Not only that, current studies indicate that behavior and life experiences can alter the biochemistry of certain genes and these changes can be encoded into our DNA and passed on to our children."

"Are you saying that Paul Courtland's killer was born with an evil gene? Is that where this conversation is going?" Evangeline asked with open skepticism.

"No, not at all. Just the opposite, in fact."

"Then I'm afraid you've already lost me."

"Just bear with me. You'll soon understand." Lena paused, as if to gather her thoughts. "The subject of my current book is a woman named Mary Alice Lemay. Have you ever heard of her?"

"Doesn't ring a bell."

"I'm not surprised. She's been confined to a state psychiatric hospital for more than thirty years. Her name has long since faded from the public consciousness."

"What did she do?"

"She killed her three small sons. Two were hanged, one was stabbed and drowned. The boys were five, three and eighteen months. When the authorities arrived at the house, they also found evidence that Mary Alice had recently given birth to her sixth child, although they never found the infant's body."

Evangeline suppressed a shudder. "You said her sixth child. What about the other two?"

"Both girls, ages six and eight at the time. They didn't have so much as a scratch on them. In fact, there was some indication that the youngest daughter, Rebecca, may have helped with at least one of the slayings. But at six years old, she could hardly be held accountable for her actions, especially if she believed, as her mother apparently did, they were carrying out God's will."

"Is that what she claimed? It was God's will that she murder her sons?"

"She said she killed her sons to save their souls from eternal damnation."

"Did it work?"

"I beg your pardon?"

"Her motive. Did the jury buy it?"

"She was found not guilty by reason of insanity and sent to a state psychiatric hospital rather than to death row, so yes, I suppose it worked."

Evangeline knew it happened, mothers killing their own children, but it was something she would never be able to fathom. She certainly couldn't lay claim to any mother-of-the-year awards, but she'd sooner take her own life than harm J.D.

"Mary Alice's husband was a man named Charles Lemay," Lena continued. "When he was just five years old, his father, Earl, was convicted of raping and murdering three young women in East Texas and burying their bodies on the family farm. He was sent to the Walls Unity in Huntsville and was executed some years later. Charles's mother moved the family to Texarkana where she remarried and her three children took their stepfather's last name."

"I don't blame them," Evangeline murmured.

"So far as I've been able to determine—and I've been researching this case for nearly a year now—the family lived a fairly normal and middle-class life until the older boy, Carl, was arrested for the murder of a female classmate when he was seventeen. Her body was found buried in a vacant lot adjacent to the family's backyard. The girl had been raped and beaten to death, just like his father's victims."

"The evil gene," Evangeline murmured.

"Carl Lemay was also sent to Huntsville. He remained incarcerated for more than forty years before he was finally paroled as an old man."

Lena bent forward and picked up her cup. But the

coffee had cooled by this time, and she set it back down with a grimace.

"After the mother and stepfather died, Charles and his sister, Leona, moved to Louisiana. They both settled in New Orleans, but some years later, Charles got a job as a sales rep with a chemical company in Houma. Around that same time, he started using the name Lemay again. And this is when he met Mary Alice."

"Did she know about his past?"

"Probably not at that time. But I think she must have found out about it later. I'm certain that was a factor in what she did to her sons."

"So she married this Charles Lemay."

Lena nodded. "Yes, against her family's wishes, apparently. He was older. Very handsome and charming and by all accounts, it was love at first sight for Mary Alice. But right from the start, there were disturbing signs. Charles Lemay was cunning and manipulative, and Mary Alice's family and friends were put off by his controlling nature. But she ignored their warnings and married him anyway."

"They almost always do," Evangeline said.

"Yes, I've known women like that, too," Lena said. "What's that old saying? They can't see the forest for the trees. Mary Alice couldn't see past her husband's charm and good looks. Not at first anyway. He bought a place on the bayou in Lafourche

Parish, and he and Mary Alice settled in. The house was out in the country, miles from the nearest neighbors, and since Charles's job required extensive travel, Mary Alice was alone much of the time."

"He isolated her," Evangeline said.

"Exactly. And then the babies started coming. Before she was thirty, Mary Alice had five young children for which she was almost solely responsible. When the two girls reached school age, she homeschooled them at Charles's insistence. You see, he not only isolated his wife, he also isolated the children. The only time any of them were allowed to socialize was at worship services. They attended a nondenominational charismatic church, and if you've never attended one of these services, the intensity can be a shock to your senses. The power of those sermons and the concepts of prophetic manifestations and demon chasers must have had a compelling impact on Mary Alice. On her children, as well, I would imagine."

"By charismatic, you're talking about snakehandling churches, right?" Evangeline felt both dread and impatience for what she suspected lay ahead.

"There are only a handful of small congregations that observe this practice," Lena said. "But, yes. The church where Mary Alice and her children worshipped believed in taking up serpents."

Lovely, Evangeline thought with a shiver. "Please

go on," she said. "I didn't mean to interrupt your train of thought."

"No, that's fine. You're bound to have questions. Believe me, I know how all this sounds. But as I said, context is everything." She paused, as if trying to remember where she left off. "One day Charles left on a business trip and never returned. He just simply vanished. Everyone assumed he'd walked out on his family. But when the police arrested Mary Alice for the murder of her children, she also confessed to killing her husband. She claimed she'd discovered that he was abusing their young daughters. She also feared that he may have been responsible for the disappearances of at least two young women from towns that were along his sales route."

"Were her claims substantiated?"

"The records involving the children are sealed," Lena said. "So I can't speak to that. As for the disappearances…no bodies were ever found. But I suspect Mary Alice was right. However, given what she did to her own children, you can understand why the authorities were skeptical. I doubt her claims were ever properly investigated. What I do know is that Charles's behavior fit the pattern of his father and brother, and I think Mary Alice was aware of that. Which is why she had to kill her children in order to save their souls."

"That's a hard sale," Evangeline said. "Because what you're saying is that she killed her sons so they wouldn't grow up to be like their father and grand-father. That's a huge assumption to make, especially where your children's lives are at stake."

"For Mary Alice it wasn't an assumption, though. It was a matter of faith. Even so, her dilemma must have been heart-wrenching. Think about it." She leaned forward, forearms on her knees as her gaze burned into Evangeline's. "How far would you go to protect your son? Would you willingly sacrifice your own soul in order to procure his eternal salva-tion?"

"Now you're making an assumption," Evange-line said. "You're assuming she told the truth about her motivation."

The blue eyes darkened. "What is truth? Your truth? My truth? Mary Alice's truth?"

"I'm not much on moral relativism," Evangeline said. "It's hard for me to get past the fact that she murdered her children in cold blood. That's the only truth that matters to me."

"You're not alone." Lena sat back against the sofa. Some of her energy seemed to have drained away. "Most people thought Mary Alice should have gone to the electric chair. Instead, she's spent the past thirty-some years in a mental hospital. I don't know which would have been the kinder fate."

"What happened to the little girls?"

"They were separated and put in foster care. The older girl, Ruth, was adopted by a family in Baton

Rouge. Her name was changed, of course, and from what I've been able to learn, she grew up in a stable, loving environment. Rebecca wasn't so lucky. She's been under psychiatric care since she was a teenager. Three years ago, her doctor committed her to Pinehurst Manor, in East Faliciana Parish."

"I know where Pinehurst Manor is," Evangeline said.

"Then you probably also know that up until a few years ago, it was a low- to medium-security facility. When Katrina hit, some of the patients in maximum-security units were evacuated and sent to places like Pinehurst. Mary Alice was one of those patients."

"You're saying she and her daughter ended up in the same mental hospital?"

"For a short while, yes."

"Did they come into contact with one another?"

"Almost certainly they did. And you can imagine the impact such a meeting would have had on someone as fragile as Rebecca Lemay. She'd had no contact with her mother or sister for years, and it's my belief that seeing Mary Alice unleashed a flood of suppressed memories—her father's abuse and her complicity in at least one of her brother's deaths. Those memories would have devastated her. Perhaps the only way she could justify what she'd done was by convincing herself that she, too, had been carrying out God's will. And if she'd been recruited as one of His soldiers, then her mission wasn't yet over. It would be her spiritual duty to finish what her mother had started."

"Meaning?"

"The only way to destroy the evil embedded in the Lemay family DNA would be to destroy all the male progeny."

"But her mother had already done that by killing the father and sons," Evangeline pointed out.

"Not completely. A few weeks after Rebecca left Pinehurst, Carl Lemay was found murdered in an old farmhouse on the outskirts of Texarkana, where he'd relocated after being released from prison."

Evangeline rubbed the sudden tingles at the back of her neck. "You think Rebecca was responsible?"

"Yes, I do. And I think she was responsible for two other murders, as well. Remember I told you that Charles Lemay's sister, Leona, moved to New Orleans? She married a man named Robert Courtland and they had two sons, Paul and David."

Evangeline stared at her in speechless shock.

Lena inclined her head slightly. "Now you see where all this has been leading. David and Paul Courtland are the direct descendants of Earl Lemay. They are the first cousins of the little boys who died more than thirty years ago at Mary Alice's hand. Paul and David were, so far as I can determine, the last male members of the Lemay family."

"If all that's true—" which was a very big if in

Evangeline's book "—Rebecca Lemay's mission would be over, wouldn't it?"

"Yes, except for one thing."

"And that is?"

"Carl Lemay was stabbed to death in his bed," Lena said. "But the use of snakes with Paul and David Courtland—"

"Wait a minute," Evangeline said with a frown. "How did you know about the snakes? It wasn't in the paper."

Lena shrugged as if how she'd obtained the information was of no consequence. Evangeline remembered what Lapierre had said about the woman. She was well-connected in the NOPD.

"I think Rebecca is now working with an accomplice," she said. "The Courtland brothers weren't just killed. There was an element of torture involved. I think Rebecca Lemay has hooked up with someone who has his own calling."

Evangeline thought of the blond woman who had supposedly been following Paul Courtland just before he died.

"Do you know what Rebecca looks like?"

"I have a picture of the girls before they were separated, but I have no idea what they look like now." Lena bent forward and pulled a photograph from the pages of a book lying on the coffee table. She handed the picture to Evangeline.

The shot might have come from the pages of a

Southern magazine, Evangeline thought. In the background, cypress trees dripped with Spanish moss, and in the foreground, two breathtaking little blond girls in white dresses clung to one another's hands as they smiled for the camera.

"They look exactly the same," Evangeline said. "How do you know which is which?"

"If you look closely, you'll see the one on the right is a smidgen taller than the other one. I believe that's Ruth."

For the longest time, Evangeline couldn't tear her gaze from those angelic faces. It was hard to imagine that one of them would grow up to be a cold-blooded killer, no matter her motivation.

"Do you have any idea of Rebecca Lemay's whereabouts?"

"It's possible she's gone back to where she grew up in Lafourche Parish. The nearest town is Torrence. I've been in contact with the sheriff's department down there. The old Lemay house has been abandoned for years, but a few days ago, a fisherman spotted someone in one of the upstairs windows. They actually thought it was Mary Alice, but of course, that's impossible. I think they may have seen Rebecca."

"Did anyone from the sheriff's department check it out?"

"I haven't been able to verify that. People in that area are still a little touchy about what happened. I doubt anyone's all that anxious to go out there to that old house. Too many ghosts."

When Evangeline handed her the photograph, Lena took a moment to carefully tuck it back into the book.

"I would very much like to speak with Rebecca Lemay," she said. "I would go down there and check that sighting out for myself, but as Captain Lapierre probably explained, I don't leave my house much these days. I'm afraid I wouldn't get very far. That's where you come in."

"You want me to go down and check it out for you," Evangeline said. "I can't do that. Like I told you on the phone, I'm no longer working this case. I was sent here today to hear what you have to say and report back to Captain Lapierre. What she does with the information is out of my hands."

Lena bent forward, her eyes very direct. "I have a proposition for you, then. It'll need to be off the record, I'm afraid."

"No way," Evangeline said bluntly. "I don't work like that."

"Johnny was right," she said with a wry smile. "You are a tough nut to crack."

It was still weird to hear her talk about Johnny so casually. Even more weird to think that he might have been in this house, might have sat in the very chair that Evangeline now occupied. In the course of one day, her husband had begun to seem like a stranger to her.

Lena studied Evangeline's face for a moment. "All right," she said. "I'll lay all my cards on the table. If you want to tell your superiors what I'm proposing, that's up to you."

"And just what are you proposing?"

"I want you to find Rebecca Lemay for me. In return, I'll do everything I can to help you find out what really happened to Johnny."

Seventeen

Mitchell called right after Evangeline left Lena Saunders's house. She could tell something was wrong by the tense sound of his voice.

"Where are you right now?" he asked.

"I'm on my way back to the station," she said. "Why? What's wrong?"

"Nathan Mallet's body was found at Mount Olive Cemetery this morning. He was shot to death."

Evangeline was so shocked and distracted by the news, she almost failed to brake for a red light. She clutched the steering wheel as she came to a fast stop. "My God," she muttered.

"It's a real shocker, all right." He paused, then said, "Look, I gotta ask you something, Evie."

"The answer is yes. I saw Nathan yesterday." Her heart started to hammer against her rib cage. Evangeline knew she'd done nothing wrong, but she had a feeling this wasn't going to go down well.

"What time did you see him?" Mitchell asked.

"It was right after you called. Somewhere between seven-thirty and eight. I saw his Mustang parked at the cemetery so I went inside and looked around for a bit. Then I came back out and waited for him by his car. We spoke for a few minutes and then I got back in my car and drove off. That's it, Mitchell. Nathan was alive when I left him."

"I wasn't implying otherwise. I just wanted to make sure you know how you're going to answer if someone else asks you that question."

"If?"

"However you want to handle this is fine by me. As far as I'm concerned, we never talked yesterday."

"Thanks." Evangeline was touched by his loyalty. Of all the things that had been turned upside down in her life lately, Mitchell's friendship was a staple. "I would never ask you to do that," she said. "Besides, I've got nothing to hide. Like I said, Nathan was alive when I left him."

"How did he seem?"

"He was nervous. He kept looking around, as if he was afraid to be seen with me. But I figured I'd just caught him by surprise." The light changed and she started through the intersection. "Have they found anything yet?"

"Right now, they're concentrating on what they

haven't found. His wallet is missing and there's no sign of his car."

"You think it was a robbery?"

"Maybe. Or maybe someone just wanted it to look that way. Evie…" He paused and lowered his voice. "I think you should know something. Nathan was shot three times. Once in the face and twice in the chest. What does that sound like to you?"

"Overkill, for a robbery, but we've seen a lot worse—" She stopped, her heart going crazy inside her chest. "My God," she breathed. "Two shots to the chest and one to the face. Just like Johnny."

"Might just be a coincidence," Mitchell said.

"If you really believed that, you wouldn't have said anything."

"You know what? I don't know what to believe. Something about this whole setup doesn't feel right to me."

"How so?"

"Nathan's gun was found underneath his right leg. Out of sight, but within easy reach, like maybe he was expecting trouble."

"What else?"

"You say you waited for him to come out of the cemetery and the two of you talked in his car. Then you left. So why did he go back inside? And when? The caretaker said everyone was gone when he locked the gates. It's possible he didn't see Nathan, but I think it's more likely that Nathan came back later, after the gates were already locked."

"You think he came back to meet someone."

"All I know is something about this stinks to high heaven. It has the feel of a professional hit, and now I'm starting to wonder why in the hell someone would go to the trouble of taking out a mullet-head like Nathan Mallet."

As soon as Evangeline spoke with Lapierre, she came clean about her meeting with Nathan. The captain took the news better than Evangeline had anticipated, possibly because she had the notes from the meeting with Lena Saunders to distract her.

How Lapierre planned to pursue the information was anyone's guess. It was a far-fetched story to say the least, and Evangeline wasn't even certain how much of it she believed. The only thing she left out of her report was Lena's proposition. The captain didn't need to know about that, especially considering that Evangeline didn't yet know what she planned to do about it.

After she left Lapierre, her first instinct was to drive out to the cemetery and take a look at the crime scene. But that might be pushing her luck, she decided, so instead, she hunkered down at her desk to get caught up on some paperwork.

It was hard to concentrate, considering everything that had gone down in the past twenty-four hours. Finally, Evangeline had had enough pencil-pushing for one day and she headed over to the lab to see if the analysis on the snakeskin had come back yet. A frazzled tech warned her that it could take up to six weeks, they were that backed up.

Evangeline wanted to ask about a ballistics report on the Nathan Mallet shooting, but she figured that would also be pushing her luck. And, anyway, it was too soon.

On her way back to the station, she stopped by the Mission of Hope, a halfway house on North Rampart, at the edge of the Quarter. Her brother, Vaughn, had been the director there for the past several years.

Vaughn was an ex-con. He'd been convicted for the robbery of a convenience store when he was nineteen years old. He'd been sentenced to ten years in Angola, but he'd been released for good behavior after six.

Before his conviction, Vaughn had been in and out of trouble for years. Sometimes when Evangeline looked back on those days, she wondered how any of them had survived it. How had her parents put up with the drinking and the drugs and the all-night parties and managed to keep their sanity?

But those days were long gone. Vaughn had come out of prison a changed man. For the past ten years, he'd devoted himself to helping others at the Mission of Hope, where he was sometimes the last, best hope for ex-cons like himself who truly wanted a fresh start.

Evangeline found him in the tiny cubicle he called an office, seated behind an old battered desk stacked high with file folders and papers. He'd been a good-looking charmer as a kid, but now at thirty-eight, his handsome face bore the scars of a prison-yard brawl and his eyes never seemed to light these days, even when he smiled.

He looked up in surprise when she rapped on the door. "Hey," he said. "Didn't expect to see you here."

"I try not to come around because I know I make you guys nervous. Cops and ex-cons are like oil and water."

He tossed his pen to the desk and folded his hands behind his head. "So what brings you by?"

"A couple of things, actually. Nathan Mallet's body was found at Mount Olive Cemetery this morning. He was shot to death sometime last night or early this morning." She nodded toward the door behind her and the large rec room beyond where three or four men sat watching *Days of our Lives* on an old console set. "People talk," she said. "I just thought if you heard something…" She trailed off on a shrug.

"You know I can't do that. The whole philosophy of this place is based on trust."

"What happens in Vegas, stays in Vegas," she

said. "I get that. But we are talking about murder."
She lowered her voice. "It's possible his death is
connected to Johnny's."

"Connected how?"

"I don't know yet. But I intend to find out."

He shook his head. "Maybe you should just put
all that behind you. Move on with your life."

"People keep telling me that," she said. "It's starting to make me a little paranoid. Like maybe there's
something I'm not being told."

"That does sound paranoid."

She stared at him for a moment. "You never liked
Johnny very much, did you? You or Dad."

He shrugged. "As long as he treated you right, I
had no beef with him."

"That didn't exactly answer my question."

"What do you care whether I liked him or not?
What difference does it make?"

"Because I want to know," she insisted. "Why
didn't you like Johnny?"

"Oil and water," he said with another shrug.

"And Dad?"

"You'll have to ask him, but I don't think it was
personal. I doubt anyone is ever going to be good
enough for you in his eyes. Not Johnny Theroux,
not anyone."

"Something tells me Dad has other things on his
mind these days. Have you talked to him lately?"

"We had dinner one night last week."

"How did he seem to you?"

Vaughn leaned forward. "He seemed fine. Why?"

"Did you know that he and Mom are separating?"

"I knew he was thinking about it. I didn't know it was a done deal."

"You knew and you didn't say anything to Mom? How could you keep something like that from her?"

"Because it's none of my business. It's none of yours, either. This is something they have to work out for themselves."

"There's another woman, isn't there?" When Vaughn didn't answer, Evangeline said in outrage, "I *knew* it. Who is she?"

"Stay out of it, Evangeline."

"You better tell me or else I'll just go ask Dad."

"You go over there half-cocked, you'll just make things worse."

"Worse for who? Besides, I can't just sit by and let him treat Mom like dirt." She got to her feet. "I can't do that."

As she turned toward the door, something caught her eye in one of the bookcases. She walked over for a better look. "Where did you get this?" she asked.

"What, that bird? It's origami," he said.

"I know what it is. I want to know where you got it."

"Someone must have given it to me."

"You don't remember who?"

"It just turned up there the other day."

"And you didn't wonder where it came from?"

"It's just a paper bird," he said. "Why the third degree?"

"Because I'm seeing these damn things everywhere," she said. "I'm starting to think it's not a coincidence."

"Any kindergartener can make them," Vaughn said. "All you need is a square of paper."

"I wish I thought it was a kindergartener who'd been sending them to me," Evangeline muttered.

"What do you mean?"

"Someone sent a mobile to the house made out of these things. Then I found one out at the cemetery. I know this sounds strange, but…"

Vaughan searched her face. "What?"

"I'm wondering if someone is trying to send me a message."

But what that message was, Evangeline had no idea.

Eighteen

❧⟨◦⟩❧

It was midafternoon when Evangeline made the trek out to Pearl River in East Tammany Parish to visit Kathy Mallet, Nathan's widow. The air cooled as she drove across the lake, and a light wind rolled whitecaps across the green surface of the water.

The two-story brick house was in one of the newer subdivisions along Highway 41. It looked much like all the other houses in the neighborhood, but a pair of wicker rockers and a hanging basket of impatiens on the tiny front porch gave it a homey touch that was in keeping with Evangeline's memory of Kathy Mallet—an attractive, unpretentious woman who taught second grade.

She pulled to the curb behind two squad cars and got out with the pecan pie she'd bought on her way over. Several cops milled about in the front yard and on the porch, and they nodded as Evangeline walked up to the front door. A couple of them spoke, but most seemed to go out of their way to avoid eye contact with her, and she wondered if word had already spread about her meeting the night before with Nathan.

Kathy's mother opened the door and as she led Evangeline through the crowded foyer and living room into the kitchen, Evangeline told her who she was.

The woman turned in surprise. "You're Detective Theroux? Kathy wondered if you'd be dropping by."

Evangeline glanced around all the strange faces, but didn't spot Kathy. "Is she here?"

"She's in her bedroom. If you have a minute, I'll go back and tell her you're here."

"Of course."

While she was gone, Evangeline made small talk with one of Kathy's neighbors. Yes, she'd known Nathan. Yes, it was certainly tragic. The consensus seemed to be that, whatever his faults, Nathan had been a good guy.

When the mother came back, she asked if Evangeline would mind going back to Kathy's bedroom. "She's not up to facing all these people right now, but she really wants to see you."

She pointed to a closed door at the end of a narrow hallway. Evangeline knocked once, didn't get an answer, then knocked again.

"Come in."

Kathy was standing at the window, looking out on the backyard. She turned at the sound of the door, and Evangeline could tell the woman had been crying.

"I'm so glad you came," she said and crossed the room to give Evangeline a quick hug. "I was hoping you would."

"How are you holding up?"

"I'm fine. I have to be, don't I? There are so many things to take care of. The arrangements. All the phone calls." She paused and drew a breath. "But I don't have to tell you about all that. You've been through it, too."

"Yes."

She took Evangeline's hand and squeezed it. Her reaction surprised Evangeline. The woman was acting as if they were old friends, but in truth, Evangeline barely knew her. They'd met and talked a few times at parties, but that was about it. Now Kathy seemed to feel some sort of closeness or kinship with Evangeline, but perhaps that was only natural, considering their husbands had worked so closely together and now they were both dead.

Shot three times—once in the face, twice in the chest.

Still clutching her hand, Kathy pulled her down to sit on the edge of the bed. She turned, her dark eyes searching Evangeline's face. "I need to ask you something. And I hope you won't take any offense."

"What is it?"

The woman's face darkened. "All those times you called here looking for Nathan…why did you want to talk to him so badly?"

"I explained all that. I just wanted to ask him some questions about Johnny."

"But you didn't think Nathan had anything to do with the shooting, did you?"

"No, of course not. But they worked a lot of cases together that last year. I thought he might know if Johnny was working on something dangerous."

"But why now? Johnny's been dead almost a year. Why did you wait so long to get in touch with Nathan?"

"I didn't. I've been trying to talk to him since Johnny's funeral. He would never return any of my phone calls. And I had a lot on mind. Like you said, there was a lot to take care of. The baby came and I went on maternity leave. Time passed in a daze for me. When I came back to work, it hit me again that something wasn't right about that shooting. So I started asking questions."

Kathy still clutched Evangeline's hand, and now she squeezed her fingers reflexively. "Don't you find it strange that right after you started asking those questions, someone killed Nathan?"

Evangeline stared at her for a moment. "Are you saying you think my asking questions is what got Nathan killed?"

"It seems too much of a coincidence to believe anything else. I'm not blaming you," she said quickly. "Please don't think that. I'd want answers, too. I *do* want answers. That's why I wanted to see you today. We're in the same boat now. I think our husbands were killed because of something they knew."

"What?"

Kathy bit her lip. "I don't know. But I want to help you find out if I can."

Evangeline hesitated. What if her questions about Johnny's shooting really had gotten Nathan killed? The last thing she wanted was to drag his widow into danger.

"There's something I need to tell you," she said. "I saw Nathan last night at the cemetery."

Kathy's head snapped up. "Last night? When?"

"It was early evening. Around seven-thirty or eight. I went out there to see him."

"How did you know he'd be there?"

Too late, Evangeline remembered the reason Nathan had gone to Mount Olive—to visit his first wife's tomb.

"I know why he was there," Kathy said softly. "I know all about his visits to Teri's grave. I'm just surprised…" She broke off, her gaze dropping to her hands. "I'm a little surprised that he went out there before coming here."

Evangeline didn't know what to say to that. "I'm sorry. We only spoke briefly."

"Was he able to tell you anything about Johnny?"

"Yes." Evangeline's gaze fell away. "He told me Johnny had gone to that parking garage to see a woman."

"Do you believe that?"

Evangeline shrugged. "I don't want to believe. But I just don't know anymore."

Kathy got up and walked back over to the window. "Since we talked last week, I've been thinking a lot about what happened. Things went south in my marriage right after Johnny's shooting. Nathan started acting really strange. I thought at first he was just upset about Johnny's death. But after a while, I realized it was more than that. He was scared of something."

"Do you have any idea what it was?"

"No, but I overheard something one night that scared me, too. Nathan was on the phone in the living room. He thought I was taking a bath, but I picked up the extension in here not realizing he'd already answered. I heard a man tell him that he needed to keep his head and not do anything stupid. As long as they stayed cool, they were home free."

"Do you know who this man was?"

"I couldn't place the voice. It sounded like he was on a cell phone, and wherever he was, the signal was really weak. The call kept breaking up. But right after that phone call is when Nathan decided to go stay with his uncle in New Iberia."

"What reason did he give you?"

"He didn't. He just walked out. Which wasn't like Nathan. He had problems and plenty of them. But he wasn't a cruel man."

"Do you think he may have come back last night to see the person who called him that night?"

"Maybe." Kathy turned from the window, her face pale and drawn. "But there may have been another reason he came back." She went over to the closet, slid back the door and rummaged through the boxes stacked on the floor. Pulling out a large manila envelope, she came back to the bed. "I found this one day when I was cleaning out the attic. I'm sure Nathan never expected that I would come across it."

"What is it?"

She undid the fastener, then upended the contents on the bed. Several wads of hundred-dollar bills tumbled out, along with a passport and a snapshot of someplace tropical.

"There's twenty-five thousand dollars here," she said. "We've never even had that much in our savings account at any given time. Where did he get so much cash? And take a look at this."

She handed Evangeline the passport. The booklet contained Nathan's photograph, but it had been issued to someone named Todd Jamison.

"It looks like Nathan was preparing for a time when he might have to leave the country quickly," Evangeline said.

"That's what I thought, too," Kathy said. "But I can't figure out why he didn't take it with him when he moved to New Iberia."

"Maybe he thought it would be safer here." Evangeline picked up the photograph. "What's this?"

"It was in the envelope with the money and the passport."

Evangeline scrutinized the snapshot. It looked as if it had been taken from a boat off the shore of some tropical island. The focus was a crowded marketplace filled with tourists in loud shirts and Bermuda shorts. Between the lens of the camera and land was an expanse of azure sky and turquoise water.

"Looks like someplace in the Caribbean," Evangeline said.

"Maybe that's where he was planning on going with the money and the new identity," Kathy said with a quiver in her voice.

There was something about the photograph that bothered Evangeline, though she had no idea why. Maybe it was the idea that Nathan's plans for a quick getaway might have had something to do with Johnny's shooting, and now she would never know the whole truth about that night.

She held up the photograph. "Would you mind if I borrow this for a little while? I'd like to see if I can figure out where it was taken."

Kathy shrugged. "That's why I showed you all this stuff. I thought you'd want to know. Like I said, we're in the same boat now. If Johnny and Nathan were shot because of something they knew…then you and I could be in danger, too, I suppose."

After Evangeline left Kathy's house, she called Mitchell to find out if there'd been a break in Nathan's case. Then, as an afterthought, she called her mother to ask about the mobile in J.D.'s room.

"I've ordered a lot of stuff lately," Lynette said with a sigh. "But no mobile. Do you remember the store it came from?"

"No, not offhand. I may still have the box at home if Jessie hasn't thrown it away."

"I bought the baby a few things from Dillard's," Lynette said. "Maybe they got the order mixed up."

"This didn't come from Dillard's. And anyway, it doesn't matter." Evangeline didn't want to worry her mother. She had enough on her mind. "I was just wondering who I need to thank."

"Check with your dad. Although that doesn't sound like something he'd do." Lynette's voice was surprisingly devoid of the bitter edge that Evangeline had grown accustomed to lately.

"Are you okay, Mom?"

"I'm fine," she said. "I've decided to have another go at spring cleaning. There's a lot of junk I want to get rid of around here. I've been thinking about doing some painting, too. How do you think the living room would look in chartreuse? They use it a lot on HGTV. Your father would hate it, of course, but his opinion isn't something I have to worry about anymore, is it?"

"Mom…"

"I'm fine, Evangeline."

"Okay. Look, I have to go. I'll call you later."

So she was no closer to solving the mystery of the origami cranes.

As Evangeline ended the call with her mother, she thought about the scarred man at the cemetery. Given her suspicion that he'd dropped the bird on the pathway for her to find, she was starting to get a little freaked out.

She thought about J.D. and Jessie all alone in the house. They were perfectly safe. Jessie was very good about keeping the doors locked. Evangeline knew she was letting her imagination get the better of her, but she called home just to check anyway. When she didn't get an answer on the landline, she called Jessie's cell.

"Hey, it's me. Everything okay there? I just called the house and didn't get an answer."

"We're sitting out on the porch," Jessie said.

"Sorry. I didn't hear the phone. Is everything okay with you? You sound a little worried."

"I'm just checking in. I'll be home in a little while."

"That's odd," Jessie murmured.

"What is?"

"The car that just went by…the driver keeps circling the block. That's the third time I've seen him. I wonder if he's lost."

"Why kind of car is it?"

"Some old Cadillac. Looks about a hundred years old."

"It's probably nothing, but why don't you go ahead and take the baby inside. Make sure all the doors are locked," Evangeline said. "Watch out the window and if you see the car again, try to get a license plate number. I'm heading home right now to check things out. I'll be there in a few minutes."

But by the time she arrived, the car was long gone. After checking in with Jessie, Evangeline spent several minutes driving around the neighborhood. She even stopped and asked a couple of neighbors if they'd noticed the car, but, of course, no one had.

She was still overreacting, Evangeline decided later as she sat out on the front porch with her gun. The house was locked up tight and the baby monitor beside her was so sensitive, she could hear J.D.'s soft breathing from his crib.

Still, she was uneasy. A strange car in the neighborhood was only one of a number of things preying on her mind tonight.

Sometime after she'd met with Nathan Mallet at the cemetery, he'd turned up dead. Shot three times. Once in the face and twice in the chest. Just like Johnny.

And on the day before her meeting with Lena Saunders, Evangeline had learned that Paul Courtland had suspected he was being followed by a strange blond woman a few days before he went missing.

According to Lena Saunders, Paul Courtland and his brother were related to Mary Alice Lemay, a woman who had killed all her male children because she feared they'd inherited their father's evil gene.

Also according to Lena, Mary Alice's youngest daughter, Rebecca, had not only helped in the execution of at least one of her brothers, but she might also be responsible for the slaying of Paul and David Courtland.

To call Lena's theory bizarre was an understatement, but Evangeline had done enough research that afternoon to know that the gist of what the writer had told her was true.

Whether Nathan Mallet's death was somehow connected to Paul Courtland's, she couldn't yet say. But one thing was certain. Something strange was going on. And for whatever reason, Evangeline seemed to be a part of it.

The night was hot and humid, but she found herself shivering as she got up and went inside. The house was secure and she had her weapon nearby. There was no real reason for her to be so on edge, Evangeline told herself as she got ready for bed.

Besides, she knew how to defend herself. Anyone trying to break in would find themselves on the wrong end of her .38. She was a crack shot, too, with a steady hand and a firm resolve. And she was fully prepared to do whatever was necessary to protect her home and her child.

Too wired to sleep, she stayed up for a long time watching an old movie, but exhaustion finally claimed her and she fell asleep to the flickering screen.

When she woke up sometime later, she thought the noise from the television had awakened her, even though the volume was turned low.

She clicked off the power, and it took her a moment to realize that the sound she'd heard wasn't coming from the TV.

It was coming from the baby monitor.

Evangeline shot upright in bed. The tinkle of music through the speaker was as clear as if the mobile were in the same room with her. In her mind's eye, she saw the tiny paper cranes circling over her baby, and a dark chill crept over her.

Reaching for her weapon, Evangeline quietly swung her legs over the bed and got up. Wincing at the squeak of the old hardwood floors, she padded across the room and slipped out into the hallway. Gun gripped in both hands and pointed downward, she eased along the wall, eyes and ears alert for any movement or sound.

The door to the nursery was open, and the night-light revealed a peaceful scene. J.D. was asleep in his crib, undisturbed by the soft jingle of the music box as the mobile circled slowly, the cranes barely adrift.

Standing beside the crib, Evangeline felt the cool gush of air from the air-conditioner vent. She put up a hand to still the mobile. The music stopped. The room fell silent. There was no sound at all in the house except for J.D.'s breathing.

Evangeline waited, and a moment later, the draft from the vent stirred the cranes again, the movement activating the music box. A few bars of the tune played out before the room fell silent once more.

Mystery solved, Evangeline thought with a breath of relief. She felt a bit foolish clutching the gun, but she didn't return it to her nightstand until she'd made a complete round through her house.

Satisfied that nothing was amiss, she settled back down to sleep. But every little noise, every movement of shadow and light, brought a new shiver, and she couldn't seem to shake the notion that out there in the dark, someone was watching.

Evil had slithered into her life and now lay coiled and waiting.

Nineteen

❧⟨⟨⟨❧

Ellis Cooper squatted on the slick, mossy bank and watched moonlight glisten off the bayou. He loved coming out here at night. The swamp was the playground of the nighttime predator.

Like him, he thought as he kept his eyes trained on the water.

Amidst the trills and croaks and chirps of the small, harmless creatures came the occasional bellow of a bull gator. All around him, he could sense the scurry of tiny feet through dead leaves, the watchful eyes deep within the shadows.

After a while, his patient vigil was rewarded, and he spotted the telltale ribbon of silver in the water. A snake swam, head up, toward the bank and a moment later, the thick body glided through the moss and underbrush mere inches from where Ellis perched.

The serpent must have sensed his presence for it stopped, hidden in the shadow of a rotting log. Ellis had a stick in one hand, and, rising, he struck it against the ground where the reptile lay concealed.

Most snakes would have slithered even farther under the log for protection, but not the cottonmouth. Water moccasins were stubborn and aggressive, and Ellis knew only too well that they would sometimes come at you if you weren't careful.

The snake reared up out of the shadows, mouth wide open, fangs bared and ready. It sprang forward, whether to strike or to frighten, Ellis didn't know. Or care. He was ready for it. His hand shot out, grasping the moccasin behind the fist-sized head. Laughing softly, he lifted the serpent up high.

In the moonlight, Ellis could see the thick bulge of the poison sacs beneath the gleaming eyes. The odor emitted from the open mouth was dank and foul, like stagnated water, but Ellis didn't mind it.

The thick body curled and writhed, and he laughed again. "You'll not get away from me," he said. "I have big plans for you."

He'd brought a burlap sack from home, and with one hand, he shoved the snake inside, then with the other hand, he drew the drawstring tight. The sides of the bag moved and shivered as the snake searched for a way out.

Careful to hold the bag above the drawstring, Ellis set off through the woods.

He emerged half a mile downstream where a brush arbor had been erected on the bank of the swamp. An old-timey revival meeting was in full swing, and he moved in closer to watch, though he had no intention of participating.

She was there. He could see her blond hair glistening underneath the string of lights powered by a nearby generator. While the congregation swayed and clapped and some members even passed out cold as the rapture overcame them, she remained as still as a statue.

Ellis moved to the side of the arbor so that he could see her profile. Bathed in all that light, she looked like an angel, and his heart raced as he watched her. Ellis had all the confidence in the world, but truth be told, he was still a little in awe of her.

Which was why, up until now, he'd been content to remain her follower. But over the past few days, he'd been getting antsy. All this plotting and planning… Why not just snatch the kid and be done with it?

He knew the answer, of course. The sword of God had to be wielded with both valor and discretion.

On the makeshift stage, two men held snakes high above their heads as the preacher, eyes closed, hands lifted to heaven, spoke in an unknown tongue.

His rich, baritone voice echoed through the darkness, across the swamp, and stirred something deep and primitive inside Ellis's soul.

Moving to the back of the arbor, he felt his control slip away as the power of the moment swept over him.

Against his will, he began to quiver and shake all over, and his knees turned to jelly. When he collapsed to the ground, he lay in the dirt, eyes rolled back in his head, tongue flicking in and out as he began to writhe and twist like the moccasin in the burlap bag beside him.

The spell lasted only a moment, but when he came to himself and sat up, his heart pounded in elation because he knew without a doubt that his seizure had been a sign.

Ellis Cooper was, indeed, one of the chosen. A warrior, a prophet, a demon chaser with the power of God behind him.

Twenty

As soon as she could get away the next day, Evangeline drove over to see Lena Saunders. Josh opened the door, showing not the slightest bit of surprise at her unannounced visit.

"Nice to see you again, Detective. I'll go get Lena."

This time he merely waved her into the living room as he continued down the hallway toward the back of the house.

Lena Saunders appeared a few minutes later. Today she was dressed all in white and her blond hair fell in thick, gleaming waves to her shoulders.

"Hello," she said as she glided into the room. "I wasn't expecting to see you again so soon. I'm delighted, of course." She waved toward the chair Evangeline had occupied the day before. "Please have a seat."

"I don't need to sit," Evangeline said. "This won't take long."

"What's on your mind?"

"I've made some calls, done some background research," Evangeline said. "I don't have anything to report yet on Rebecca Lemay's whereabouts, but I'm working on it. I spoke to the administrator at Pinehurst Manor and he's agreed to see me. I'm driving up there as soon as I can get away. It's possible the hospital will have a forwarding address for Rebecca."

"What about the old Lemay house?" Lena asked. "I'm convinced someone saw Rebecca there a few days ago."

"I'll have a look around," Evangeline said. "But it's out of my jurisdiction. All I can do is ask a few questions. The sheriff down there is under no obligation to cooperate."

Lena nodded. "I understand. But hopefully you'll be able to get more out of him than I've been able to. You'll give me a call if you find out anything?"

"Yes, but don't expect a daily report. This could take a while. It's not like I can devote myself to it full-time. Unless Lapierre sees fit to put me back on the Courtland case, I'll have to do most of the legwork on my own time."

"How will you explain your absence when you drive up to Pinehurst?"

"I'll take a personal day," Evangeline said. The first one since she'd returned from maternity leave.

"I've made some calls, too," Lena said as she crossed the room to a sleek black writing desk. Opening a small notebook, she ripped off the top sheet. "I was afraid at first I wouldn't have much to report. My sources at NOPD were reluctant to talk about Johnny's case. Now I know why. Were you aware that the FBI has taken over the investigation?"

"What?" Evangeline stared at her in shock. "Why would the FBI have Johnny's case? That doesn't make any sense."

"I agree," Lena said. "But that's a question for this man." She handed Evangeline the slip of paper she'd ripped from the notebook. "As I understand it, he's the one who's been put in charge of Johnny's case."

Evangeline looked down at the name neatly written in black ink.

Special Agent Declan Nash.

Nash could have refused to see Detective Theroux, but he suspected she would camp out in the parking lot until he left for the night.

Might as well let her have her say, he decided.

He went downstairs and got her himself. She had to sign in and surrender her weapon before passing through the metal detector, and as she walked toward him, clipping the visitor's badge to her lapel, he could see that her eyes were burning with anger.

She was absolutely furious and he wondered what she'd managed to dig up in the short time since he'd last seen her. Her resolve was pretty formidable.

"Let's go upstairs to my office," he said as he headed for the elevators.

She was silent on the way up. Facing forward, she glanced neither to the right nor left, and when they reached his floor, she disembarked and stepped aside so that he could lead the way.

Once they were in his office, he closed the door and motioned to a chair as he settled in behind his desk. "What can I do for you, Detective Theroux?"

"You can start by telling me why the FBI has taken charge of my husband's murder investigation. Or more specifically, why *you've* taken charge of it."

"You've obviously been misinformed. Again."

"And you obviously still think I'm an idiot. You've been manipulating this whole thing right from the start. What I can't figure out is why. I'm guessing Johnny had something to do with the Sonny Betts operation, am I right? Did he—how did you put it?—blunder in over his head and you failed to wade in and pull him out in time?"

Nash studied her from across his desk, wondering who in the hell at NOPD was leaking information to her.

He didn't like loose lips and he liked mistakes even less, especially when they were of his own making. He'd made a gross miscalculation with Detective Theroux. He'd done the one thing he'd sworn he wouldn't do. He'd underestimated her.

In spite of her impressive record, in spite of everything he knew about her, he'd never expected her to get this far.

He'd used bad judgment, including his failure to bring in Nathan Mallet when he had the chance. Now the poor bastard was dead, and some of his blood might arguably be on Nash's hands.

But not Johnny Theroux's blood.

That situation had already been set in motion before Nash had ever even arrived in New Orleans. His job had been the cleanup.

He was still cleaning up.

Rising, he walked over to the window to stare down at the parking lot. Some view, he thought.

"You've got some of it right," he finally said as he turned back to face Evangeline.

Her blue eyes burned with anger. "Which part?"

"It does have something to do with the Betts operation. Johnny walked in on a buy."

"You mean a drug deal?"

"Drugs, arms. Like I said, Sonny Betts has his fingers in a lot of pies these days. Whether Johnny knew what he was walking into or not, we don't know. Maybe he was tipped off, maybe he was just at the wrong place at the wrong time."

Her eyes were still blazing, but her voice was unnaturally calm. "Nathan Mallet told me that Johnny went to the parking garage to meet a woman that night."

"I wouldn't put too much stock in anything Nathan Mallet had to say. I'm sure his main interest was getting you off his back."

"Why?"

He turned back to the window for a moment, frowning into the sunlight. "Mallet was a dirty cop. He'd been on the take for years." When she didn't respond, he glanced over his shoulder. "You don't seem surprised."

"About Nathan? I guess I'm not. The way he behaved after Johnny's shooting…I knew something was wrong. Was he working for Betts?"

"That's a reasonable assumption."

She looked annoyed by his parsing. "Is that a yes or a no?"

"I can't give you a definitive answer."

"Can't or won't?"

He shrugged.

She decided to try another tack. "Did Nathan lure Johnny into the parking garage that night?"

"He might have, if he thought Johnny was onto him."

She got up and came over to the window where he stood. "You do know Nathan's dead?"

"Yes."

"Of course you do," she said ruefully. "You probably knew before we did. You probably also know that he was killed the same way Johnny was. Three shots—two to the chest and one to the face."

"Sounds like somebody wanted to make sure he didn't talk."

"You think Betts had him killed?"

"I think there were a number of people who wanted Nathan Mallet to go away."

"Including you guys?"

"We're not in the extermination business," he said.

"Not lately, anyway," she muttered. She walked back over to the chair, but she didn't sit. She was too amped for that. "Why wasn't I told any of this before?"

"You weren't asking questions before. When you came back to work after your baby was born, you started shaking things up. That's when you got our attention. We couldn't allow you to take things too far."

"*Allow?*" Her outrage flared. "That's why you had me removed from the Courtland case. You didn't want me connecting it to Johnny."

"We didn't want you going anywhere near Sonny Betts with some half-cocked notion of revenge."

"I'm not into revenge," she said. "What I am into is justice."

"You'll get it," he said. "It may take a while, but you'll have your justice."

"And why should I believe that?" she asked coldly. "When I haven't been able to trust a single word out of your mouth yet."

Nash stood at the window and watched her stride across the parking lot to her car.

He'd done a piss-poor job of containing this whole situation, but at least now he was dealing with Evangeline Theroux face-to-face.

He'd never had much of a taste for the machinations that came with his job. He preferred a much more straightforward approach, though he didn't delude himself into thinking this was over. Evangeline Theroux was now a woman on a mission, and he knew she wouldn't give up without a fight. She'd keeping digging and digging until she uncovered the truth.

But truth was a relative term.

The question now wasn't so much *if* she found out, but when and how. It was a matter of degrees and increments. Control was the key.

His phone rang and he removed it from his pocket to glance at the name on the display: Louisiana Correctional Institute for Women.

He closed his eyes and drew a breath. "Hello?"

"Dad?"

At the sound of his daughter's voice, Nash's chest tightened and he felt a familiar wave of helplessness wash over him even as he tried to keep his voice calm and normal. "Hi, baby. How are you today?"

"Not so good. This place is awful, Dad. I don't think I can stand it here one more day. I'm going crazy. Sometimes I wish I could just…" Her voice caught as she trailed off. She sounded like the lost little girl that she was. "I just want to come home."

"I know you do." He drew another breath as he ran a hand through his hair. "But that's not going to happen anytime soon."

"I know."

"I'll try to come up there to see you this weekend," he said. "Would you like that?"

"Yes. But, Dad…when's Mom coming? It's been so long since I've seen her. Is she mad at me?"

"No, baby. She's just busy. New husband and all that. I'll give her a call and see if we can stagger our weekends. That way it won't be so long between visits. Would that help?"

"I guess so. I just want to get out of here. Please, Daddy. *Please.* There must be something you can do."

She started to sob quietly into the phone.

Nash looked out over the sun-baked parking lot as his throat tightened and his chest felt ready to explode. "You killed someone, Jamie. I can't make that go away."

Twenty-one

Evangeline called Mitchell as soon as she got back to her car. While she waited for him to answer, she lifted her gaze to the building in front of her and idly counted the floors. For a moment, she thought she spotted Nash in the window of his office. Then she lost him in the glare of sunlight off the glass, and she decided it probably hadn't been him anyway.

"Hebert," Mitchell said on the other end.

Evangeline leaned forward and started her car. "Where are you right now?"

"I'm at the station," he said. "What's up?"

"I thought we might take a drive out to the lake."

"I'm all for that," he said. "But something tells me we're not going out there for lunch."

"We're going to see Sonny Betts again," Evangeline said.

"Wait a minute. I think we have a bad connection. Because I could have sworn I just heard you say something about going to see Sonny Betts. And I know you didn't actually say that because you're not stuck on stupid."

"What's stupid about wanting to ask him a few more questions regarding the murder of his former attorney?"

"What isn't stupid about it? One, you're not even on the case, and two, you heard what Lapierre said about Betts. We don't make another move on a guy like that unless we have got some heavy-duty artillery to use against him. Right now, we've got squat."

"I'm not suggesting we go in with guns blazing," Evangeline said. "I'm talking about a friendly little chat. I'm headed out there right now. I was kind of hoping you'd meet me."

"And then Lapierre can kick both our asses, is that it?"

"What do you care about Lapierre? You're moving to Houston."

"That's not a done deal, and it's beside the point anyway."

"What if I told you that Betts had something to do with Johnny's death?"

He gave a loud, exasperated sigh. "Based on what, Evie?"

"Based on what Special Agent Declan Nash of the FBI just told me in his office. Johnny's death wasn't random, Mitchell. There's a good chance he was set up."

"By who?"

"Nathan Mallet."

"Why would Nathan set up Johnny?"

"Because I think Johnny found out Nathan was dirty. He worked for Betts."

"And just what do you hope to prove by going out there and rattling Betts's cage again?"

"This time, it's not Betts's cage I'm trying to rattle," she said. "It's Declan Nash's."

Evangeline was five minutes from her rendez-vous point with Mitchell when she realized she was being followed. Earlier she'd spotted a red Mustang behind her when she left the federal building, and she'd thought at first it might be Nathan's stolen car.

But the driver made a right at the first traffic light, and Evangeline hadn't caught sight of the car again.

The vehicle behind her now was a black Lincoln with heavily tinted windows.

Keeping an eye in the rearview mirror, Evangeline made a quick left on a red light, hoping to lose the tail, but the Lincoln shot up behind her, tapping her bumper just as a car approaching from the other direction swerved in front of her.

Evangeline had no choice but to hit the brakes as the two cars wedged her between them. Heavily armed men spilled out of the vehicles and surrounded her car with enough artillery to start a small war. Guns were suddenly pointed at her from every direction.

"Get out of the car now!"

A dozen different actions raced through Evangeline's head, none of them viable at the moment. She had no choice but to do as she was told.

Pushing open the door, she slowly climbed out.

"Throw your weapon on the ground. Do it now!"

Rough hands seized her then and her arms were pulled behind her back and cuffed. Dragging her over to one of the cars, they shoved her into the backseat and slammed the door.

By the time Evangeline could struggle to a sitting position, the car was already moving. The whole confrontation had taken less than thirty seconds. So fast any onlookers probably wouldn't have even realized what was going on until it was too late.

"Who are you people?" Her heart thudded against her chest and she tried to ignore the pain that streaked across her shoulders.

"You have no idea what you've been meddling in," the man on the passenger side said.

"What are you talking about? Who are you?" she asked again.

But he merely gave her a withering look and turned back to face the front.

She glanced out the window at the passing scenery.

She thought at first they were going to Sonny Betts's place, but instead they cut back and traveled a maze of side streets and alleys until they reached a warehouse. The overhead door was activated by a remote and the big car slid inside. A moment later, the door rumbled closed behind them.

Evangeline glanced around, trying to get some sense of her surroundings, but they were in total darkness. She was taken out of the car and led to the back of the building, where her cuffs were removed and a gruff voice instructed her to sit. When she failed to comply, she was pushed down on a wooden, straight-back chair, and her wrists were once again fastened behind her.

"What do you want?" she asked.

No response.

"Who are you?"

Only silence.

"If you people think you can snatch a New Orleans homicide detective without consequences, I suggest you think again."

Someone laughed this time.

"You should be worrying about the consequences of your own actions, Detective Theroux. You just don't know when to quit, do you?"

She tried to get up, but a hand on her shoulder pressed her back down.

"You may as well get comfortable," a second voice said behind her. "You've got a wait ahead of you."

"What am I waiting for?"

"If I told you that, it'd take all the fun out of it, now wouldn't it?"

The room fell silent. No one spoke again until a side door opened and a third man stepped into the warehouse. Evangeline could hear the low murmur of voices in the dark, but she couldn't make out what any of them were saying.

The door opened again and for a moment, Evangeline thought they had left her. Then an overhead light came on and she squinted, momentarily blinded by the brilliance.

When her vision cleared, she saw Declan Nash standing in front her.

"I figured it would come to this," he said. "But I didn't think it would be this soon."

"Come to what?" she asked angrily. "Kidnapping?"

"A lot of people went to a great deal of trouble to keep this day from happening," he said. "You have no idea."

"Why don't you stop speaking in riddles and tell me what the hell is going on." Evangeline tugged at the handcuffs. "And while you're at it, how about taking these things off me?"

He reached behind him and plucked a key off a small wooden desk. Then he walked around the chair and unfastened the cuffs.

Evangeline jumped up and whirled to face him

as she massaged her wrists. "Was that really necessary?"

"With you, yes." His glance traveled over her and she thought for a moment he looked anxious. "You're not hurt, are you?"

She was still rubbing her wrists. "I'll live."

He moved around to the front of the table.

"What's going on?" she demanded. "Why did you bring me here?"

"This seemed as good a place as any to give you what you want."

"And that is?"

"The truth," he said, "About Johnny."

Her heart skipped a beat as she walked toward the desk. "And why should I believe you this time?"

"You don't have to believe me." He lifted the lid from a cardboard crate on the table and removed a thick file folder, which he plopped down in front of her. "You can reach your own conclusions."

Her gaze dropped to the folder. "What is this?"

"Your husband's file. If you're not convinced by the time you've reached the end, there's more where that came from."

When she made no move to open the folder, he said, "Go on. Take a look." He grabbed a wooden chair and shoved it toward her. "Here," he said. "You better sit. This could take a while."

Reluctantly Evangeline pulled up the chair and sat down. She placed her hand on the folder, but for some reason, she couldn't bring herself to open it. She didn't understand fully what was going on here, but she instinctively knew she wasn't going to like what she found inside that file.

She glanced up. Nash had moved over by the door and was on his cell phone.

Again her gaze dropped to the folder. *Open it. Just get it over with.*

She flipped it open and the first thing she saw was a picture of Johnny.

Her heart almost stopped.

There he was. Just the way she remembered him.

Her Johnny. The love of her life.

She drew a shaky breath as she made herself study the photo. The shot had been taken through a window using a telephone lens. Johnny was standing in an unfamiliar room conversing with another man that Evangeline recognized as Sonny Betts.

She looked up, saw that Nash was watching her, and she quickly glanced back down.

Johnny…and Sonny Betts?

No. No.

No.

Another photo had been shot poolside with Johnny, Betts and several other people Evangeline didn't recognize. Drinks in hand, they were all laughing and smiling and totally oblivious to the camera.

By this time, Evangeline's hands were shaking so

badly she could barely pick up the photographs. There were dozens. Shots of Johnny with Betts, shots of Johnny with men she didn't know, shots of Johnny in his car emerging from the parking garage where he'd been killed.

There were surveillance notes, too, all carefully stamped with the date and time. Some of the notes were nearly two years old.

Evangeline scrutinized every photo, read every note, scoured every report. And when she was finished, she closed the folder and sat for a moment, not trusting herself to speak.

"Do you want to see more?" Nash asked quietly. He left his spot by the door and came over to the table.

She shook her head. "I've seen enough for one day."

"I'm sorry."

"Are you really?" She didn't know why her anger was still directed at Nash.

"Like I said, no one wanted it to come to this."

Johnny's betrayal was as heavy as an iron cloak on her shoulders. She felt small and beat down. "Who's no one? Who else knows about this?"

"Apart from my team, a few people at NOPD."

She closed her eyes. "Why wasn't I told?"

"It's a sensitive issue," he said. "There's still an ongoing investigation. I'm only telling you now because your questions were creating an uncomfortable situation."

"Uncomfortable," she repeated numbly.

"I really am sorry you had to find out—"

"How long?"

"How long—"

"How long was he working for Betts?"

"At least two years. He was already under surveillance when I took over the operation. He was probably approached when Betts returned from Houston and started building his network. Johnny and Nathan Mallet were both on the payroll."

"That's what I don't understand. If Johnny was on the take, where did the money go? We didn't lead a lavish lifestyle. Far from it. We barely made ends meet. The only reason I've got some breathing room now is because of his life-insurance policy."

"He probably funneled everything into an offshore bank account. He was a smart guy. He knew the only way to avoid suspicion was to keep a low profile."

And just what was he going to do with all that money? Evangeline wondered. Had she and the baby figured into his future plans at all?

"He wasn't smart enough to keep himself alive, was he?" she said harshly. "What happened? Did he fall out of favor with Betts?"

"We think a rival syndicate took him out. A power play, most likely."

"What about the woman he went to see?"

"She worked for Betts. She handled the money. I doubt there was a personal relationship between them. We never saw any evidence of it."

"Well, that's something I guess." Evangeline pushed aside the folder and stood. "I'd like to leave now if you don't mind."

"I'll drive you home."

"Don't take this personally," she said. "But right now, you're the last person I want to be with."

That evening, Evangeline carried the baby monitor out to the front porch and sat down on the top step. She remembered sitting there the night before when all she had to worry about was a strange car in the neighborhood and whether or not to believe the outrageous story that Lena Saunders had told her.

She still didn't know whether to believe that story. But one thing was certain. Lena Saunders had led her to the truth about Johnny.

Her eyes burned with fatigue and unshed tears, but she wouldn't give in to her emotions. She'd never been the type to wallow in despair, not even in the aftermath of Johnny's shooting. She had J.D. to think of. She was all he had left.

Down the block, a car door opened and closed, and Evangeline watched as a man crossed the street and started up the sidewalk toward her house. Her gun was on the porch beside her, and she put her hand over the weapon and kept it there until he'd turned up her sidewalk and she recognized who he was.

Nash paused as their gazes met in the twilight. Then he slowly closed the distance to the porch and climbed the steps.

She turned her head up to him. "How long have you been sitting out there?"

"A while. I wanted to make sure you'd gotten home all right."

"Don't your agents give you a report?"

"I guess I wanted to see for myself." He hesitated. "I'll leave if you want."

"Suit yourself. I don't care one way or the other."

He still hesitated before finally lowering himself to the step beside her. "Do you want to talk about it?"

"What's there to talk about? My husband was on the take and I never suspected a thing. All I want to know now is how I could have been so blind."

"Don't beat yourself up. You didn't do anything wrong."

"Good thing stupidity's not a crime."

He planted his forearms on his thighs and gazed out into the gathering darkness. "For what it's worth, I understand a little of how you must be feeling. I know what it's like to be disillusioned about the person you trusted most in the world."

"You don't know how I feel right now."

"I know about betrayal. I was married to a woman for fifteen years," he said. "I thought we had the perfect marriage. Then one day, out of the blue, she told me she wanted a divorce. She said she hadn't been happy for a really long time, and she needed to find herself while she still had her youth. That's actually what she said to me."

Evangeline turned to stare at him.

He gave her a little sideways smile. "That's not the worst part. I thought with a little time, a little space, we'd be able to work things out. A few weeks after she left, I found out she was already living with her boss. They'd been having an affair for nearly a year. He was married, too, and he and his wife went through a nasty divorce because of Deb. Both families got dragged through the mud before it was all said and done. The fallout nearly ruined my career. The bureau tends to frown on a messy personal life."

"How did you get over it?"

"It took a long time and I made a lot of stupid mistakes along the way. But the worst part is what all that did to our daughter. She's still paying the price for what we put her through."

"How old is she?"

He turned back to the darkness. "She just turned twenty a couple of months ago. We celebrated her birthday at the Louisiana Correctional Institute in Saint Gabriel."

Evangeline turned in surprise. "She's an inmate?"

"For her eighteenth birthday, she and her friends went out partying. They were all well over the legal limit, but Jamie was the one driving that night. She veered into the wrong lane and hit a car head-on. The other driver was killed instantly. Two of the girls in the car with Jamie were critically injured. Jamie suffered a concussion and a broken leg. She was still on crutches when she was convicted of vehicular manslaughter and sentenced to ten years in prison. She'll be eligible for parole in another two."

Evangeline had no idea what to say to that. "My brother's an ex-con. He served nearly seven years in Angola for robbing a convenience store. My parents were devastated. I don't think they ever got over it."

"I don't think I ever will, either," he said quietly.

They fell silent for the longest time as night settled over the neighborhood. Heat lightning shimmered in the distance as the breeze off the river kicked up. It was the kind of night that always made Evangeline feel lonely and lost.

"I should go," Nash said beside her. It was almost a question.

She nodded.

"Are you going to be all right?"

She tried to smile. "I guess that's the upside to having someone knock on your door and tell you your husband is dead. I've already survived the worst night of my life. I'll get through this, too."

He fished a card from his pocket and laid it on the porch beside her. "This is my number. If you need anything…"

"I won't. But thanks."

He rose and walked down the porch steps. When he got to the bottom, she said his name and he turned to glance up at her.

"Why did you really come here tonight?"

He hesitated, glanced out over the yard and then his gaze came back to her. "Because I wanted to see you."

And then he turned and walked off into the darkness while Evangeline sat hugging her knees, an odd little catch in her chest.

She didn't think she'd be able to sleep, but it was funny how exhaustion and mental anguish could sometimes be your best friend.

After checking on J.D., Evangeline curled up in bed, staring into the darkness as her thoughts tumbled one over another.

She thought about all those pictures of Johnny and Sonny Betts, the meticulous surveillance documentation, the tapped phone conversations that the FBI had assembled against her husband.

She thought about her parents' troubled marriage and the hell that Vaughn had put them through.

They'd survived untold heartache over the years only to end up separated because her father was restless and her mother was not an easy woman to love.

She thought about the night J.D. had been born and the day she'd brought him home from the hospital, and she wondered if she would ever be able to love him the way he deserved to be loved.

She thought about the bizarre story Lena Saunders had told her about two little girls named Ruth and Rebecca. One innocent, one a murderer.

She thought about origami cranes and the man with the scarred face.

And just before she fell asleep, she thought of Declan Nash. He had a daughter named Jamie and an ex-wife named Deb.

And he had come to Evangeline's house tonight because he wanted to see her.

Sometime later, Evangeline awakened to a strange sound. This time she knew it wasn't the television because she hadn't turned it on. The sound was again coming from the baby monitor on her bedside table.

But there was no music this time. What she heard was the sound of J.D. fretting and a strange woman's voice soothing him that chilled her blood.

"Shush. She'll hear you."

Twenty-two

A woman leaned over the railing of J.D.'s crib. She was on the opposite side from the door, away from the night-light, and for a moment she seemed no more than a ghostly outline that blended seamlessly into the shadows.

Evangeline blinked, praying the mirage would disappear even as she gripped her weapon in both hands and took aim. Her heart hammered so hard she could scarcely breathe, but her finger on the trigger was steady.

"Move away from the crib!"

Slowly, the woman looked up, but she didn't step away or even straighten. Her face was hidden by a cowl of blond hair that fell forward from a center part. There was something strange and otherworldly about her featureless visage, and Evangeline felt the coldest kind of dread settle in the pit of her stomach.

"Step back," she said, "before I blow your fucking head off."

The woman's hands were inside the crib, and as she straightened, she lifted J.D. over the rail and held him in front of her. "There, there," she crooned.

Panic exploded in Evangeline's chest. She wanted desperately to keep a clear head, but even after hearing the woman's voice coming from the baby monitor, she had never expected to find anything like this. She didn't know what to do. Terror had momentarily disabled all her training and common sense.

Think, Evangeline. For God's sakes, use your head.

Okay, options.

Without a clear shot, the gun was useless. Besides, she would never dare chance even a warning shot with the baby so close. Nor could she risk trying to get to the phone. Any sudden move might set the woman off.

So at the moment, there were no options, Evangeline quickly concluded. She and J.D. were at this person's mercy.

The baby roused and whimpered, then dropped his little head against the woman's shoulder as she began to massage his back. She hummed the music-box tune, and the haunting melody sent a chill up Evangeline's already frozen spine.

"Please," she whispered. "Just give me the baby and leave. I don't know who you are or what you want...." Her voice cracked and she took a moment to get herself under control. "Just put him down and walk away."

"You don't have to be afraid. I'm not going to hurt him. I would never do that."

"Prove it," Evangeline pleaded. "Give him to me."

As she took a step into the room, the woman eased farther back into the shadows. "Not yet." Her hand continued to make circles on J.D.'s back. He sniveled in his sleep, and she held him even closer then kissed the top of his head. "Put your gun on the dresser and move back to the door."

When Evangeline hesitated, the woman said, "Please, just do as I say. Guns are so dangerous. If anything were to happen to this precious baby, you'd never be able to live with yourself."

"Okay, okay. I'll do anything you say. Just please don't hurt him." Evangeline put the gun on the dresser and then stepped back into the doorway.

The woman moved over to the window and the nebulous silhouette that had been almost invisible in the shadows took on a real form in the glow of moonlight that seeped in through the glass. She was only a few steps away, and Evangeline wondered if she could rush her and grab J.D. before she had time to hurt him.

It was a chance she wasn't willing to take. Not yet.

Evangeline scrutinized the intruder. She was

pale and thin, and she wore a plain, dark skirt, shapeless cardigan and tennis shoes. With her free hand, she pushed one side of her long, thick hair from her face, and it tumbled in a tangled, blond mess over one shoulder.

"What do you want?" Evangeline asked in a calm, reasonable tone. "Tell me so we can end this."

"I have a story to tell you."

Evangeline swallowed. "Okay. But why don't you put the baby in the crib. We can talk in the other room."

She smiled over the top of J.D.'s head. "I think it would be better if we talk in here."

"We might wake up the baby. You don't want to do that."

"But without the baby, you won't listen to me. And if you don't know the whole story, you won't be able to understand. So far, you've only heard *her* side."

"Her?"

"My sister." She looked up and the light from the window caught her in such a way that Evangeline saw another face, also thin and pale, but more refined. More elegant.

The resemblance in that moment was so uncanny, she didn't know why she hadn't seen it right off.

"You're Rebecca," she said softly. "And Lena Saunders is your sister, Ruth."

Why hadn't the woman told her the truth? Evangeline wondered. Why pretend she was someone else? Lena Saunders and Ruth Lemay were one and the same. And now Evangeline stood facing Rebecca Lemay. What kind of strange game were the sisters playing with her?

Rebecca Lemay nuzzled the top of J.D.'s head and drew a deep breath, as if trying to drink in the very essence of the sleeping child.

And Evangeline went weak in the knees. *Dear God.*

According to Lena Saunders—Ruth Lemay— this was a woman who, as a child, had helped her mother murder one of their young brothers. This was a woman who, as an adult, had killed at least three men in cold blood.

And now she held Evangeline's sleeping son in her arms. Her cheek was against the baby's head as she rocked him back and forth.

Chill after chill swept over Evangeline. The scene before her seemed surreal. It couldn't possibly be happening, and yet…it was.

Outside the window behind Rebecca Lemay, the sky darkened to cinder and Evangeline could see heat lightning in the distance. Her gaze lit on the weapon she'd placed on the dresser. It was so close and yet as useless as a severed limb.

"How did you get in here?" she asked.

"The girl who watches the baby…I saw her put the key underneath a rock by your front porch."

So she'd used Jessie's key to let herself into the

house. Evangeline thought about the molted snake-skin she'd found, and her heart pounded even harder. "Have you been in here before?"

"It doesn't matter," Rebecca said. "The only thing that matters now is that you hear my side of the story."

"Okay. I'm listening."

Her cheek still rested on J.D.'s head as she cradled him snugly against her bosom. "It was a long time ago, but I still remember everything about that day. Mama was acting so strange. I didn't understand why, but I sensed something bad was about to happen. For days, I'd had this awful tightness in my chest. It was like trying to breathe underwater. I even dreamed one night that I was drowning…." She cuddled J.D. even closer and he whimpered again in his sleep.

Please, Evangeline prayed. *Please, please don't hurt him.*

"Mama hadn't really been herself since Daddy left, but this was different. It was like…something had taken hold of her. Possessed her…" She paused to draw a long breath. "She started cleaning the house like a mad woman. I thought company might be coming, but we never had visitors. Even the church people stopped calling. Mama always kept a spotless home, but that day she scrubbed and mopped and dusted until every room sparkled. She worked at it for hours, on into the night. I could hear her downstairs after we'd put the boys to bed. Working and working. She and my sister. When I went down to see about them, they were on their hands and knees, scrubbing the same floor Mama had mopped that very afternoon. She didn't even look up at me, but my sister told me to go on back to bed and leave them alone. They had work to do and I was too little to help."

Her voice had gotten slightly higher as she told the story, and the years seemed to melt from her face so that Evangeline could see clearly the child from the photograph. A little girl whose innocence had been so fractured by her mother's obsession that she was never going to be whole.

She was still looking at Evangeline, but her eyes were losing their focus as she slipped back into the past.

"I woke up just after dawn and my sister's bed was empty. I figured she and Mama were still working. I got up and dressed. When I came out into the hallway, I heard a sound from Mama's bedroom. Like a moan or a soft cry. I didn't know what to make of it. I was scared to go in there and see, and yet I couldn't stay away. I thought Mama might need me. So I eased down the hallway and opened her door."

Evangeline stood motionless in the doorway. Their gazes made contact, but somehow she knew the woman couldn't see her. Her features were slack and her voice had taken on the numb monotone of someone under hypnosis.

"The sheets were covered with blood. I thought Mama must have hurt herself and now she might be dying. But then I saw my sister at the foot of the bed. She had a doll in her arms, and I couldn't understand why she would be playing house with Mama lying there hurt so bad. Then I heard the doll cry and I realized that it was a baby. Mama had just given birth. That seemed so strange to me because I didn't even know she was…that way. I wanted to see the baby, but my sister said no. That would just make everything so much harder. She told me to go back to our room and close the door. She'd come get me when it was over."

"When what was over?" Evangeline asked in a hushed voice. Because she knew. She already knew what was coming.

Rebecca Lemay fell silent for a moment, her face in silhouette as she half turned to the window. "When Mama…when it started, I didn't understand what was happening at first. Not until I saw…" She trailed off on a deep shudder that racked her whole body. "Then all I could think about was saving that baby. So I took it downstairs and crawled into the whispering room."

"What's the whispering room?" Evangeline's heart was still thudding against her chest.

"It was a little space underneath the stairs where

Mama used to make us go when she needed some peace and quiet. We weren't allowed to make any racket in there. All we could do was whisper. I stayed in there for a long time with the baby. Until all the screaming finally stopped."

Until all the screaming stopped.

The taste of bile filled her mouth as she pictured that horrifying scene.

Rebecca Lemay took a step forward, her eyes wide and shimmering and childlike. "You understand what I'm telling you, don't you? It didn't happen like she said. It wasn't me. It was her. My sister, Ruth. She was the one who always helped Mama take care of the boys."

It took a moment for Evangeline to fully comprehend her meaning. "How did she help take care of them?"

"She dressed them in the morning and combed their hair for church and listened to their prayers at bedtime. She even read them Bible stories when Mama had the headache. She was Mama's little helper. God's little warrior. That's what Mama always called her."

"What else did she do?"

Rebecca Lemay's eyes gleamed with madness. "She helped Mama save them."

Twenty-three

Evangeline could see the swirl of blue lights outside her living room as she leaned a shoulder
against the wall, feeling oddly detached from the
chaos inside her house.

Two uniforms stood just inside the front door,
one scribbling on a clipboard while the other was
on his cell phone. Another two were outside can-
vassing the yard while crime scene techs were busy
dusting for prints in the nursery and at the back
door where Rebecca Lemay had made her escape.

NOPD always turned out in full force for one
of their own.

Even an outsider like me.

Although maybe she wasn't as much of an
outsider as she'd always thought. Nash had said
there were those within the department who had
tried to protect her from the details of Johnny's

death. And right now, Evangeline would be hard-pressed to make the argument that these guys were treating her with anything but camaraderie, sympathy and the utmost respect.

Mitchell arrived a few minutes after the first squad car, and J.D. had been screaming at the top of his lungs by then. All the commotion and Evangeline's adrenaline had terrified him, and it had taken her a long time to calm him.

Finally, after a bottle, he'd gone back to sleep and she'd put him down on her bed and barricaded him with pillows. She'd left the door ajar and planted herself just outside so that she would be able to hear him if he so much as whimpered.

As soon as the tech came out of the nursery, she motioned him over.

"Did you find anything?" she asked anxiously.

"I lifted some prints off the crib. Once we eliminate yours and the sitter's, we can run them through the computer. We can also check for a match with the prints we found at the Courtland crime scene. Who knows? We might get lucky." He didn't sound too hopeful, though.

Mitchell, who was standing beside Evangeline, shook his head in disbelief. "Just when you think a case can't get any more peculiar, now we've got a pair of twisted sisters to deal with."

"Yeah, no kidding."

After the tech left, Evangeline glanced up at

Mitchell. "Look, I'm really sorry I didn't tell you earlier about the interview with Lena Saunders. Ruth Lemay. Whoever the hell she is." She shook her head in confusion. "It's your case and you deserved to know. But Lapierre specifically told me not to say anything to anyone until she had a chance to evaluate Saunders's story. You know how she is."

"Hey, don't worry about it. It wasn't your call to make. I can't help wondering why you were the one singled out, though."

"Lena Saunders knew Johnny. At least, that's what she claims. When she saw my name in the paper attached to the Courtland case, she decided I was the one she wanted to talk to."

"And the nut-job that showed up here tonight?"

"Evidently, she wanted to set the record straight. She basically disputed everything her sister told me. She says that Ruth is the one who helped their mother."

"So which sister is telling the truth?"

"What is truth?" Evangeline murmured.

"Huh?"

"Nothing. I was just remembering something Lena told me."

"If her story checks out and we find Rebecca Lemay's prints at the crime scene, I guess we can pretty much eliminate Sonny Betts's involvement in all this."

"It's starting to look that way," Evangeline agreed. The memory of everything she'd learned the day before suddenly came rushing back and she felt exactly the way Rebecca Lemay had described her premonition—like trying to breathe underwater. Her chest tightened and for a moment, panic bubbled in her throat. Johnny had been on Sonny Betts's payroll. She'd seen the evidence with her own two eyes, and yet Evangeline knew it would take a long, long time before she'd ever be able to fully accept his betrayal.

"I found out some other things about Sonny Betts," she told Mitchell.

"Oh, yeah?" He turned and studied her face.

She glanced around. The living room was clearing out, but she still didn't want to take the chance of someone overhearing her. "I want to talk to you about it, but not here."

"Sure, kiddo. Just name the time and place." His gaze was still on her and he frowned. "You sure you're okay?"

"I will be. I have to be, don't I?"

"Oh, I don't know. Even a tough girl like you deserves a day off now and then."

Evangeline knew he was trying to tease her out of the dark space she'd crawled into that night and she appreciated the effort. She did. But she was still too shaken from finding out about Johnny, and then seeing J.D. in Rebecca Lemay's arms. She didn't want to think about what could have happened, how she might have failed her son yet again.

Mitchell glanced over her shoulder at the front door, and his playful grin vanished. "What the hell is he doing here?"

Evangeline turned and saw Declan Nash on her front porch.

She couldn't believe it. What *was* he doing there?

He opened his ID for the officers at the door, then stepped inside her house and glanced around. The way his gaze swept over her belongings so intently stirred a curious mix of anger and vulnerability in Evangeline.

He was still dressed in a suit even at this hour, and she thought, *Jeez. Doesn't the man ever sleep?*

And then he spotted her and she felt that same blend of anger and vulnerability as their gazes briefly locked.

He said something to one of the cops, then walked over to where she stood with Mitchell. She made the introductions, the two men shook hands briefly, and with a curious scowl, Mitchell drifted away.

"Your partner isn't exactly the friendly sort, is he?"

"Most of the time he is. You just took him by surprise showing up here like this. I have to admit…" She finally let her eyes meet his again. "I'm a little taken aback myself."

"Sorry," he said. "Under the circumstances, I didn't think it appropriate to call first. Besides, I wasn't sure you'd take my call anyway."

"Probably not," she freely admitted. "I guess that's a moot point now, though, because here you are. So why don't we dispense with all the crap and you just tell me how you heard about what happened here tonight?"

"I can't do that."

She folded her arms in annoyance. "Let me guess, then. You either have someone watching my house or your contact at NOPD put a little bug in your ear. Either way, you're not wanted or needed here."

"Thanks."

"No offense, but this isn't any of your concern. It's a local matter, and as you can see—" she motioned toward the cops at the door "—NOPD has the situation under control."

"What about you?"

"What about me?"

"How are you holding up? How's your son?"

"We're both fine. Now if you don't mind—"

"Did you know the woman who broke into your house?"

She rolled her eyes and pushed herself off the wall. "God, you're relentless, aren't you?"

"About some things, yeah."

Their gazes met again, and Evangeline thought, what the hell? He'd find out sooner or later anyway. Evidently, he had a pipeline straight into the police department. "Her name is Rebecca Lemay. She may have been the same woman who was following Paul

Courtland before he was murdered. Looks like you were right about that one."

"What's her connection to Courtland?"

"Nothing you need to be concerned about."

He gave her a bemused smile. "You guys give new meaning to the word *territorial*."

"Oh, really? Wait until I run you off the road and cuff you to keep you away from Sonny Betts. Then we'll talk about territorial."

Mitchell came back over to have a quick word with Evangeline. "We're wrapping things up," he said. "But I don't think you and J.D. should stay here until you get these locks changed. Why don't you two bunk over at my place tonight. Lorraine won't mind."

"Thanks, but we'll be fine here."

"You sure? Better safe than sorry," he warned.

"We'll be fine," Evangeline insisted. "She won't come back tonight." But she wished she was as certain as she sounded.

She walked Mitchell out to the porch where they conversed for a few minutes with some of the other cops. When she came back into the house, Nash was standing at the bedroom door, gazing in at her son.

Nash watched as she closed the distance between them. She looked dead on her feet, and he had the strongest urge to pull her into his arms and hold her close. Where that idea came from, he had no idea, but suddenly he remembered the scent of lavender that had drifted up from her hair that day in the park.

She was tired, but he could still see a spark of defiance in her eyes, as if she'd somehow read his mind. "What are you doing?"

"I thought I heard him cry," he said.

She brushed him to the door. Pausing for a moment on the threshold, she quickly crossed the room and stood by the edge of the bed for a long time before she finally came back out.

"He must have been dreaming." She pulled the door behind her. "It's been a rough night."

"For both of you."

"I don't care about myself. I'm just glad…" He saw her shiver. "It'll be daylight soon. I really don't think we'll have any more trouble tonight."

"I don't think so, either. But I'd really like to hear what this woman said to you."

"Why? I already told you, it's nothing to do with you."

"Maybe I want it to be."

She turned at that. "Why? What are you talking about?"

"Maybe I want to be involved because…I like you."

He punctuated the confession with a little smile, but her face suddenly looked sad and distressed in the glare of all the lights she'd turned on earlier.

Nash knew he shouldn't have said anything. You don't reveal a dead husband's devious past to a still-grieving widow, then turn around and hit on her. Any moron knew that.

But out on the porch the evening before, something had passed between them. A moment, nothing more, but Nash couldn't get it out of his head. All night long, he hadn't been able to stop thinking about her. And when he got the call earlier, he hadn't been able to get here quick enough, even though there was no good reason for his presence. No reason at all except he'd wanted to see her. He'd wanted to see for himself that she and her son were okay.

It was strange, this fascination he had for Evangeline Theroux. She was very different from the other women who'd passed through his life. She was tough as nails on the outside, but every once in a while, she'd slip up and the chinks in her armor would show. It was those tiny cracks in her poise that made Nash stop worrying about things like propriety and restraint.

"Do you know anything about the concept of an evil gene?" she asked suddenly.

He was caught off guard by her abrupt question and it took him a moment to catch up. "I know there's research being done, but no real evidence has been found that a violent gene exists. Why? What does that—as you say—have to do with the price of tea in China?"

"Thirty years ago, a woman named Mary Alice Lemay killed her three young sons because she thought they had inherited the propensity for evil from their father. Their grandfather and uncle had both been convicted on multiple counts of rape and murder, and Mary Alice believed that her husband had followed in their footsteps. She claimed she killed her little boys in order to save their eternal souls from damnation. In other words, she killed them before they had a chance to sin."

"What's this woman to do with you?"

"She's nothing to me. But Paul Courtland's mother is Mary Alice Lemay's sister-in-law. I think the blond woman who was following Paul is his cousin. It's possible that one of Mary Alice's daughters is systematically exterminating all the remaining male members of the Lemay family."

"In order to eradicate this evil gene?"

"That's the theory."

"Your theory?"

"No. A true-crime writer named Lena Saunders. I talked to her yesterday morning. She claimed she had information regarding Paul Courtland's killer, so Captain Lapierre sent me over there to take her statement."

Nash started to point out that she'd been taken off the case, but given the circumstances, he decided to withhold any comment.

"I found out tonight that Lena's real name is Ruth

Lemay. According to Ruth, her younger sister, Rebecca, helped their mother murder at least one of their brothers. And now she's going after the male family members that are left. But Rebecca tells a different story. She says it was Ruth who assisted their mother in the killings."

"And now you don't know which sister to believe."

"Or if I even believe either one of them."

"What does your gut tell you?"

"That Lena—Ruth—may have played me. She could be setting her sister up to look guilty. But on the other hand…Rebecca broke into my house. She took my son from his crib and deliberately used him as a shield. I don't think those are the actions of a rational mind. When I think of what might have happened…" She shivered and wrapped her arms around her middle. "Thank God, nothing *did* happen. I would never forgive myself if J.D. had been hurt. I can't think of anything worse than not being able to protect your own child."

"Neither can I," Nash said quietly.

She looked up, stricken. "I'm sorry. I wasn't talking about you."

"I know that."

But it was true. Letting your child down was not an easy thing to live with.

Nash remembered the day Jamie had been born, holding her for the first time. That soft, sweet-smelling bundle that had charmed him from the moment she opened her little eyes. He'd made so many promises to her and to himself that day, but in the ensuing years, he'd too often put work and his own interests first. He'd failed her as a father and there was no going back and making up for his mistakes. No way to get back all those moments, big and small, that he'd carelessly let slip through his fingers.

And now his twenty-year-old daughter sat in prison for taking the life of someone else's child.

"I should get going," he said. "Let you get some sleep."

"I'm too wired for sleep," she said. "I know I was rude to you earlier, but I wouldn't mind if you stayed. It would probably do me good to have someone to talk to."

"If you're sure I won't be in the way."

Her smile was wan. "You won't be. I really would like the company."

"Okay. I'll stay, then."

"You want something to drink? Coffee? Dr Pepper?"

"No, I'm fine."

She waved toward the couch. "Have a seat. I'll be right back."

While he waited, Nash picked up a photograph from the coffee table and gave it a casual glance, then a more thorough scrutiny. He was still studying the picture when she came back into the room with her drink.

"Do you have any idea where that might have been taken?" she asked, nodding toward the photo.

"Looks like someplace in the Caribbean."

"Yeah, that's what I thought, too." She took a sip of her drink, then placed the glass on a coaster on the coffee table. "Nathan Mallet's wife found it in an envelope he'd hidden in their attic, along with a wad of cash and a passport under the name Todd Jamison. She thinks he put it there just in case he had to make a quick getaway."

"Sounds plausible."

She nodded. "I can't help wondering if Johnny had a stash hidden somewhere. Maybe he had a contingency plan, too. One that didn't include me and the baby."

Nash didn't know what to say so he remained silent.

"I still find it hard to believe that he would do something like that. I thought I knew him. We were close, you know? How could I be so blind to what he was doing? There must have been clues and I just didn't see them. But look at this place." She waved a hand, encompassing the small, modestly furnished room. "We weren't exactly living it up. If he was on the take, where did all that money go?"

"Like I said, he probably had an offshore bank account somewhere. If you look through his papers, you might even find an account number."

"That's not exactly a pressing concern of mine at the moment."

"No, I guess not."

She stared off into space, her face an open book of pain and betrayal, and Nash once again felt the need to wrap his arms around her, bury his face in her soft, sweet-scented hair. He couldn't do that, of course. Not knowing what he knew.

"I just don't understand how he could do that to us." Slowly, she glanced up. "And I can't help thinking that maybe there's another shoe waiting to drop."

Twenty-four

~~~❧❧❧~~~

Evangeline was banging on Lena Saunders's door bright and early the next morning. She'd dropped J.D. off at her mother's house, then called the station to say that she'd be taking a personal day. Lapierre was actually very gracious and understanding, although Evangeline couldn't help wondering if she'd just gone down a notch or two in her captain's estimation.

She couldn't worry about that now, though. Through a strange set of circumstances, her house had been invaded, her son threatened, and now she had to do whatever she could to make certain nothing like that happened again.

Josh let her in and she was pacing the living room when Lena finally came downstairs. This morning she was dressed in icy blue with a wide silver cuff that reflected the sunlight streaming in through the

French doors. Her hair was loose about her shoulders, and for a moment, the resemblance to the wildhaired woman of last night was so striking that Evangeline wondered if there might be only one sister with a split personality.

"Hello, Ruth."

The woman stopped in her tracks, her eyes going wide with surprise. "How did you know?"

"Did you not consider that I would figure it out the moment I laid eyes on your sister?"

Something shifted in her eyes and she put a hand to her heart. "You found her."

"She found me. And let me just say, her recollection of the past is not exactly in sync with yours."

"What do you mean?"

Evangeline lifted her gaze to the ceiling. "How do I put this delicately? She claims you're the one who helped your mother murder your brothers."

"She said that?" The woman walked over to the windows to stare out at the sparkling pool. "Rebecca is a very disturbed young woman."

"Just to be clear—should I call you Lena or Ruth?" Evangeline asked with a trace of sarcasm.

"I'm not Ruth Lemay. I haven't been in years. In every way that counts, I'm Lena Saunders."

"Well, then, I guess it was Ruth's sister who broke into my house and threatened my son."

Lena whirled. "She what?"

Evangeline took a few steps toward her. "She let

herself in using a key that my babysitter had hidden underneath a rock by my front porch. Which means that she not only found out where I live, but she also had my place staked out. Now, why would she do that? How would she even know who I am?"

"I don't know."

"Are you sure she didn't find out from you?"

Lena's eyes widened in distress. "Of course not. I haven't seen or spoken with her in years. She must have seen you leave here and followed you." The woman tugged nervously at the pearl necklace around her throat. "Which means she also had my house staked out."

"Why would she do that?"

"Our relationship has always been very complicated."

"But you just said you haven't seen or spoken to her in years."

"That's true. You have to remember, though, that in Rebecca's mind, things that happened thirty years ago may still seem like yesterday. And as children, she and I were very close. But being the oldest, I had more responsibilities on my shoulders. Mama counted on me, not just to help out with the house and the boys, but as moral support. After Daddy left, she leaned on me even more, and Rebecca grew jealous. She wanted to be Mama's little helper, and sometimes I think…" She broke off and turned back to the window. Her fingers tangled in the pearl necklace as she closed her eyes. "I think that's why she did what she did. To show Mama that she could count on her, too."

What a twisted family, Evangeline thought. Even considering Vaughn's problems with the law when he was younger and her parents' impending separation, their family seemed positively normal by comparison.

"You told me when the authorities got to the house, they found evidence that Mary Alice—your mother—had given birth. Who was the baby's father?"

"Our father. Charles Lemay."

"Rebecca says she took the baby and hid in the whispering room until it was all over."

Slowly, Lena turned. Something in her eyes sent a shiver down Evangeline's spine. "She told you about the whispering room?" She walked away from the windows and sat down heavily on the silver sofa.

Evangeline followed her. "What's the big deal about the whispering room?"

Lena closed her eyes. "It was a secret. We were never supposed to talk about it."

"Why?"

"Because that's where Daddy used to make us wait for him. That's why we were never allowed to talk above a whisper. He didn't want anyone to hear us."

"By anyone, you mean your mother?"

She nodded and dropped her eyes to her hands, as if an old shame kept her from meeting Evangeline's gaze.

In Evangeline's mind, she saw the two little girls in the photo, huddling together, clutching hands and whispering to one another in the dark. Waiting for their father to come and claim their innocence.

"Rebecca would never go in there after Daddy left. She was scared to death of that place. She didn't hide in there," Lena said. "I did."

"What happened to the baby?"

"I left it in the whispering room. I never even knew if it was a boy or a girl. Mama had it wrapped in a towel when I found it, and I never saw it again after that day. But even after all these years, I still dream about that little face. I still sometimes think I hear that tiny cry." The hand that she touched to her wet cheeks was trembling.

Evangeline said softly, "Why didn't you just tell me the truth before?"

"I never lied to you. Everything I told you was the truth."

"But you neglected to tell me your real name."

"My real name *is* Lena Saunders. I haven't been Ruth Lemay since I was eight years old. I'm not part of that family anymore. I got out a long time ago."

"You can change your name but you can't change who you are," Evangeline said. "Ruth is still in there somewhere. You can speak of her in the third person all you want, but that won't make her go away. Ruth's story is your story. Ruth's truth is your truth."

"But I can't let it be. I have to keep myself

detached in order to write about it objectively. And more than that, if I let myself become Ruth again…" She swallowed and blotted a tear on her cheek with the back of her wrist. "How would I be able to turn my own sister in for murder?"

"Is that why you told your story in the third person?"

"It wasn't my story. It was the truth. And, yes, when I talk about that day…when I even think about it…it does feel like it happened to someone else."

Her eyes suddenly turned desperate. "We have to find her. You see that, don't you? Now that you're onto her…now that she knows who you are…"

Evangeline's heart thudded at the look of sheer terror on Lena's face.

"If she feels threatened by you…" Lena Saunders turned, but it was Ruth Lemay who searched Evangeline's face. "I don't want to think about what she might do."

Ellis Cooper cut across the yard and climbed the porch steps. Placing the wriggling burlap bag on the floor beside him, he sat down in an old cane rocker and fanned himself with his cap. The morning was hot and sticky, but it was cool here on the porch. The house was shaded by pecan and oak trees, and he could feel a slight breeze off the water.

The South Louisiana landscape that surrounded him was a far cry from the North Georgia hills where he'd grown up, but Ellis had taken to the swamp like a duck to water. His vista from the porch was as primordial as it was darkly beautiful, and he felt one with the elements here.

He drew in a long breath and the earthy scent of the bayou filled his senses, stirring something deep inside his soul. Ancient cypress trees grew thick along the banks, their limbs heavy with curtains of Spanish moss that dragged across the lily pads, abloom now in the spangle of light that filtered down through the leaves.

Resting his head against the back of the rocker, he let his mind drift as he idly watched the last of the early morning mist swirl among the treetops. After his first stay in the mental hospital, Ellis had spent the remainder of his youth in foster care, but the moment he turned eighteen, he'd returned to his father's house, where he lived until the old man dropped dead in the kitchen one morning.

Ellis had stayed on for a while, had even toyed with the notion of taking over his father's congregation, but the charismatic movement was slowly dying out in Georgia. He knew of active churches in Missouri and Kansas, but Ellis saw no appeal in moving North. And by that time, he'd already determined that his particular calling had little to do with preaching. The gospel could be spread by others. God had another purpose for Ellis.

After all, it was His hand that had guided Ellis

here, to the swamp where he had met a blue-eyed angel that had further shown him the way.

From the moment he'd first seen her in church, he knew she was someone special. Like him, she was on a mission, and the fire that burned in her eyes that night ignited a primal lust deep inside Ellis. When he had taken up the serpent, lifting it high over his head, he could feel her eyes on him and the passion that pumped through his veins was so powerful, the experience so profound, he'd been afflicted with the aftershock for days.

That was the night it all started. That was the night when she had first approached him. That was the night Ellis Cooper had first answered his calling.

He had learned from her that evil could take any form. It could inhabit the bodies of the elderly and the infirm, could even threaten the innocent souls of children. He couldn't allow himself to be thwarted by the package. He couldn't afford to be weakened by the humanly concepts of guilt or conscience or remorse while evil remained afoot in the world. She knew that and so did he.

After a while, Ellis rose from the rocking chair, picked up the burlap sack and went inside the house. He opened a door off the kitchen and a dank, putrid scent rose from the bottom of the stairs.

For obvious reasons, it was rare to see a house with a basement in the swamp, but the space underneath Ellis's kitchen had been a pleasant surprise. He had no idea what the original purpose might have been. A storm cellar maybe. A place to ride out a hurricane.

But even in dry weather, there was always standing water. It smelled of musk, rotting fish and other creatures that had wandered in and gotten trapped.

A high window at the far side of the room allowed in just enough light so that Ellis could catch glimpses of the swimming bodies and raised heads, the occasional gleam of the vipers' catlike eyes.

He came halfway down the stairs, toeing a moccasin off the steps as he squatted and untied the burlap bag, then upended it over the water. The black body fell with a plop into the water, and for a moment, there was a scurry of movement at the foot of the stairs.

Ellis watched, as he always did, with an almost hypnotic fascination.

Twenty-five

❧❧❧

The sky grew darker as Evangeline headed north later that morning, and a light rain began to fall by the time she arrived at Pinehurst Manor. She pulled into the visitors' parking area and sat for a moment, admiring the impressive facade.

Surrounded by twenty acres of dense scrub oak and pine, the hospital more closely resembled an old plantation home than a modern psychiatric facility—except, of course, for the fifteen-foot perimeter wall topped with razor wire and the guard kiosks that were stationed at regular intervals around the property.

As Evangeline studied the manicured grounds through the windshield, she saw a uniformed guard appear at the corner of the building. He waited at the edge of the parking area for her to climb out of the car.

"Detective Theroux?"

She produced her ID and he nodded. "They just called up from the gate to let us know you'd arrived. I'll walk with you from here," he said. "You'll have to surrender your weapon and sign in."

The formalities completed a few moments later, another guard led her down a long corridor and opened a door. "Betsy," he said to the plump redhead seated behind a large desk. "Is he in?" He nodded toward a door behind the redhead's desk. "This is Detective Theroux with the New Orleans Police Department." He pronounced *police* with the emphasis on the first syllable.

"He's expecting you, Detective. Right this way." She stood and smoothed a hand over her brown skirt as she motioned for Evangeline to follow.

She was ushered into a large, pleasant office with long windows that looked out on a pretty garden of azaleas and flaming hibiscus. "Dr. Carlisle, this is Detective Theroux."

He got up from the desk and offered his hand, then waved her to the chair across from him. He didn't look the way Evangeline had pictured him after their brief phone conversation. For one thing, he was younger than she expected. Around thirty-five, she would guess, with longish hair and wire-rimmed glasses. He was dressed casually in jeans and an open-collar shirt, which also took her by surprise.

"So you're here about Mary Alice Lemay."

"That's right. As I told you on the phone, we have reason to believe there's a possible connection between Mary Alice and a recent homicide in New Orleans."

"You know that she's been incarcerated for over thirty years," he said.

"We don't think she was personally involved. But as I said, there could be a connection. Have you been able to verify whether or not her daughter Rebecca was also a patient here?"

"I checked the records. I won't go into the details of her diagnosis or the treatment, but I can tell you that she was here for several months in 2005. She was admitted in June and released the following December."

"And Mary Alice was transferred here during the evacuation."

"That's right."

"Do you know if she and her daughter had contact during that time?"

"That I don't know. I only came on board last year. But I can let you talk to some of the staff who were here at that time."

"Thanks. That could be helpful." She paused. "Do you know if Rebecca ever comes to see her mother?"

"Oh, yes. She comes at least once a month."

"What about her other daughter?"

"I wasn't aware that she had another daughter."

Evangeline reached in her bag and hauled out one

of Lena Saunders's books. She turned it over so that the author's photograph was face up.

"You've never seen this woman before?"

He studied the photograph for a moment, then glanced up with a bewildered frown. "I don't understand. Isn't this Rebecca Lemay?"

"No, this is a picture of her sister, Ruth. They do look alike. Probably could even pass for twins. But that's not Rebecca Lemay."

His gaze dropped again to the book. "I'm rarely mistaken about these things. Are you sure?"

"You think this is the woman who has been coming to see Mary Alice?"

"If they look as much alike as you say, I suppose I could be wrong. But the resemblance to her sister is uncanny. Even the way she holds her head…" He studied the picture for a moment longer, then handed the book to Evangeline.

"Is it possible for me to see Mary Alice?"

"Yes, of course. But that's about all you'll be able to do, I'm afraid. She hasn't spoken a word to anyone in over thirty years."

A few minutes later, they were standing outside the door to Mary Alice's room.

"Is she allowed out?" Evangeline asked.

"The doors in this wing are only locked at night. The patients are free to come and go in the secured areas."

He swung open the door and stepped aside for

Evangeline to enter. A woman was seated in a rocking chair in front of a barred window. She gave no indication that she was aware of their presence until Dr. Carlisle spoke to her.

"How are you today, Mary Alice?"

She turned then and the first thing that struck Evangeline was how young the woman looked. She had to be well into her fifties or early sixties, but the skin on her face was still smooth and supple, and her blue eyes—the color of hyacinths—were clear and lucid.

Her blond hair was chopped off just below her ears with a fringe of uneven bangs across her forehead. It was an odd cut, and Evangeline wondered if she'd somehow gotten hold of a pair of scissors and whacked it off herself.

"I've brought you a visitor," Dr. Carlisle said. "This is Detective Theroux. She's come all the way from New Orleans to see you."

The woman's unblinking stare unnerved Evangeline.

"Hello," she said as she knelt before the woman.

Evangeline's first instinct was to recoil when Mary Alice put out a hand, as if to touch her face. This was a woman who had brutally murdered her own children. But Evangeline forced herself to remain still, and the hand that brushed against her cheek was surprisingly gentle.

Mary Alice reached out with her other hand, and

for a moment, Evangeline thought she meant to cup her face. Then she realized the woman was holding something out to her.

In her palm was an origami crane.

Twenty-six

After Evangeline left Pinehurst Manor, she headed south through Baton Rouge, deep into Bayou country.

Leaving Highway One, she continued her southward trek on a two-lane blacktop that wound through a long corridor of oak, cypress and willow trees. White clouds drifted across a soft blue sky, and as the light shimmered down golden through the leaves, a lush drowsiness settled over the canebrakes and along the flooded ditches, thick with lily pads, cattails and drooping stalks of water iris.

Just on the outside of Torrence, Nash called.

"You're breaking up," Evangeline said as she pressed the phone to her ear. "I can't hear you."

There was a long pause before he came back on. "Is that better?"

"Some." She could hear the roar of an engine in the background. "Where are you?"

"In a plane on my way back to New Orleans. I was wondering if we could meet this afternoon. I have something I want to talk to you about."

"I'm not in the city. I asked for a personal day so that I could take care of some things."

"Are you okay? Is the baby okay?"

"J.D.'s fine. He's with my mother. I'm in the Bayou Country just outside Torrence."

"What are you doing down there?"

"It's where the Lemay family used to live. I'm trying to get a lead on Rebecca Lemay's whereabouts. Lena Saunders said that her sister may have been spotted recently at the family's old house. I want to see if the local law enforcement knows anything about it."

"Is there anything I can do?"

"Maybe. I've asked someone at NOPD to look into both Ruth and Rebecca Lemay's backgrounds, but you've a lot more resources than we do."

"I'll see what I can find out."

"One more thing. Lena Saunders told me that she thinks Rebecca may be working with an accomplice now. She also told me that she and her sister were raised in a charismatic church, so that could be why snakes were used to kill Paul and David Courtland."

"You think that's how she and her accomplice hooked up?"

"I have no idea, but I thought I'd throw it out

there in case you run across anything in either of their backgrounds."

"Anything else?"

"No, that's it. I'm just entering the city limits so I need to go."

"Evangeline?"

"Yeah?"

"You run into any trouble down there, you call me."

"I don't anticipate any trouble, but thanks."

The concern in his voice made her uncomfortable. After last night, she knew Nash was interested in her, but no matter what Johnny had done, she still wasn't ready to move on yet. Especially with a man who had been so instrumental in shattering her illusions.

In Torrence, she located the sheriff's office near the courthouse and parked beneath the tangled limbs of a water oak. The sun was boiling overhead, but the breeze in the shade was so cool on her damp back, she found herself shivering as she pushed open the glass door and stepped into the air-conditioned police station.

After giving her name to the receptionist, she was shown into Sheriff Arnie Thibodaux's office, a small, square room encased in glass on two sides to provide a view of the street, as well as the outer office.

Thibodaux was about fifty, with a thick black mustache and tiny eyes that seemed to disappear into folds of skin the color and texture of sun-baked mud. He was dressed in a pressed blue uniform that looked so fresh, Evangeline had to wonder if he'd set foot outside his office all day.

Boots propped on his desk, he sat reared back in his chair reading a fishing magazine, but as soon as he saw Evangeline, he tossed the periodical aside, dropped his feet to the floor and waved her in.

"So tell me something. What's a New Orleans homicide detective doing all the way down here?" he asked when she'd settled into a hard plastic chair across from his desk.

"I'm hoping you can give me some information on an old case."

"Well, that all depends on how old we're talking about." His voice was flat and reserved and he didn't seem overly anxious to be of service.

"Over thirty years ago."

He whistled as he adjusted the belt around his ample waistline. "That could be a problem. Most of the files that go that far back were destroyed in a fire. Floods got the rest."

"Well, that's not what I wanted to hear," Evangeline told him. "Maybe you can help me anyway. I'm looking for information on Mary Alice Lemay. She killed—"

"I know what she did." The good-ol'-boy facade

slipped for a moment as something unpleasant flitted across his weathered features.

"You were around back then?"

"I was a deputy," he said grimly. "Still wet behind the ears when we got the call that day, but what we found out there at that old house seasoned me real fast."

"I can imagine."

"I never saw anything like it, and hope I never do again. I couldn't sleep for a month. What that woman did to those li'l' ol' kids..." He trailed off, shaking his head, still, after all these years, unable to fathom how a mother could take the lives of her own children. His dark eyes fastened on her, and she could see his natural curiosity warring with the small-town cop's wariness of his big-city counterpart. "What's your interest in that case, anyway?"

Evangeline decided to be up-front with him. The last thing she wanted was to alienate local law enforcement. "We think there may be a connection to a recent homicide in New Orleans."

He cocked a dark brow in surprise. "I don't see how that's possible. Mary Alice has been locked up in the loony bin ever since it happened."

"I realize that. But I'm interested in her daughters."

"You think one of them is involved? How?"

"It's a long story."

He folded his hands behind his head. "I'm not going anywhere. Besides, cooperation is a two-way street in my book. Let's hear what you got."

Evangeline paused, glancing out the window as she wondered where to start. Across the street, a woman pushed a baby carriage along the hot, steamy sidewalk.

"Rebecca Lemay may have been involved in the murder of a prominent New Orleans attorney named Paul Courtland. Have you ever heard of him?"

"Can't say I have, no."

"Mary Alice's husband, Charles, had a sister named Leona. Paul Courtland was her son."

Thibodaux stroked his soft chin. "Well, let's see, then. That would make Rebecca Lemay this Courtland fellow's first cousin, wouldn't it? And you think she killed her own kin?"

"Right now, she's a person of interest. Which is why I need to talk to her. Do you know if she's been seen around these parts lately? I heard someone was spotted at the old Lemay place not long ago."

He dropped his hands to the arms of his chair, drumming his fingers against the scarred wood. "I wouldn't put too much stock in that story if I were you. Stevie Ray Wilson claims he saw Mary Alice looking out one of the upstairs windows, but we know that can't be true. Knowing Stevie Ray, he probably just saw his own reflection or something. That boy's never been the sharpest knife in the drawer, plus, he likes to hit the sauce pretty good. So he's not exactly what I'd call a reliable witness."

Evangeline nodded absently. "Could I ask you some questions about that case?"

"Thirty years is a long time, and my memory's not what it used to be. Don't know how much help I'll be. I'll answer what I can, though."

"Can you tell me if all the bodies were recovered?"

"Yep. We found all three of the little boys. And that's all I want to say about that."

"What about the baby?"

He stared at her for the longest moment. "How did you know about that? It's not common knowledge, even around these parts."

"I've talked to Ruth Lemay. She goes by the name of Lena Saunders now. She's a writer. She said she spoke to you on the phone recently about the sighting at the old house."

He shook his head. "I don't know who she talked to, but it wasn't me."

"You're sure?"

"My short-term memory is just fine, so, yeah, I'm sure."

He looked a little peeved by her question, so Evangeline decided not to press him on it. "So what about the baby?"

He turned his head and stared out the window for a moment. "All we found was a bunch of bloody sheets and the severed umbilical cord wrapped in an old towel. After we took Mary Alice into custody, she was examined by a doctor, and he confirmed that she'd recently given birth. My guess is she threw that baby into the swamp. A body that size wouldn't last long out there."

"Who called the sheriff's office that day?"

"Mary Alice's cousin. A woman named Nella Prather."

"Does she still live around here?"

"Nah, she's been gone for years. She married an old boy name Mike Blanchard, and last I heard, they'd moved up to New Orleans. Shouldn't be too hard for you to locate her."

Evangeline took a moment to jot the woman's name in her notebook. "When Mary Alice was brought in, did she say why she'd done it?"

"She said something about wanting to save them. That doesn't make any more sense to me now than it did back then. How did killing those little boys in cold blood save them?"

Evangeline knew it was a rhetorical question. "What about the girls? Did they have much to say about what happened?"

"I remember the oldest girl was all torn up about it. Just kept crying for her mama and her brothers. They finally had to ask the doctor to give her something to settle her down. But the youngest…" His eyes were dark and troubled as he gazed at Evangeline across the desk. "That girl had ice water in her veins. Never showed a lick of emotion. And the way she'd look at you…" He broke off on a shudder. "I don't mind saying, that one gave me the creeps."

Evangeline thought about the woman in her house the night before, the way she'd cradled and hummed to J.D. The way she'd kissed his head and hugged him to her breast.

Evangeline felt panicked and sick just thinking about it.

"I'd like to go out to the house and take a look around myself, if that's okay," she said.

"Well, technically, you'd be trespassing, but nobody's lived out there in years. I don't reckon it'd do any harm. If you can wait a spell, I'll ride out there with you. Otherwise, all I can do is point you in the right direction."

"That might be best," Evangeline said. "I'll be heading back to New Orleans soon."

"I better write it down for you, then." He scribbled the directions on a piece of paper and slid it across the desk. "Keep to the main road as much as you can. You don't want to get lost out there in the swamp. Might take us days to find you and I don't want to have to postpone my fishing trip."

Evangeline couldn't tell if he was joking or not. "I'll remember that."

"One other thing." He rose and walked her to the door. "Folks around here are still a mite skittish about that old place. There's always been a lot of talk about ghosts and such. It's all just superstitious hogwash, but I don't know that I'd mention going out there to anyone if I were you. No sense stirring up talk and bad memories if we can help it."

She held up the paper. "Thanks for the directions."

"You bet. Y'all take care. If you're packing a piece, keep it on you." He pointed to the ankle holster on his desk. "Even off duty, I don't ever go into the swamp unarmed."

Evangeline missed the turnoff and had to double back twice before spotting the narrow gravel road that cut through a heavy forest of oak trees and scrub brush. The canopy of tangled limbs across the road was so dense that half a mile in, the light disappeared and the wind blowing in through the open car window felt cool and moist.

As Evangeline cleared the dripping trees, she caught her first glimpse of the house. The two-story clapboard rested on stilts, and on first glance, it seemed to have held up remarkably well over the years. But as she got out of the car, she noticed the sagging porch and peeling paint, the screen door that drooped on one hinge.

Slowly she climbed the steps, testing the planks on the porch before moving to the door. Turning, she surveyed her surroundings before going inside. She was miles from anywhere and the silence was so deep and pervasive, she could feel an uneasy chill beginning a slow crawl up her backbone.

She was starting to wish she'd waited for Thibodaux to come with her, but then she told herself to buck up. She had a .38 in one hand and her flashlight in the other. The sun was shining in the clearing, but without electricity, the interior was bound to be dim and shadowy.

Stuffing the flashlight in the back pocket of her jeans, Evangeline pulled open the screen door and stepped inside.

She'd expected the house to be dank and smelly and layered with years of grime, but instead of cobwebs hanging from the ceiling and creepy-crawlies rustling around in dark corners, the scent of lemon oil clung to the silent rooms. Which was odd. According to Thibodaux, the place had been abandoned for years.

But in the light that filtered in through the broken windowpanes, the house looked freshly scrubbed from top to bottom.

It made Evangeline think of something Rebecca Lemay had told her:

Mama always kept a spotless home, but that day she scrubbed and mopped and dusted until every room sparkled. She worked at it for hours, on into the night.

Mary Alice had been preparing the house for

what was about to happen. And now Evangeline couldn't help wondering if someone had made preparations for the same reason.

As she stood just inside the door, a deep foreboding settled over her. She didn't want to stay in that house a moment longer. It was as if some invisible force tugged her back outside, into the sunlight and safety of the clearing.

But Evangeline ignored the warning and instead of retreating, she pulled back the receiver on her gun, easing a round from the clip into the chamber. Steadying her nerves, she slowly walked through the house, checking each room and finding the next as spotless as the last.

Most of the furniture had long since been destroyed or stolen, but the classroom at the back of the house looked just as it must have all those years ago when Mary Alice had homeschooled her children. The chalkboard was wiped clean and an eraser and fresh chalk rested in the tray.

The books were stored neatly in the shelves, but underneath the lemon oil, Evangeline could smell the invasive scent of mildew and rot.

Retracing her steps, she ended up back in the front hall, her gaze lighting on the latched door beneath the stairwell.

The whispering room.

I stayed in there for a long time with the baby. Until all the screaming finally stopped.

That's where Daddy used to make us wait for him. That's why we were never allowed to talk above a whisper. He didn't want anyone to hear us.

Those little-girl whispers seemed to echo through the empty house as Evangeline reached for the latch. Taking a deep breath, she threw open the door to the light.

Something rushed out at her and she screamed as she jumped back. Losing her footing, she fell with a hard thud against the wood floor.

The flashlight flew out of her pocket, but somehow Evangeline managed to cling to her gun, and now she swung the .38 from side to side, her heart pounding inside her chest.

Something dark circled the room, and as it swooped toward her, Evangeline ducked her head under her arms and squealed. When she looked up, the bat had flown into the screen door and clung like blight to the torn mesh.

Struggling to her feet, she brushed off the seat of her jeans and retrieved the heavy Maglite that had rolled away. She switched it on, relieved to find that the bulb still burned steadily, and walked back over to the door. As the beam prowled the close space, Evangeline's mind once again conjured an image of two little girls huddled inside, whispering words of comfort as they clung to one another in the dark.

She could still hear those whispers, and as the

hair lifted at the back of her neck, she glanced over her shoulder.

No one was there.

The whispers were all in her head.

An oppression she couldn't explain settled over her as she closed and latched the door, then moved to the stairs. The house had a very dark history and the weight of those memories pressed down on her with each step that she climbed. The whispers in her head turned to screams as she reached the top of the stairs.

This was where it had happened. Up here, in one of these rooms.

Evangeline paused, her legs suddenly leaden. She didn't want to go on.

Then just leave. What did you think you would accomplish by coming here anyway?

She had been hoping to find Rebecca Lemay. The woman had invaded her home, threatened her son, and Evangeline needed to know why. She needed to make sure that it never happened again.

Taking a deep breath, she continued her search. As she entered the largest bedroom, she kept her weapon at the ready, both hands sweaty on the grip. She moved quickly to the closet, threw back the door and glanced inside.

Satisfied that neither bat nor human would jump out at her, she walked over to the window and stared out at the water. A lone heron circled above the swamp grass, its wings gilded by the late afternoon light. Through the broken window, Evangeline could hear the matinee song of the cicadas and bull-frogs drifting up from the bayou, and the metallic tinkle of an old wind chime.

She started to turn away, then froze.

Someone stood beside her car.

He remained so still that Evangeline had to stare for a long moment to assure herself he was real and not a shadow. Then his head tilted and she knew that he'd spotted her in the window.

Even from a distance, she could feel the impact of his eyes, the shock of his unwavering scrutiny.

He was tall, thin and very pale. His black hair gleamed like a raven's wing in the light, and as their gazes clung, Evangeline felt the thrill of familiarity charge through her veins.

He was the man from the cemetery.

She couldn't see the scarred side of his face, but she knew he was the same man.

But what would he being doing way out here?

Unless he'd followed her.

Maybe he'd followed her to Mount Olive that day, too.

Whirling away from the window, Evangeline sprinted across the room and rushed down the stairs. Weapon still clutched in both hands, she lunged across the front hall to the screen door, paused to glance out, then bolted onto the porch, the gun sweeping from side to side.

He was gone.

She checked both sides of the porch to make sure he wasn't lying in wait for her. And as she turned back to the yard, she spotted him again, this time at the edge of the woods.

He stopped and turned, as if waiting for her to come after him. It was the same cat-and-mouse game he'd played with her at the cemetery.

"Hey!" she shouted as she clamored down the steps. "What the hell do you think you're doing?"

He waited until she'd closed some of the distance between them before turning to disappear into the trees.

"Stop! I'm a police officer!"

She tore after him, but the moment she plunged into the forest, Evangeline knew she was out of her element. The dense trees provided too many hiding places, and she'd already lost sight of her quarry. If she'd learned anything in her years as a cop it was to never knowingly put herself at risk of an ambush.

She retraced her steps to the clearing and walked over to her car. The thought crossed her mind as she opened the door that while she'd been in the house, the man had had plenty of time to tamper with her engine. She hadn't locked the car, so he would have had easy access to the hood release. He could have removed the fuel pump fuse or disconnected the coil input wire. There were a number of ways to disable a car quickly for someone who knew what they were doing.

Evangeline climbed into the car and started the ignition. The engine turned over immediately, and she breathed a sigh of relief as she backed to the end of the driveway and turned the car toward the road.

By the time she reached the highway, the sun had dropped below the treetops and the sky turned crimson on the horizon.

As she turned into the sunset, a flash of fire hit her in the eyes, temporarily blinding her. Her sunglasses had fallen to the floor on the passenger's side, and as she leaned across the console to reach them, she saw the dull gleam of a black tail protruding from underneath the front seat.

Evangeline jerked her hand back just as the snake slithered onto the floorboard. It was huge, the body as thick as a man's arm and the head the size of a fist. A musty smell filled the car, along with the dank odor of the swamp and something far more foul.

Sensing danger, the diamond-shaped head lifted nearly a foot into the air, and the slitted eyes focused on Evangeline, paralyzing her with a cold, stark terror. The mouth gaped, revealing the cottony interior and the long fangs that were as sharp as needles.

She tried to tell herself not to panic. She'd read somewhere that adult pit vipers rarely released all of their poison on humans. They reserved it for prey that it could more easily kill.

But tell that to the huge moccasin on her floorboard.

Trying not to make any sudden moves, Evangeline carefully eased her leather bag toward her on the seat. The car careened off the road and she tried to swing it back on the pavement. But the tires spun on the wet shoulder, and before Evangeline could gain control, the vehicle plunged down the steep embankment, bumping over the wild terrain at a terrifying speed before plowing through swamp water into a tree.

Evangeline had no idea where the snake was, whether it had coiled for a strike or slithered back under the seat. She didn't take time to find out. Fighting off the deployed air bag, she tumbled out the door into ankle-deep water.

Her bag was still in the car and the last thing she wanted to do was reach back inside. But she needed her phone and her gun.

She was stranded in the middle of nowhere with a psycho and a cottonmouth water moccasin on the loose.

Twenty-seven

T he tow truck dropped Evangeline and her car off at the nearest garage and, while the lone mechanic checked the extent of the damage, she called Sheriff Thibodaux to let him know what had happened.

"You sure you didn't leave your door open? Maybe that's how the dang thing got inside."

"I didn't leave my door open and I only had my window cracked. Someone put the snake in my car," Evangeline said.

"This fellow you said you saw out there…what did he look like?"

"Tall and thin with black hair and a big scar on one side of his face. Have you seen anyone around town lately that fits that description?"

"No, but there's a lot of fishing cabins back in the swamp. Could be somebody staying in one of those. I'll keep an eye out for him. Meanwhile, I'll send a deputy out there first thing in the morning to have a look around."

"Thanks. I'd appreciate a call if you find out anything."

"You bet."

As she hung up the phone, the mechanic came around to give her the bad news.

"Two words," he said as he rubbed at a grease streak on the side of his nose. "Busted radiator."

"Oh, man, I was afraid of that. Any chance you can fix it?"

"You mean tonight? 'Fraid not. It's already past closing time. I can get to it tomorrow after lunch, but that's the best I can do. You need a ride somewhere?"

"You're not headed to New Orleans, are you?"

"That's a long way from here."

"Yeah." She gave him her card. "I'll need an estimate before you start to work."

"No problem. You sure you'll be all right here?"

"Don't worry about me. I'll figure something out."

What that something would be, she wasn't sure. She could call her mother, but Lynette would worry herself sick the whole way. Besides, she had the baby today. As for the rest of her family, Vaughn's old Plymouth probably wouldn't even make it out of New Orleans, and at the moment, Evangeline wasn't all that anxious to spend time cooped up in a car with her dad. She'd probably end up saying something she'd later regret.

So she called Nash.

When the black sedan finally pulled up beside Evangeline, she got up slowly and walked over to the car. The side window came down, and she leaned down to peer inside.

"Thanks for coming."

"No problem," Nash said.

"No, seriously, this is a huge imposition, and I'm really sorry to put you out like this. But I didn't want to call my mother. She has the baby today and my brother's car—"

"Evangeline?"

"Yeah?"

"Just get in."

She opened the door and climbed in.

The interior of his car smelled of leather and aftershave, and Evangeline drew a long breath. She still had the fishy odor of the swamp in her nostrils, but this helped.

She turned to Nash. "I really am sorry to trouble you. This is a lot to ask of someone you hardly know. I'm a little surprised you agreed to come." When he merely shrugged, she said, "You could have said no. Why didn't you?"

"You know why."

Dusk was drifting into night, and the lights from

the oncoming cars polished his dark hair and reflected like pools of moonlight in his eyes.

Evangeline's heart beat even harder as he reached
for her hand. He held it until she slid hers away on
the pretense of pushing her hair out of her face.

She turned back to the window because she
didn't want to look at him, didn't want to acknowledge the attraction that suddenly smoldered between
them. She wondered if he realized what it had cost
her to reach out to him. If he knew, even now, how
hard she had to fight an overwhelming sense of guilt
and betrayal.

No man had tempted her since the moment she
met Johnny, but now when she thought of him, remembered what he'd done, she wondered if her love
for him could even be real because the man she'd
married had never really existed.

"You okay?"

She turned, met his gaze, then glanced away
again. "I'm fine."

"What did you find out?"

"Not a lot more than I already knew, but one
thing's certain. Something really creepy is going on
here." She took a few minutes to tell him about the
man she'd seen beside her car and the snake that had
crawled out from underneath the front seat.

"I know he put that snake in my car," Evangeline
said. "It didn't just crawl in there by itself. Luckily,
I had a fingerprint kit in my trunk and I managed to

lift some latents from the door handle while I waited for the tow truck."

"Give them to me," he said. "I'll run them through our computer."

"Thanks." She paused for a moment, watching the dark landscape flash by. "And then there's the trail of origami cranes that someone has been leaving me."

He turned with a puzzled frown.

"On the same day that Paul Courtland's body was found, someone sent my son a mobile made out of origami cranes. I thought my mother had sent it, but she didn't. Later, I saw one at the cemetery near Johnny's vault and another in my brother's office. Earlier today I drove up to the psychiatric hospital where Mary Alice Lemay is incarcerated. She tried to give me a crane that looked identical to all the other ones. The doctor I spoke with said she makes them all the time. It's almost an obsession. At first, I thought the cranes were some kind of message, but now I think someone has been leading me to Mary Alice this whole time."

Nash scowled at the road. "For what purpose?"

"I'm starting to wonder if all this could somehow be connected to Johnny."

He gave her a startled glance. "Johnny? How so?"

"He knew Lena Saunders. According to her, he's the reason she insisted on talking to me. When I saw her that first day, she said if I'd locate Rebecca

Lemay for her, she'd help me find out what really
happened to Johnny. She's the one who gave me
your name."

Nash's gaze seemed frozen on the road. "How
did she know about me?"

"She claims to have a lot of contacts in law enforcement. And evidently she does because she was
right about you."

When he didn't respond, Evangeline shrugged.
"The point is, maybe she struck the same deal with
Johnny. Maybe he went to the parking garage that
night looking for Rebecca Lemay."

"You saw the files," Nash said softly. "You know
what he was into."

"I can't accept that's all there is to it."

He waited a beat, then said, "You're not going to
let this go, are you?"

"I'm not very good at letting things go," she said.
"It's a weakness. When Johnny died, I would catch
glimpses of him everywhere. I'd wake up in the
middle of the night, so certain he'd been standing
over me, I'd get up and search the house. He was on
the other end of any hang-up call. Hidden behind the
tinted windows of every car that drove by the house.
Sometimes his presence was so strong, I thought I
must be going crazy."

Nash's eyes were dark and penetrating as he
turned to stare at her. "You're still in love with him,
aren't you?"

They were crossing over the Huey Long Bridge, and the lights dancing off the dark surface of the river looked like stars twinkling against a black sky.

They were heading back into the city, back to the world Evangeline had shared with Johnny.

"A part of me will always be in love with him," she said.

"Even after everything you know about him."

"Yes. I still want him back. If I had the power, I'd still turn back the clock. No matter what." She paused and drew a breath. "So with all that considered... maybe this wasn't such a good idea."

He shrugged. "You're probably right."

She turned back to the window, strangely disappointed that he had acquiesced so easily.

Nash dropped her off at her house and waited while she went across the street to her neighbor's to pick up the keys to the new locks that had been installed on both front and back doors earlier that morning.

Letting herself in, she stood at the window and watched as he drove off. Then she showered and grabbed a bite to eat while she waited for Lynette to bring the baby home.

After she fed him, she filled his little bathtub and washed the pureed carrots out of his hair as he splashed in glee. He loved bath time and the warm water seemed to relax him. By the time Evangeline lifted him from the tub and wrapped him in a big, fluffy towel, he was already rubbing his eyes. Freshly diapered and dressed in a sleeper, he lay cuddled against her shoulder as she rocked him to sleep.

As she placed him in his crib, her shoulder bumped the mobile, setting the cranes in motion. A shiver streaked up her spine, and for the longest moment, she stood gazing down at her slumbering son, wondering why she'd suddenly been drawn into Mary Alice Lemay's dark and troubled life.

Walking over to open the window, Evangeline stood gazing out. The evening was soft and dreamy, with moonlight pooling on the grass and the scent of her neighbor's roses filling the dusky heat.

It was very still out. No movement at all in the yard except for the subtle shift of shadows as the moon floated across the sky.

Evangeline leaned a shoulder against the window frame. Loneliness settled over her, but she welcomed it tonight. The desolation was like an old friend. Familiar and almost comforting.

She closed her eyes and tried not to think of Declan Nash.

A little while later, Evangeline curled up on the couch and closed her eyes.

For the longest time after Johnny's death, she'd felt helpless and broken, so lost and lonely, she wondered how she would be able to get through another night. She knew that some women in her situation turned to other men, but the momentary solace of a stranger's warmth was not for her.

Still, on some of the long, sleepless nights, she would allow herself to remember the comfort of a man's arms around her, the erotic thrill of a gruff whisper, a shared laugh in the heat of the night. The intimate look that passed between a man and a woman when they wanted one another.

As she rolled onto her back, a soft knock sounded on the door. Evangeline closed her eyes. This was a complication she didn't want or need in her life right now.

She swung her legs over the couch and sat for another moment before she got up to let him in.

"I'm surprised you're still up," Nash said.

"I'm too wired to sleep." She stepped back from the door. "You want to come in?"

His gaze met hers for a moment, and then he moved past her into the living room.

She followed him in. "What are you doing here?"

"I've been thinking about those origami cranes," he said. "You think someone left you a trail that led you to Mary Alice Lemay, but my question is…why you?"

Evangeline shrugged. "I guess it could be something as simple as my being assigned to the Courtland murder case." She headed for the kitchen. "I could use a drink."

She brought back a bottle of wine and a couple of

glasses. Motioning him to a chair, she poured the wine and settled down on the sofa. "Did you really come all the way back over here to talk about origami cranes?"

Light pooled in his eyes, making them seem dark and light at the same time.

He leaned forward and set his glass on the coffee table. His gaze never left hers. "I've got a lot of baggage, Evangeline."

She set her wineglass aside, too. "What am I supposed to say to that?"

He didn't answer. "Two failed marriages, a daughter in prison. In prison. A job that sometimes demands a twenty-four-seven commitment."

"Why are you telling me this?"

"You know why."

Evangeline saw the desire in his eyes before he could cloak it with the shadow of his past. She got up and went over to the window to glance out at the street.

"You're not the only one who's made mistakes, you know. We all have crosses to bear."

He got up and came to lean against the window frame. "Is Johnny your cross?"

Outside, the palm trees were like shadows against the soft violet of the city sky. A few stars twinkled out, but the moon was obscured by a bank of clouds moving in from the gulf.

She glanced up at Nash. He was staring out, too, his face calm and pensive.

"You wanted me to find out about him, didn't you?"

For a moment, he looked caught. Then his gaze went back to the darkness outside the window.

"Are you surprised I'd figured that out?"

"No, not really."

"Why did you come to the crime scene that day when you already knew you were going to have me removed from the case? You didn't even bother disguising the fact that you were the one pulling the strings."

They were so close she could smell his aftershave, could feel his breath warm against her face. Evangeline shivered, both in dread and anticipation because he had denied none of her accusations.

"You wanted me to see those files."

"I wanted you to stop asking questions about Johnny."

A silence fell between them.

"Do you want me to go?" Nash finally asked.

Evangeline shivered as she stared out into the night. She felt his hand on her neck, in her hair and something gave way inside her.

She closed her eyes and told herself this wasn't a betrayal. Johnny was dead. And before he died, he'd betrayed *her*. Maybe not with a woman, but in a way that hurt her every bit as much as infidelity. Maybe more.

Nash was watching her, and his eyes darkened as she reached up to touch his cheek, to trace the strong contour of his jaw with his fingertip, to outline his mouth with the pad of her thumb.

He didn't move, even when she wound her fingers around his neck, but his eyes dared her to forget.

She pulled him toward her and they kissed.

Evangeline couldn't stop trembling. She hadn't been with another man since Johnny. Abstinence had never been a conscious decision, but her grief had allowed no room for any other emotion. Now it was as if a fragile dam had broken and a pent-up need rushed out of her.

She tugged at Nash's clothes; ran her hands up and down his hard body; opened her mouth and deepened the kiss.

"I can't stop thinking about you," he said against her neck. "You've been driving me crazy since the first day I met you. And I swore I'd never let another woman do that to me."

"You mean this?"

She jerked his shirt apart and the buttons went flying.

He laughed softly against her mouth.

They shed clothes all the way to the bedroom, and when they fell back against the mattress, Evangeline didn't bother crawling underneath the cover. She lay naked on top of the quilt, watching him. Not caring that he watched her right back, not caring that he was seeing her in a way that no man but one had seen her in years.

A little while later, they got up and showered together, and afterward Nash brought Evangeline a glass of wine. She sipped it in bed while she watched him knot his tie in the mirror.

He looked amused by her scrutiny. "What?"

"Do you even own a pair of jeans?"

"That's an odd question to ask at a time like this."

"It seems the perfect time to ask." She studied him over the rim of her glass. "I really don't know anything about you."

His gaze met hers in the mirror. "That's not exactly true."

"You know what I mean."

"Okay. I do own a couple of pairs of jeans. I even wear them once in a while. Never at work, though."

"Are you implying this is work?"

"Hardly." He turned from the mirror and came back over to the bed. Placing one hand on either side of her, he leaned down and kissed her. "This is what I call incredible."

"It is. Was." But self-doubt filled Evangeline and she was glad when he straightened and moved away.

The phone rang, but she decided to let the machine

pick up in the other room. After her recorded message, she heard only silence and, after a moment, the soft click that severed the connection.

Her glance darted to Nash. His reflection stared back at her, and she remembered what she'd told him earlier about hang-up calls. She always imagined that Johnny was on the other end of the line.

He reached for his jacket. "I should get going. I need to put in a few more hours at the office tonight." He turned with an apologetic smile. "I'm terrible at this. I've been married to my job for so long, I make lousy company."

Evangeline drew up her legs under the cover and rested the wineglass on her knee. "I'm not so great at it, either."

He came over and sat down on the edge of the bed. "I'm no good at relationships, Evangeline. I've got two failed marriages to prove it."

"So you've mentioned."

"I just want you to know what you're getting into."

"Who says I'm getting into anything? Tonight was great, but it was just one night." She paused. "Why are you looking at me like that?"

He took the wineglass from her hand and set it on the nightstand, then draped an arm over her knees. "This may sound corny and totally insincere considering how long I've known you, but tonight meant something to me."

"It meant something to me, too, but I don't expect anything. And you shouldn't expect anything from me, either. I'm not ready for a relationship. It's too soon, and I have my son to think about and a career that also takes a huge commitment, just like yours. I don't have a lot of energy left over for anything else."

"You had plenty of energy earlier," he teased.

She felt her face heat. "I'm just trying to tell you, you don't need to worry about me. We had a nice night. I'm cool with leaving it at that."

She reached for her robe, slipped it on and walked him out. Locking the door behind him, she moved to the window and watched him leave. He strode down the walkway to his car and climbed in, but he didn't start the engine right away. Instead he sat there for so long that she wondered if he meant to come back inside. Then she decided that he must be watching the house. She was a cop, so a part of her resented the intrusion while another part felt touched by his concern.

Surely he would leave in a minute, she thought. Surely he knew that she could take care of herself.

She left the window and took her time washing out the wineglasses and tidying up the kitchen. Before she turned in, she glanced out the window again.

Nash was still out there.

Twenty-eight

It was a fairly simple matter to locate an address for Mike and Nella Blanchard. They lived in one of the subdivisions out by the lake, and as soon as Evangeline could get away from the station the next morning, she grabbed a car from the motor pool and took a run out there.

The air was cooler away from the city, and as Evangeline rolled down her window, she could smell brine and sand and flowers. The lake was slate-gray and glistening with diamonds, though farther out, a dark cloud had formed, and where the sunlight hit water droplets, a rainbow arced over the surface. The scenery was almost dreamlike, a prism of soft colors that blurred and melted into the horizon.

She found the Blanchard house tucked neatly into a landscaped cul-de-sac. It was similar to the other modest ranch-style homes in the neighborhood. A chain-link fence enclosed the backyard, and a black mutt had already started to howl by the time she climbed out of the car.

A woman in a straw hat sat on the front porch snapping pole beans into a plastic bowl. "Hush, Maggie!" she hollered at the dog, then watched Evangeline suspiciously from beneath the brim of her hat.

Evangeline came to the bottom of the steps and stopped. "Good morning."

The woman nodded and smiled. "Morning."

She was probably in her late fifties or early sixties, but her high cheekbones and dewy complexion gave her the kind of timeless beauty that only softened with age. Her fingers continued snapping the beans, but her hazel eyes never left Evangeline.

"I'm looking for a Mrs. Blanchard. Nella Blanchard."

"Well, you've found her. And who are you?"

"I'm Detective Theroux." Evangeline opened her ID and held it up.

The woman squinted as she read aloud, "New Orleans Police Department." She looked a little taken aback. "Now what in the world would the New Orleans Police Department want with me?"

"I'm hoping you can answer some questions for me," Evangeline said. "I was down in Torrence yesterday. The sheriff there told me that you're related to Mary Alice Lemay. A cousin, I believe he said."

The hazel eyes flickered as the silence stretched out like a thin, quivering wire.

"He said you're the one who made the call to the station that morning."

A subtle change came over the woman's features then. It was like watching a storm cloud sweep across the sun. "I don't like thinking about that day, much less talking about it."

"I can understand that," Evangeline said softly.

"Not many days go by that I don't think about it, though."

"It must be a painful memory for you."

"You have no idea." She glanced down the steps, her eyes wary beneath the brim of her hat.

"All that happened a long time ago," she said.

"I know. But the murder of those little boys may be connected to a more recent homicide here in New Orleans."

She tried not to react, but Evangeline could see the shock in her eyes, and then the confusion. "I don't see how that could be."

"There were two little girls left alive that day."

"Ruth and Rebecca."

"That's right."

Nella looked out over the yard. Evangeline could see her eyes moving along the sidewalk, lifting to the sky, watching the dark cloud coming ashore. A few drops splattered against the porch steps and on Evangeline's bare arms. The rain was cool and bracing and, closing her eyes, she turned her own face to the sky.

When she glanced at the porch again, Nella was staring back at her. She had the strangest look on her face, as if something had caught her by surprise.

"Can you tell me about them?" Evangeline asked.

Nella's eyes searched her face. "They were beautiful," she said. "Like angels."

"Could you walk me through what you saw that day? I know it's been a long time, but just tell me what you remember."

She set the plastic bowl on the porch and straightened. For a moment, Evangeline thought the older woman had chosen not to speak with her, but then she realized that Nella was lost in thought. Her eyes grew distant and her facial muscles slackened as she worked her way back in time. And then she shuddered deeply.

"The first thing I noticed was the silence. All those children and there wasn't any racket at all. It was unnatural, like the stillness of a tomb."

Slowly, she took Evangeline through the story, her recollection of that day so vivid that Evangeline could picture the scene in her mind as they walked from room to room, searching for some sign of the children.

Evangeline had been in that house the day before,

so she knew those rooms. She knew the quiet of that house, the eerie echo of all those tormented whispers and screams.

"When I came back into the hallway, I heard a sound coming from the room beneath the stairs. I opened the door and found one of the girls inside. I didn't know which one she was, though. They looked so much alike, I was never able to tell them apart."

"Where was the other girl?"

"I didn't see her until I went upstairs. She was at the end of the hallway, and when she came toward me, I noticed that she had blood on her clothes. I asked her if she was hurt, but she said Jacob had got the blood on her when he grabbed her dress. I asked her then if Jacob was hurt, and she said—I'll never forget this—she said, 'Jacob doesn't hurt anymore.' That's when it hit me. The realization of what Mary Alice had done. And all I could think was that I had to get those two little girls out of there before she came back. No matter what, I had to save them."

"What about the baby?" Evangeline asked.

Nella's face went deathly white. "What do you know about the baby?"

"I know the body was never found. The sheriff in Torrence seems to think that Mary Alice threw him in the swamp."

Nella put her hands to her face.

"I'm sorry," Evangeline said. "I know this is upsetting to you. Maybe it'll help if I tell you the reason I need to know about that baby. Someone is killing off all the male members of the Lemay family because they think evil is being passed on through the genes. I know it sounds crazy, like some weird science fiction movie or something, but three men have been murdered in cold blood. An uncle and two cousins. If that baby lived, his life would be in danger. And if he had male children, their lives would be in danger, as well. I don't want any more bloodshed in that family. I don't think you do, either."

Nella's hands dropped and she slowly looked up. "You have it all wrong."

"I do?"

She searched Evangeline's face. "What makes you think that baby was a boy?" she finally asked.

"Just an assumption, I guess. Are you telling me it was a girl?"

"Yes. The baby Mary Alice gave birth to that morning was a little girl."

Evangeline frowned. "And she lived?"

Nella closed her eyes and nodded. "She was alive the last time I saw her."

"When was that?"

"I found her in the room beneath the stairs with one of her sisters. I left them there while I went upstairs to look around. When I came back down, the baby was alone in the room. Ruth and Rebecca had vanished."

"What did you do?"

"There wasn't a phone at the house so I took the baby with me to go call for help. When the sheriff got there, he found Mary Alice and the girls sitting on the front steps, all dressed up as if they were ready for church. It was a sight he said he would never forget as long as he lived."

"And the baby?"

"I took her."

Evangeline felt a punch of dread in her stomach. "What do you mean, you took her?"

"The sheriff asked me to find her a good home. We were both afraid of what would happen to her if she was put in the system. Who would adopt a child coming from that kind of background? With that kind of stigma? My best friend's sister had been trying for years to have another baby. She'd suffered one miscarriage after the other. When I told the sheriff about her, he said to make the arrangements and he would see to a birth certificate."

Evangeline could feel something dark growing and swelling inside her. The dread started in the pit of her stomach and mushroomed up through her chest. "What was the woman's name?"

"I'm trying to remember her married name. It's been years since we kept in touch."

But she knew. The truth was in her eyes, in the tremble of her lips. She knew.

And so did Evangeline.

"The woman's name was Jennings," Nella whispered. "Lynette Jennings."

* * *

Evangeline's heart was in her throat as she drove like a bat out of hell to her mother's house.

To Lynette Jennings's house.

Her real mother was Mary Alice Lemay. Her veins were tainted with Mary Alice's blood. Her DNA was encoded with Charles Lemay's genes.

And now those same genes had been passed down to her son. And because of his heritage, his life could be in danger.

Evangeline pressed the cell phone to her ear, willing her mother to pick up. When she heard Lynette's voice, a myriad of emotions swirled through her head. Anger. Betrayal. Disbelief. No time for any of that now, though. Later, there would be reckoning, but the only thing that mattered now was her son.

"Mom?" How strange it seemed to call her that now. "Listen to me. I think J.D. could be in danger—" Evangeline gripped the phone as a string of questions erupted from Lynette. "No, Mom…just listen. I don't have time to explain." She realized she was yelling into the phone, and she drew a quick breath, trying to calm herself. "You need to make sure all the doors are locked, and don't let anyone inside. I'm calling Mitchell as soon as we hang up. He may get there before I do."

"Evangeline, honey, what is going on—"

"Mom, please, just do as I say. I'll explain everything as soon as I can."

Evangeline's mind raced as she accelerated through the busy streets. All she could think about at the moment was making sure J.D. was safe.

But a voice kept pounding away inside her. *Mary Alice Lemay is your mother. A woman who murdered her own sons gave birth to you. You carry the genes of Earl, Carl and Charles Lemay.*

Jesus. Christ.

She came from a long line of cold-blooded murderers.

How the hell was she supposed to wrap her head around that?

Don't think about that now. Don't!

J.D. was all that mattered. She couldn't let herself think of anything but saving her son. Her precious little boy.

"I'm coming," she whispered.

Lynette didn't need a premonition to warn her something bad was about to happen. Her daughter's fear had been palpable. Someone wanted to hurt J.D., but they'd have to get past Lynette first. She might not be the best mother in the world, but she was no coward when it came to her children and their children. She would fight to the death to protect any of them.

She ran down the hallway to the bedroom where she kept J.D.'s crib. Flinging open the door, she froze on the threshold, her heart in her throat.

A woman glanced up as she lifted J.D. into her

arms. She was blond and thin and pale, and something that might have been a memory wormed through Lynette's terror. Did she know this woman?

"What are you doing?" she said on a gasp. "Give me my grandson."

She started across the room, but the woman moved away from her. "Stop right there. Don't come any closer."

Lynette shivered at the woman's threatening tone. "Dear God, how did you get in here? Who are you?"

"My last name is Lemay," the woman said. "Now do you know who I am?"

Lynette's knees almost buckled. "Mary Alice," she whispered.

"I'm her daughter."

"What do you want?" Lynette's heart pounded so hard she couldn't think. She had to do something… but what? She was terrified the woman would hurt the baby if she tried to take him by force. But there was no way in hell she would let a stranger walk out of this house with her grandson. *No way in hell.*

A shadow fell across her and she whirled.

A tall, pale man stood behind her. The man with the scarred face and gleaming eyes. As Lynette watched in horrified fascination, he lifted his right hand over his head so that she could see the wriggling water moccasin he clutched behind the thick head.

As he clung to the serpent, his lips moved silently,

his eyes beginning to glow with the righteous fire of madness.

Then he began to speak in a strange tongue, his body writhing in imitation of the snake that was trying to get away.

Lynette had never been so frightened in her life, but the only thing that kept her from collapsing in terror was J.D. He had started to cry, and she half turned her head toward the sound while keeping her gaze fixed on the creature before her.

"It's okay, sweetie. Nana's here. It's okay."

His cries grew louder, tearing at Lynette's heart. If anything happened to that baby…

"What do you want?" she asked frantically. "I have some money in my purse. Take it. Just don't hurt that baby. Please."

The woman behind her said, "We're not here to steal from you. Although it might be justified. After all, you took something once that didn't belong to you. Didn't you, Lynette?"

Stall. That was the only thing Lynette could do. Mitchell should be here soon. Any minute now…

"Please don't hurt him," she whispered.

The snake writhed over the man's head. The mouth opened and the scent of musk filled the room.

Dear God, please help me. Help me protect J.D.

"I'm not here to hurt him," the woman said. "I've come to save him."

And with that, the man flung the snake at Lynette.

It struck her in the chest, then fell to the floor with a loud thump. What happened next was only a blur. The snake struck so quickly Lynette had no time to brace or protect herself.

It caught her just above the knee and when she tried to fight it off, the fangs sunk into her hand. For the longest moment, the serpent hung suspended, and then with a scream, Lynette flung it away. The snake thudded against the wall and slithered into a corner to hide.

Evangeline saw the flashing lights of the squad cars the moment she turned on her mother's street.

Her heart started to pound in terror.

Oh, God.

Something was wrong. She could believe that Mitchell would call out the cavalry, but this many cops could only mean one thing.

Evangeline parked in the street and tore through the yard, nearly colliding with one of the officers. He caught her by the shoulders. "Whoa, wait a minute, miss. You can't go in there. This is a crime scene."

Crime scene?

"I'm Detective Evangeline Theroux," she screamed. "This is my mother's house. My baby's inside."

The officer exchanged a glance with his partner. "Your baby's inside?"

She didn't answer. She tore herself loose from his grasp and lunged for the door.

Just beyond the foyer, her mother lay convulsing on the floor. A uniformed officer knelt beside her, and he looked up when Evangeline burst into the room. "Where are the EMTs?" he asked angrily.

Evangeline was on her knees beside him in a flash. "How bad?"

"She's been snakebit," he said. "I think she's going into anaphylactic shock."

Evangeline bent over her mother. "Mom, can you hear me?"

No response.

"Mom, what happened? Where's J.D.?" she asked desperately.

Lynette's mouth opened and closed, but no sound came out.

Evangeline got up and raced down the hallway to the small bedroom where her mother kept a crib. It was empty.

Panic hammered her chest as she stumbled from one room to the next, checking every corner, every closet, even though she already knew the awful truth.

Her son was gone.

Twenty-nine

Evangeline was already on the phone by the time she reached her car. She called Nash first, then Mitchell, then Vaughn. By the time she hit Highway 90, she was on the phone with Sheriff Thibodaux in Torrence.

"I sent a deputy out there earlier to have a look around," he said. "Everything was all clear. I'm just about to leave on a little trip, but I'll swing by there before I take off. I see anything suspicious, I'll give you call."

Evangeline pressed the accelerator to the floor, but she was still a good forty-five minutes away. And the clock was ticking.

She had no idea what she would find at the Lemay house once she got there. Rebecca? Ruth?

Her sisters.

Her own flesh and blood.

And one of them wanted to kill her son.

It hit Evangeline then just how far she was willing to go to protect J.D. from their madness. One sister was innocent, the other guilty, but in order to save her son, she would kill them both if she had to.

Cell phone clutched in her hand, she sailed along sugarcane fields and through tunnels of willow trees with the sun at her back. Every now and then when the road curved, she could see sunlight dancing on the bayou and the graceful prance of herons through the swamp grass. It was a paradise of water lilies, buttercups and wild roses. Of gilded wings and rippling water. And into this paradise, evil came with blond hair and blue eyes.

What would she do if J.D. wasn't at the house?

He could be anywhere. The swamp offered a million places to hide. She wouldn't have a clue where to start looking.

But Nash would. *This is what the FBI did best,* he'd told her.

She wanted desperately to believe that, but with each passing moment...

Don't. Don't!

Her son would be fine. She would find him in time, and by nightfall he would be safely back in his own bed. Evangeline would stand guard over him night and day if she had to. She would never again let him out of her sight. He was so tiny and innocent....

She blinked away hot tears as her knuckles whitened on the steering wheel. She would find him. She would.

The phone rang and she pressed it to her ear. "Yes."

"This is Nash. Listen, I've got some news for you."

Her heart bolted to her throat. "J.D.?"

"No, I'm sorry. I didn't mean to get your hopes up. This is about Rebecca Lemay's accomplice. We got a match on the prints you lifted from your car. They belong to a former psychiatric patient named Ellis Cooper. This guy sounds like a real nutcase. You be careful down there."

"Don't worry about me. I've already notified the sheriff in Torrence. He'll provide backup if I need it."

"Evangeline?"

"Yeah?"

"Hang in there. We're going to find him."

Her eyes burned with tears, but she had no time for emotion. No time for a breakdown. She had to find J.D. Nothing else mattered.

"I can't lose him," she whispered.

"I'll do everything in my power to make sure that doesn't happen."

"I know, but he's so little. So helpless…" She trailed off. "He's all I've got."

And at that moment, the revelation of how much

she loved her son humbled and staggered her. And shamed her because she hadn't realized it before.

She loved that little boy more than her own life. She would do anything to protect him. *Anything.* "We'll find him," Nash said again, and Evangeline tried to take comfort in the steadiness of his tone.

By the time she drove into Torrence, terror was a cold vise around her heart.

She parked in front of the police station and bolted inside.

The officer behind the front desk was on the phone, but he hung up the minute he saw Evangeline. "Detective Theroux?"

"Yes."

"We've been expecting you. The sheriff called a little while ago on his way out of town. He said to tell you the place is all clear. He didn't see hide nor hair of anyone out there."

"How long ago was this?"

"Half an hour maybe. He also said to tell you he thinks you're on a wild-goose chase."

The last was shouted at Evangeline's back as she raced back through the door.

Twenty minutes later, she turned off the main highway onto the gravel road. The shade of the forest seemed deep and oppressive, the whisper of wind through the leaves the worst kind of omen. But when she finally pulled into the clearing, the sight of the sheriff's car filled her with hope. Maybe he'd come back for a second look.

Evangeline parked beside the squad car and got out. Checking her weapon, she clutched the grip in both hands as she slowly climbed the stairs. Opening the screen door with her foot, she quickly stepped inside and swept the air with her gun.

The house was quiet.

Too quiet.

She should be able to hear the creak and moan of the wooden floors as the sheriff moved through the house, but she heard no sound at all. Nothing but the drone of mosquitoes that swarmed through the broken windows and sagging screen door.

Evangeline swatted one from her eyelashes as she eased through the house. "Sheriff Thibodaux? You in here? It's Detective Theroux."

She hated to give away her position, but she also didn't want a startled lawman shooting her. Retracing her steps into the front hall, she started up the stairs.

"Sheriff? I'm coming up."

At the top of the stairs, she heard something in the front bedroom, and as she pushed open the door, a scream rose to her throat.

The sheriff lay on his back on the floor, his eyes open and staring. Yellow fluid oozed from a wound on his neck and another on his arm where the skin had split from the rapid swelling.

As Evangeline stepped into the room, she saw something slither across the floor and disappear into the shadows. She froze, her heart pounding fiercely, and then she took another careful step inside.

Kneeling beside Thibodaux, she felt his wrist. She couldn't find a pulse, and she feared he'd gone into cardiac arrest.

A floorboard creaked out in the hallway, and she jumped to her feet. She edged back to the door, glanced out, and then realized too late that the danger was already in the room behind her.

She saw a movement out of the corner of eye. Before she could whirl, something slammed into the side of her head, and she dropped to her knees, then pitched face-first to the floor.

Thirty

When Evangeline came to, she was lying in water.

The smell of dead fish and stagnant water clogged her nostrils, and as she struggled to open her eyes, she thought she must still be in the swamp.

Her hand lifted to the throb at the side of her head and gingerly she probed the goose egg she found there. As everything slowly came back to her, fresh panic bloomed in her chest.

She wasn't in the swamp. She was in a room, like a cellar. Several inches of smelly water covered the floor where she lay, and to her left, she could see daylight. As she turned her head to the window, she saw something swim by her face.

Choking back a scream, she tried to remain motionless, but she couldn't stop trembling and her heart was pounding so violently, she thought it must surely be sending out vibrations in the water.

As she watched, the snake glided around and came back toward her. The head was up out of the water, and in the light from the window, she could see the gleam of its eyes. Could even make out the vertical pupils.

And then she saw another. And another.

They were everywhere.

Evangeline lay paralyzed as a black body slithered over her legs. Another touched her bare arm. She closed her eyes and tried not to scream.

When she dared look again, she counted at least a half-dozen diamond-shaped heads swimming in the water.

Ever so carefully, she turned her head away from the window. She could see a set of steps leading up to a door. Between her and the stairs, Thibodaux lay facedown in the water.

His body was still now, and Evangeline knew that he was dead. She'd read somewhere that death by snakebite was more often the result of heart failure than from the venom.

Evangeline could believe it. Her heart even now pounded so hard she was afraid her chest might explode.

Her head throbbed, too, and she thought of her mother, lying helpless on her own living room floor. She thought of J.D., missing from his crib, and an image of his little face materialized behind her closed eyelids. His sweet, innocent smile. The eyes that looked so much like Johnny's. How could she ever have doubted her love for that baby? Her need to find him and protect him was like a raging wildfire inside her chest.

She had to find a way out. She couldn't allow herself to remain frozen by terror. Her son needed her. She was all he had left.

And he was all she had left.

Hold on, J.D. I'm coming, baby.

Evangeline lay very still and tried to work out a plan. Would it be better to spring quickly to her feet or take the slow approach?

She had no idea. She wasn't even sure she could move quickly, given her injury and the numbness in her arms and legs. She flexed her muscles to try and warm them up.

Bracing herself, she counted to three, then leaped to her feet, jumped over the sheriff's body and let panic hurl her up the steps.

Too terrified to think about what might wait for her beyond the door, she seized the knob and twisted, then threw her shoulder against it. When that didn't work, she tried to kick it open, but the lock held and she turned to frantically scan her surroundings as she stood shivering at the top of the steps.

She was trapped.

The only other way out was the window, and

even if she could wade through the water without getting bit, the opening was too high for her to reach.

Her gaze lit on the body at the bottom of the steps. She needed to search through Thibodaux's pockets, see if she could find something with which she could jimmy the door.

But that meant going back into the water.

That meant wading through all those sinewy bodies.

Slowly, she went down the stairs, put one foot into the foul-smelling water and then the other, telling herself the snakes were as afraid of her as she was them. Not moccasins, though. They were very territorial. How many times had she heard stories of how they would turn and come at you if they felt threatened?

She first checked for his weapon, but he wasn't wearing a holster. Made sense, since he wasn't in uniform. Evangeline searched through the pocket nearest her, then reached across his body and slipped her hand into the water. Something cold touched her wrist and she waited a beat, then slid her hand in farther.

Nothing.

Fighting off another wave of terror and frustration, Evangeline started to turn back to the stairs. Then a memory came floating up through that black fog of fear. What was it Thibodaux had told her that first day in his office when she'd noticed the ankle holster on his desk? *"Even off duty, I don't ever go out into the swamp unarmed."*

Carefully, easing herself through the water, she reached under his pant leg, terrified that a snake might come slithering out. Instead, she felt the soft nylon of his holster, and a moment later, she had the small .38 special in her hand.

Eyeing the water around her, she turned and sprinted toward the steps. At the top, she stood back from the door and fired three shots into the lock, splintering the wood enough so that she could kick open the door. It took her several tries, but finally she was through.

Gripping the gun, she walked through the cabin and out the front door. The sheriff's SUV and her car had been brought here from the Lemay house.

Evangeline ran down the steps and checked inside each vehicle, praying the keys would be inside.

They weren't.

Helplessly, she surveyed her surroundings. There was nothing but woods and swamp all around her. She had no idea where she was, and for a moment, succumbed to the panic and terror clawing at her lungs. Where was she? Where was J.D.?

She couldn't bear to think about what might have already happened. What she had let happen.

But it was important not to dwell on that. She had to blot out the images racing through her head. Her baby at the mercy of a madwoman...

Please, please let me find him. Please let him be okay.

A path at the edge of the yard led back into the woods. Into a trap for all Evangeline knew, but what other choice did she have?

As she hurried through the trees, mosquitoes swarmed her face and nettles tore at her skin. By the time the path ended, the flesh on her arms was raw and bleeding and she was hopelessly lost.

She bent down, hands on knees, gulping air as her breath came in sobs.

Then, through the maddening drone of the mosquitoes came the distant tinkle of a wind chime.

A wind chime!

She'd heard it the day before through the broken upstairs window of the Lemay house.

She was close.

No more than a hundred yards away, if that.

All she had to do was follow the sound.

Ten minutes later, she was back in the clearing. Another two minutes had her crossing the yard toward the house.

A woman opened the screen door and came out on the porch to meet her. It was the same woman she'd seen in J.D.'s nursery. Rebecca Lemay.

She was dressed much the way she had been that

night—long skirt, tennis shoes and shapeless sweater, which she pulled tightly around her even though the day was scorching hot.

Evangeline lifted the gun. "Where is he? Where's my baby?"

"You don't need to worry. He's safe now."

Evangeline's heart dropped to her stomach as terror clawed at her heart. She started to run. "Where is he?" she screamed. Her finger pressed against the trigger. The rage that mushroomed inside her was hard to control. "Tell me where he is or I swear to God, I'll kill you."

"Evangeline, no!"

Lena Saunders—Ruth—was suddenly running across the yard toward her. Evangeline had no idea where she'd been hiding. She came forward now with her arms outstretched. "Please don't hurt her."

"I don't want to hurt anyone." Evangeline kept the gun leveled on Rebecca. "I just want my baby back. Tell me where he is."

"I told you," Rebecca said. "He's safe."

"Where is he, damn you!"

"Evangeline…" Lena came slowly toward her. "Please…just put the gun down before someone gets hurt."

"She took him," Rebecca said, pointing down the steps toward her sister.

Evangeline swung the gun toward Lena. "Stop right there. I'll kill you both if I have to."

Lena's blue eyes widened in alarm. "Evangeline, listen to me. Rebecca's sick. She needs help." She turned to her sister. "Please, just tell us where you put the baby."

Rebecca took a step back. "No."

"We just want to help you," Lena said.

"You'll send me away again."

"I never sent you away. It wasn't my fault what happened. It wasn't your fault, either. You didn't know any better. You just wanted to help Mama, didn't you?"

"You were her helper," Rebecca said. "You were her favorite."

"I was the oldest. She depended on me. You can depend on me, too. I'll get you help. Whatever you need. All you have to do is tell me what you did with the baby."

At that moment, Evangeline heard J.D.'s cry. It was coming from somewhere inside the house.

She and Lena moved at the same time. Before she reached the steps, something hit her hard between her shoulder blades. The force of the blow catapulted her forward and she fell with a hard thud to the ground. The gun flew from her hand as she lay dazed and shocked in the dirt. With an effort, she lifted her head and glanced behind her, saw the man with the scarred face standing over her. He had a club in one hand and a burlap sack in the other.

"I've got her," he said and laughed.

Evangeline lunged for the gun, grabbed it, but he was just as quick. Straddling her, he rolled her over and tried to pin her left arm to her side while he grappled for the gun in her right hand.

A shot went wild and she heard one of the sisters scream. She couldn't worry about that now, though. She had to get free. She had to find J.D. No matter what, she had to find her son and save him from these lunatics.

She fought viciously. With her free hand, she raked her nails across the tender skin of his scar. She clawed at his eyes, dug her knee into his groin. Nothing seemed to faze him.

One hand was at her throat, squeezing, squeezing while his other hand pried loose the gun in her hand. He flung it aside and then, his fingers tightening around her neck, he reached for the burlap bag.

As he upended it, a black, ropey body tumbled to the ground. As quick as lightning, his hand flicked out and he snatched the snake behind the head. He brought it close to Evangeline's face, and when he poked the snout with his club, the mouth widened, revealing the cottony interior and the long, razorlike fangs.

The swampy stench of the snake filled her nostrils as a cold, black terror dropped over her. Was this what he had in store for J.D.?

Adrenaline surged through her veins as her hand

scrabbled across the dirt, searching for the gun. Her fingers closed around a stick, and when he lifted the snake high over his head, mumbling words she could not understand, Evangeline reared up and drove the makeshift weapon into his eye with all the strength she could muster.

He screamed and dropped the snake.

The thick body fell hard against Evangeline's chest, then sprang forward in a blur. The fangs sunk into the man's neck and hung for the longest time as he fell backward to the ground, writhing in pain.

Evangeline grabbed the club and scrambled to her feet. Flinging the snake aside, the man, on hands and knees now, tried to get up, too, but Evangeline was ruthless now. She swung the club and connected with his temple, then the back of his neck. He fell face forward into the dirt and did not move again.

Dropping the club, Evangeline turned. Rebecca lay on the ground at the foot of the porch steps, blood gushing from a wound in her chest. Her sister was on her knees beside her.

"She's been hit," Lena said on a sob. She lifted Rebecca's slim body in her arms and rocked her back and forth. "I'm sorry," she whispered. "I'm so sorry." She looked up with shimmering eyes. "I never meant for this to happen."

"I know."

"She's my baby sister. I'm supposed to take care of her, but I couldn't help her. I couldn't save her."

Evangeline turned from the weeping woman and bolted up the steps. As she stepped inside the house, J.D.'s cries seemed to surround her and she knew where he was.

She opened the door to the whispering room, where she herself had once lay hidden.

A ray of sunshine fell on J.D., and for a moment, Evangeline's breath caught in her throat as the light haloed his hair. The dark history of the house whispered through the silent rooms as she bent and gently picked him up, cradling him to her heart.

"It's okay. Shush. It's okay. I'm here now."

Something in her voice must have reassured him because he calmed almost instantly. His little fist tangled in his mother's hair and he held on for dear life.

"I'm here," she whispered over and over. "I'm finally here."

Outside, the woman who called herself Lena was still on her knees beside Rebecca, her face buried in her sister's hair. There was nothing Evangeline could do for either of them now.

As she started down the steps, the weeping woman looked up. There wasn't a tear in her eyes or on her face.

"I can't let you leave here," she said.

Evangeline's heart began to pound as she clung to J.D. There wasn't a trace of Lena Saunders on her face. She was Ruth now.

"Give me the baby, Evangeline. You know I have to do this. It's the only way."

"It was you." Evangeline's gaze went to Rebecca's still form on the ground. "She was telling the truth. It's always been you. You're the one who visits Mary Alice at Pinehurst. You pretended to be Rebecca to give yourself cover. Everyone knows she's been in and out of psychiatric hospitals for years. She wouldn't be held responsible for her actions, but you would be. You—Lena Saunders—could face the death penalty for what you've done."

"Give me the baby, Evangeline."

"You were very clever, too. Oh, so concerned about your sister. You left all those cranes for me to find, the snakeskin in my house. You laid the groundwork, had it all planned out." Evangeline glanced down at the scarred man's prone body. "You even found someone to share in your delusions, didn't you? Someone who didn't mind doing your dirty work."

"Give the baby to me!"

"Go to hell."

"It's the only way to save him. Let me do what I was meant to do."

"Murder children?"

"You don't understand. I'm guided by His hand. Just as our mother was. Rebecca wanted to be, but she was too weak. You're strong like me, Evangeline. You're my only sister now. My blood is your blood. Our father's blood is his blood." She nodded toward J.D. "You have to let me save him."

"You'll have to kill me first."

Ruth's blue eyes darkened. "Think what Johnny would have wanted."

"Don't you dare even speak his name," Evangeline said furiously. "You used his memory to get to me. You never even met him, did you?"

"What does it matter? All that matters is this child. You know what he'll grow up to be. Do you really want that for him? Think about it, Evangeline. How much do you love your son? Johnny's son. How far are you willing to go to protect him, to save his immortal soul from eternal damnation?"

"I'll go as far as I have to," Evangeline said, backing across the porch. "Even if it means killing you."

"You can't run away from who we are. You told me that once, remember? You said Ruth was still inside me somewhere. Her story is my story. Her truth is my truth. And you were right, I am Ruth Lemay. And you're my sister. The DNA, the blood… it's a part of us. And now it's a part of your son."

Evangeline kept backing away from her. Ruth was still standing at the foot of the steps when the bullet caught her in the back. The punch drove her forward and she dropped to her knees, her gaze locking with Evangeline's.

The gun slipped from Rebecca Lemay's fingers as her sister's body fell across hers.

* * *

Her hand cradling J.D.'s head, Evangeline stumbled down the steps. As she started across the yard, a car emerged from the trees and slammed to a halt. A man got out and ran toward her. It was Nash.

A squad car came out of the woods behind him. And then another. Evangeline paid no one any mind, even when someone called her name. She kept walking until the distance between her and Nash had vanished.

He stood looking down at her for the longest moment, and then his arms came around her and J.D. and he held them both close.

Thirty-one

After two days, Lynette was taken out of intensive care and moved to a private hospital room. When Evangeline stopped by on her lunch break, her mother was sitting up in bed. She smiled when Evangeline walked through the door and started to reach out her arms for a hug, then thought better of it.

Evangeline sat down on the edge of the bed. "How are you feeling?"

Lynette was still smiling, but her eyes brimmed with tears. "Much better. The doctor said I might be able to go home in the morning."

"That's great. Will you need a ride?" Evangeline hated that her voice sounded so stilted, but she couldn't seem to help it. So much had happened. So many lies had been uncovered. It would take her a while to sort them all out.

"I don't want to trouble you. Besides…" Lynette

glanced away. "Your father said he'd come by and drive me home."

Evangeline stared down at her in surprise. "That's okay with you?"

Lynette shrugged. "It's just a ride. It doesn't mean anything." But there was a hopeful note in her tone that she couldn't quite suppress. Then her expression darkened and tears flooded back into her eyes. "Evangeline…I'm so sorry. Your dad and I should have told you the truth a long time ago. What we did was wrong, but it was for the right reason. We wanted desperately to protect you. What that woman did to her children…we never wanted you to have that burden. And over time, it just became easier to pretend that you were ours. Because you are. In every way that counts." She reached for Evangeline's hand. "Can you ever forgive us?"

Evangeline had wondered that herself over the past forty-eight hours. Now as she stared down into her mother's careworn face, the answer came easily. "A few days ago, I might have had a hard time forgiving you, but now I know how far I was willing to go to protect my own child. I would have killed an innocent woman if it had come to that. So I'm not sure I'm in any position to judge you. I have my son back. That's all that matters to me now." She bent to kiss her mother's cheek, and Lynette's arms slipped around her, holding her close for a very long time.

Later that night, Evangeline sat out on the front porch with the baby. He'd been fed and bathed and it was long past his bedtime. But she couldn't bear to put him down. She wanted him close. Wanted to be able to stare down into his little face for as long as she needed to reassure herself that he was safe.

The burnished clouds of sunset had cooled and darkened, and the sky turned lavender as twilight winged softly over the landscape.

A car door slammed down the street, and a moment later, Nash turned up the walkway to her porch. He paused on the bottom step, his face in shadows, before coming the rest of the way up. He sat down beside her, and the scent of his aftershave, the scent of *him,* filled Evangeline's senses.

"I have some news," he finally said, his gaze on the sleeping baby.

"What kind of news?"

"Remember when I promised you justice? We're moving in on Betts."

Evangeline turned to study his face. "When?"

"I can't say exactly when. But soon. I'll let you know when it's over. This time he won't walk. We'll make sure of that."

Evangeline stared down at her son. "That's good," she said.

"You don't sound too excited about it."

"Justice is a very good thing," she said. "But it won't bring Johnny back. It won't change what he did."

"No, I guess not."

Summer lightning flickered on the horizon and the soft breeze carried a hint of rain.

Nash said softly, "He's a fine-looking boy, Evangeline."

Her heart swelled with pride.

"You should see your face when you look at him." He paused, as if suddenly at a loss for words. "Don't let go of that feeling," he said. "Don't ever forget what's important."

Tears burned Evangeline's eyes. Tears of guilt and wonder and a love so fierce, her chest felt ready to explode.

"For so long, I only went through the motions," she said. "I did everything I thought a mother should do, but I thought something was missing inside me. Something that wouldn't allow me to love my son the way he deserved to be loved. Now I know it was just fear holding me back. Fear of losing him the way I lost Johnny. It took meeting that fear head-on for me to realize how much I love him. He means everything to me. I'd die to protect him."

"He's lucky to have you for a mother," Nash said. He sounded moved. Humbled.

"No," she said. "I'm the lucky one. I know that now."

They sat for the longest moment in silence while she cradled her sleeping son in her arms.

"I had the strangest dream last night," she finally said.

"Oh, yeah?"

"I was sitting out here on the porch just like we are now and I saw Johnny on the street. He was driving Nathan Mallet's red Mustang, the one he always loved. When he saw me on the porch, he honked and waved, but when I ran after him, he drove away without stopping, like he had somewhere important he had to be." She turned to Nash. "What do you think that meant?"

His eyes searched her face in the darkness. "Maybe it was his way of saying goodbye."

"I told you once that I could still feel his presence, remember?" She drew a long breath, releasing something bittersweet inside her. "I don't feel him anymore. Not with you here. So maybe that dream was my way of telling *him* goodbye."

Nash said nothing as she turned and watched the clouds roll in from the gulf. The breeze picked up and the heady fragrance of her neighbor's roses hung heavy on the steamy night air.

Evangeline couldn't look at Nash, but she didn't pull away when he slipped his arm around her shoulder.

Down the street, a car engine roared to life. It sounded like Nathan Mallet's old Mustang, and in her mind's eye, Evangeline saw Johnny wave as he gunned the motor and drove away.

J.D. whimpered in his sleep, as if he'd heard the sound, too. Evangeline lifted him to her chest and pressed her cheek to the top of his head.

"I'm here," she whispered. "Mama's here."

REQUEST YOUR FREE BOOKS!

2 FREE NOVELS
FROM THE ROMANCE/SUSPENSE
COLLECTION PLUS 2 FREE GIFTS!

YES! Please send me 2 FREE novels from the Romance/Suspense Collection and my 2 FREE gifts (gifts are worth about $10). After receiving them, if I don't wish to receive any more books, I can return the shipping statement marked "cancel." If I don't cancel, I will receive 4 brand-new novels every month and be billed just $5.49 per book in the U.S. or $5.99 per book in Canada, plus 25¢ shipping and handling per book plus applicable taxes, if any*. That's a savings of at least 20% off the cover price! I understand that accepting the 2 free books and gifts places me under no obligation to buy anything. I can always return a shipment and cancel at any time. Even if I never buy another book from the Reader Service, the two free books and gifts are mine to keep forever.

185 MDN EF5Y 385 MDN EF6C

Name	(PLEASE PRINT)

Address	Apt. #

City	State/Prov.	Zip/Postal Code

Signature (if under 18, a parent or guardian must sign)

Mail to **The Reader Service:**
IN U.S.A.: P.O. Box 1867, Buffalo, NY 14240-1867
IN CANADA: P.O. Box 609, Fort Erie, Ontario L2A 5X3

Not valid to current subscribers to the Romance Collection,
the Suspense Collection or the Romance/Suspense Collection.

Want to try two free books from another line?
Call 1-800-873-8635 or visit www.morefreebooks.com.

* Terms and prices subject to change without notice. N.Y. residents add applicable sales tax. Canadian residents will be charged applicable provincial taxes and GST. Offer not valid in Quebec. This offer is limited to one order per household. All orders subject to approval. Credit or debit balances in a customer's account(s) may be offset by any other outstanding balance owed by or to the customer. Please allow 4 to 6 weeks for delivery. Offer available while quantities last.

Your Privacy: Harlequin is committed to protecting your privacy. Our Privacy Policy is available online at www.eHarlequin.com or upon request from the Reader Service. From time to time we make our lists of customers available to reputable third parties who may have a product or service of interest to you. If you would prefer we not share your name and address, please check here. ☐

BOB08R

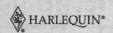

AMANDA STEVENS

32530 THE DEVIL'S FOOTPRINTS   ___ $6.99 U.S. ___ $8.50 CAN.
32428 THE DOLLMAKER   ___ $6.99 U.S. ___ $8.50 CAN.

(limited quantities available)

TOTAL AMOUNT $ _____
POSTAGE & HANDLING $ _____
($1.00 FOR 1 BOOK, 50¢ for each additional)
APPLICABLE TAXES* $ _____
TOTAL PAYABLE $ _____
(check or money order—please do not send cash)

To order, complete this form and send it, along with a check or money order for the total above, payable to MIRA Books, to: **In the U.S.:** 3010 Walden Avenue, P.O. Box 9077, Buffalo, NY 14269-9077; **In Canada:** P.O. Box 636, Fort Erie, Ontario, L2A 5X3.

Name: _____
Address: _____ City: _____
State/Prov.: _____ Zip/Postal Code: _____
Account Number (if applicable): _____

075 CSAS

*New York residents remit applicable sales taxes.
*Canadian residents remit applicable GST and provincial taxes.

MIRA®

www.MIRABooks.com   MAS0309BI